KU-263-500

Lily Herne divides her time between Cape Town and Norwich, UK, and can sometimes be found in both places at once. Her interests include chainsaws, steampunk and cake. You can follow her on Twitter at @Herne13 or friend her on Facebook – she'd love to hear from you.

Cardiff Libraries
www.cardiff.gov.uk/libraries

Llyfrgelloedd Caerdy
www.caerdydd.gov.uk/llyfrgelloe

ACC. No: 03242089

DeAdLAndS

A Deadlands Novel

LILY HERNE

Much-in-Little

Constable & Robinson Ltd
55–56 Russell Square
London WC1B 4HP
www.constablerobinson.com

First published by Penguin Books (South Africa) (Pty) Ltd 2011

First published in the UK by Much-in-Little,
an imprint of Constable & Robinson Ltd, 2013

Copyright © Sarah Lotz and Savannah Lotz, 2011

The rights of Sarah Lotz and Savannah Lotz to be identified as the
authors of this work have been asserted by them in accordance with the
Copyright, Designs and Patents Act 1988

All rights reserved. This book is sold subject to the condition
that it shall not, by way of trade or otherwise, be lent, resold,
hired out or otherwise circulated in any form of binding or cover
other than that in which it is published and without a similar condition
including this condition being imposed on the subsequent purchaser.

This is a work of fiction. Names, characters,
places and incidents are either the product of the author's imagination
or are used fictitiously, and any resemblance to actual persons,
living or dead, or to actual events or locales is entirely coincidental.

A copy of the British Library Cataloguing in
Publication Data is available from the British Library

ISBN: 978-1-47210-090-0 (paperback)
ISBN: 978-1-47210-091-7 (ebook)

Printed and bound by CPI Group (UK) Ltd, Croydon, CR0 4YY

1 3 5 7 9 10 8 6 4 2

Part One

This story begins with a funeral. I know it's a bit of a downer to start it here, but it just feels right. I could begin ten years ago when the War ended, or even start when I discovered my 'special skill', but if you don't like it, as my friend Ginger would say, 'Not my problemo, mate.'

Oh, and I should probably warn you that it ends with a funeral as well.

But I'm not going to tell you whose.

You can find that out for yourself.

1

My name is Lele de la Fontein. I'm seventeen and a bit, and the first funeral I was telling you about was my grandmother's. I don't remember exactly on which day it took place (who cares about those kind of details, right?), but I do remember the weather. Winter was in full swing; the sky pregnant with the rain that was to turn the streets into muddy rivers for days afterwards; the wind pulsing and howling around us.

Not that the biting South-Easterly seemed to bother the Resurrectionists. They were standing in a circle around Gran's shrouded body, holding hands and swaying from side to side as if they were playing the world's sickest game of ring-a-ring o' roses. Most of them were Dad's age or older, and around their necks they all wore those horrible amulets carved to look like human vertebrae. Their leader, a man with a scraggly grey beard and rickety legs, abruptly stopped swaying and thrust his arms into the air. 'Soon we shall send this woman, our dearly beloved sister, out into the world,' he said in a ridiculous booming voice. 'Yes! Out into the world beyond! For her divine resurrection in the next life.'

His followers all smiled and nodded, but I couldn't stand it any longer. 'This is crap!' I said, making sure my voice carried over the wind. 'They shouldn't be here.'

'Leletia!' the Mantis snapped. 'Keep your voice down.'

'Gran didn't believe in all this kak!'

The Mantis glared at me, and I did my best to stare her down, but it wasn't a battle I was going to win anytime soon. For the thousandth time I tried to figure out what it was Dad saw in her. It couldn't be her looks. Thanks to her bulbous eyes, spindly limbs and general twitchiness, she always looked as if she was on the verge of pouncing on something. I tried to catch Dad's eye, but, as usual, he was lost in his own world. He stared straight ahead, the empty left arm of his jacket taped to his side so that it wouldn't flap around in the wind. He didn't look even slightly sad, but that wasn't surprising. Gran wasn't *his* mother, and after Mom died he hadn't had much to do with her. Or with me and Jobe, while we're on the subject.

The wind dropped, and the moans of the Rotters floated towards us. They sounded closer to the fence than usual, as if they could sense what was about to happen.

I think it was then that Gran's death really hit me. I tried repeating the same mantra to myself over and over again – *I will not cry, I will not cry, I will not cry* – but my tear ducts weren't listening. I wasn't just crying because Gran was gone. I mean, don't get me wrong, I was going to miss her so much my stomach hurt, but there was also a selfish part of me that hated her for leaving us. Because without her, Jobe and I would be forced to stay in the stinking city enclave; we'd be stuck with Dad and the Mantis for good.

Jobe snuggled closer to me, sing-songing to himself as he often did, oblivious to the fact that our lives had taken a massive turn for the worse. He didn't seem to be feeling the chill, although his bare brown feet were turning slightly blue. The Mantis had made him leave Chinwag – his kitten and constant companion – behind, but even this didn't seem to bother him.

The Mantis pulled her fine woollen wrap tighter around her bony body and sighed, 'And *try* to get your brother to behave, Leletia.'

I ignored her. Jobe did what he wanted. Not even I had any control over him, and she knew that. I scrubbed my face with my palms, smearing away the worst of the tears, and tried not to look at Gran's body, its shape seemingly so much smaller than when she'd been alive.

We all jumped as the enclave gate clanked open behind us.

Rickety Legs gasped and clapped his hands together. 'They're coming!' he said, his followers clustering around him like a bunch of excited kids. My stomach flipped, and even the Mantis's grim expression tightened.

It was time.

I held my breath as the Guardians' wagon came over the rise towards us. The huge black horse pulling it was prancing in terror; the harness strapped too tightly across its body, foam frothing around the bit in its mouth. The wind whipped its mane around its neck, and behind the blinkers on its bridle I caught a glimpse of the whites of its eyes.

The cart shook and bumped over the patchy track, eventually coming to a stop a few metres from us. The Resurrectionists all fell to their knees, muttering prayers and clutching at their vertebrae amulets. The Mantis and Dad bowed their heads, but

I refused to look away. It was the first time I'd been so close to a Guardian and for a second I almost forgot about my grief. There were two of them – one driving the cart, hands hidden under the sleeves of its robe, and another sitting rigidly next to it. The driver turned its head towards us, and I couldn't resist peering into the dark shadow that lay under its hood. But the rough brown fabric fell too far over its head; the blank darkness where its face should be somehow creepier than anything my imagination could conjure up.

Of course, at that stage not even the bigwig embassy officials knew what the Guardians looked like under their robes. There were rumours of course – that they were highly evolved Rotters who covered up so that they wouldn't freak everyone out with their maggoty, decaying flesh; that they looked so terrifying that just one peek at their true form would send a person insane. (Of course, now that I *do* know what they look like under their robes, I'm not surprised they covered up.)

The Guardians climbed down and headed towards us, ignoring the prostrate Resurrectionists as if they also thought the cult was a pointless load of crap. The driver lifted Gran's body and flung it onto the back of the wagon as if it was nothing more than a bag of potatoes; as if she hadn't once been a living, breathing person at all. Then, job done, they climbed back on to the wagon and started heading back towards the gate.

'Let's go,' the Mantis said. 'It's freezing.'

Dad put his good arm around her shoulders and they turned away. Rickety Legs nodded at the Mantis, shook her hand, and then he and his crew started ambling away, chatting amongst themselves. 'Leletia, bring your brother,' Dad mumbled.

Jobe was crouched on the ground, fingers fanned out in the mud, and when the wind died I could hear he was speaking to himself in the strange quiet voice he sometimes used: 'Gogo,' he murmured. 'Gogo.'

I guess all the anger, grief and distress I was feeling reached a head. Or maybe Jobe's rare words finally cemented the fact that I would never see Gran again. This was it. I was really, truly on my own.

'No!' I screamed, and started racing towards the spiked metal gate. One of the Guardians was busy hefting it open, and I thudded down towards the wagon, my legs gathering momentum, unable to stop as the sloping ground fell away sharply in front of me. I skidded and fell to my knees, inches away from the wheels. The horse reared up in alarm, but neither Guardian reacted. The driver just flicked the reins again, and the horse moved on, snorting and shaking its head.

I scrambled to my feet. The gate was fully open now and I could see right through to the outside – right into the Deadlands. I'd become used to seeing the top of Table Mountain, the shells of the few remaining high-rises and the burned-out skeletons of the cylindrical buildings everyone used to call the Tampon Towers peeking over the fence, but I'd never seen into the Deadlands before. Jobe and I had been ferried to the city enclave in the middle of the night, but we hadn't even caught a glimpse of the faceless Guardian who drove our wagon. Now I could make out the rusted carcass of an overturned taxi, grass growing in and around its broken windows. And as I stared at it, something scrabbled around its side, something with raggedy grey limbs and a skull that seemed to be made up of nothing but yellow teeth and dark eyeholes.

The thing moved in rapid, jerky gestures. It was heading straight for the opening, crawling on all fours, jaw gaping impossibly wide, a ghoulish moan coming from its throat.

I knew that if I didn't move fast it would be on me in seconds, but my limbs had turned to jelly. The Rotter skittered forward, metres away from the gate, as I watched, paralysed with horror. Then, as if it was a trainer instructing a dog to sit, one of the Guardians languidly lifted its arm and the creature slunk back to its hideout in the junked vehicle. Seconds later the gate closed behind the wagon with a metallic clash.

I felt my arm being yanked roughly as someone hauled me to my feet. 'Lele!' Dad yelled at me, trying to catch his breath. 'What the hell were you thinking?'

I shrugged my shoulder out of his grasp and started walking back towards where the Mantis and Jobe were waiting. The rain was starting to fall steadily, drops the size of two cent pieces splashing down around us.

'How could you?' the Mantis hissed.

I was so overwhelmed by a spike of hatred that I actually started shaking. I know the Mantis was supposed to be a great war hero and everything, but right then, as far as I was concerned, she was an A-grade bitch. Somehow, I promised myself, I'd make a plan to get away from the city enclave. Away from Dad. Away from the Resurrectionists. And *especially* away from the Mantis.

And I'd do whatever it took.

The light was fading fast. Taking Jobe's hand, I turned back towards the fence one last time.

'Bye, Gran,' I whispered into the wind.

I was trying not to think that somewhere, out in the Deadlands, Gran was getting up.

2

I spent the next day hiding out in my room, doing my best to ignore Dad and the Mantis, whiling away the time sketching. I hated that room; I just couldn't get used to being so confined. Gran's cottage in the Agriculturals may have been little more than a glorified shack, but there were acres of farmland and veld around our fenced settlements and livestock pens – the area so vast that we could barely hear the moans of the Rotters who roamed in the faraway Deadlands. Not so in the city, where it was an almost constant background noise, ebbing and flowing at the whim of the wind.

Thanks to the Mantis's high-powered job at the embassy, she and Dad owned a squat brick-and-mortar box squeezed in between its neighbours. It was supposed to be privileged housing, but you could have fooled me. The place stank of the paraffin that fuelled the lamps at night and the windows were tiny and hardly let in any light, even on the sunniest of days.

Around dinner time, Jobe appeared at the door, Chinwag clutched in his arms. He toddled over to me and placed a cool hand on my forehead. 'Eina,' he said.

'Yeah, Jobe,' I said. 'You've got that right.'

He climbed onto the bed and curled up next to me, Chinwag squirming out of his grasp and snuggling herself into the crook of my legs.

There was a knock on the door and the Mantis entered. She was carrying a long-sleeved woollen tunic over her arm and I could tell by the look in her eye that she was about to give me one of her 'important talks'. She stalked over to the wooden chair in the corner of the room and sat down, primly crossing her ankles. 'So, Leletia,' she said, all fake cheeriness, as if we hadn't all been at a funeral the day before. 'First day at your new school tomorrow. You must be so excited.'

I wasn't in the slightest bit excited. If it hadn't been for the sorrow that was eating out my insides, I'd have been feeling a low, throbbing dread.

She held out the grey tunic. 'Isn't it gorgeous?'

'I'm not wearing that,' I said.

Her eyes flickered with irritation. 'You *will* wear it, Leletia.'

'My name's *Lele*.'

She sighed and pinched her nose with her thumb and forefinger as if I was literally giving her a headache. 'We've all got to adjust,' she said. 'I know how hard it is for you to deal with your grandmother's passing over ...'

'You don't know anything about me.'

She carried on as if I hadn't spoken. 'We all lost people during the War and we all have to learn to move on and try to make a better life for ourselves. That is why your father and I decided it was best for you to go to school tomorrow. There's no point wallowing in grief.'

'I don't want to go to your stupid Rotter-lover school!' I didn't like how my voice sounded – whingeing and weak – but I couldn't help it.

The Mantis looked me straight in the eye, but she didn't raise her voice when she spoke. 'You listen to me very carefully, Leletia. That kind of talk could land all of us into very serious trouble – you especially.'

I glared at her. 'Okay, Cleo. I don't want to go to your stupid *zombie*-lover school. Better?'

'I know you think you're being very clever, Leletia. But ignorance is no excuse –'

'Who's being ignorant? I'm not the one who treats the Guardians like they're gods!'

'The Resurrectionists are making a better life for all of us, Leletia,' the Mantis said with that same irritating calmness. 'If it wasn't for them, we'd still all be living in tents like refugees.'

'It's sick, though, making deals with them. You're sick!'

She gave me a small, icy smile and toyed with the amulet around her neck. 'You're extremely lucky to be going to school at all. Not everyone gets the chance. You know that.'

'So you've said, like, a hundred times.'

'Do you know how lucky you are? A chance at a career?'

'Whatever.'

'Not *whatever*, Leletia. You've come of age. You know the alternative.'

I hated to admit it, but she was right. And the alternative wasn't pretty. Marriage. Breeding. Two of the girls at my old school had left to get married when they were fifteen; even in the Agriculturals there were loads of young mothers and fathers, many of them not much older than me, carrying babies and pulling toddlers around by the hand.

The Mantis was really getting into her stride now. 'Besides, it's the best school in the enclave. Have you any idea how many favours I had to call in to get you in there?'

But I had one card up my sleeve. 'What about the Lottery?' I said.

She jerked back slightly. 'What do you mean?'

'What if I win the Lottery? Then it's all a waste of time, isn't it?'

'Now you're just being obtuse! You know you're not eligible. Not after ... your brother ...' Her eyes strayed to where Jobe was snuggled up close to me and I felt a small thrill of triumph. I'd suspected that mentioning the Lottery would rattle her. I'd heard that even hard-core Resurrectionists didn't like talking about it. But her discomfort didn't last long. 'You're going tomorrow, Leletia, whether you like it or not.'

I thought about telling her to stick it. But what was my alternative? Running away? Even if I did somehow make it through the Deadlands and back to the Agriculturals unscathed, I didn't want to imagine what would happen to Jobe if I wasn't around. I'd heard rumours that kids like him weren't tolerated in some parts of the city enclave.

Taking my silence as agreement, the Mantis got to her feet, pausing only to pick up Mom's old army boots from where I'd dropped them at the base of the bed. They were at least a size too big, but I'd padded them out with old socks, and they were comfortable enough. 'You can borrow a pair of my shoes tomorrow,' she said. 'We'll get you some more at the leather market at the weekend.'

'No thanks. I'm wearing those.'

'Don't be ridiculous. You'll be the laughing stock. It's bad enough that your hair ... well, at least that will grow. It's about time you learned that we do things differently in the city.'

'You mean so that I don't embarrass you?' I sat up, and Chinwag zooted to the end of the bed where she began licking a paw.

The Mantis didn't answer.

'I'll go to your stupid school,' I said, reaching over and grabbing the boots out of her grasp. 'But on my terms.'

She opened her mouth to fire back at me, but then Jobe tapped her knee and murmured, 'Shhhhh.'

So you see, right then I wasn't the happiest person in the world. I don't want you to think I'm some kind of self-pitying freak, but let's face it – things were bad. What I didn't know, and couldn't have guessed, was that they were about to get a whole lot worse.

It's weird, but I hardly remember anything about life before the War, even when I really try. I mean, I was only seven when it all kicked off, but I should still remember stuff, shouldn't I? I have only a vague recollection of the flat we lived in before the Rotters came; it was small and smelled of Mom's cigarettes, and we had to climb up several flights of steps to reach the front door. In fact, my only clear memories are of the years Jobe and I lived with Gran in the Agriculturals. We were happy there. She loved us.

But that was then. Ancient history. And, like the Mantis said, I didn't have a choice.

So that morning I put on the scratchy grey tunic and pulled the thick woollen stockings over my legs. The unfamiliar clothes were at least a size too big. I'm always getting teased about how skinny I am, but it's not my fault. I eat as much as anyone; it just doesn't stick to my ribs.

As if he'd picked up on my mood, Jobe clung to my legs as I grabbed Gran's ancient Billabong rucksack – the one she'd kept safe through the years after the War. I gently pried him loose and knelt down to face him. 'Listen, Jobe. You have to stay here. You have to behave for Dad. 'Kay?'

I gave him a hug that was really more for my benefit than his, but as I pulled away I was almost sure that I saw a flicker of understanding in his eyes. Sometimes this happened, and it made all the other times, the times he stared off into space, sing-songing to himself, bearable.

The Mantis was already ensconced in the rickshaw by the time I made my way outside. 'Leletia,' she snapped. 'Hurry up.'

I hated going by rickshaw. The men and women who pulled them along the streets all ran barefoot and that day our driver was a hefty woman with long blonde hair and ginormous shoulders. I smiled at her apologetically as I heaved myself in next to the Mantis, but she barely acknowledged me.

The Mantis's bulbous eyes skated over my body and she nodded in approval at the leather sandals I was wearing. I smiled to myself. There was no way I was going to let on that I'd hidden my boots in the bottom of the backpack.

The rickshaw driver started pulling us away from the house, hucking and jumping to get the momentum going. It was still early, but already the streets were crammed with bodies scurrying to and fro. The rain fell in steady sheets, pitter-pattering on the rickshaw's tarpaulin roof, but the wet weather didn't stop the hawkers trying to tempt us with pancakes of boiled spinach, or the sheep's heads and pigs' trotters that bubbled and frothed in drums at every corner. The smoke melded with the stench of molten tar as workers slaved away to pave the muddy roadways. I hated it. The endless greyness and people-made fakeness of it made my eyes hurt. Everywhere you looked there was concrete or mud, not a sign of a tree or even a blade of grass.

'You look really pretty in your uniform,' the Mantis said in her 'look, I'm your friend' voice. A total lie of course. I looked like a freak, and I longed for my hoody and jeans. Pretending not to hear her, I stared out at the passing rickshaws and the half-completed buildings that lined the street.

'Look, Leletia,' the Mantis said, after a lengthy silence. 'Isn't it beautiful?'

I honestly couldn't see what the hell she was talking about. As far as I was concerned not only was the city enclave as ugly as sin, but it also stank. The Mantis and Dad were always going on about the fancy-smancy sewerage system the Resurrectionists were constructing, but now we were edging into the centre of the sector and the place reeked of open drains and other foul stuff I didn't want to think about.

The rain was falling more heavily now, and the rickshaw driver paused to wipe the rivulets out of her eyes before flexing the muscles in her shoulders and moving onwards again.

We topped a rise and I got another tantalising glimpse of Table Mountain in between the spilling clouds.

The rickshaw driver slid to an abrupt stop.

'What now!' the Mantis said, looking at me in irritation as if it was my fault.

'Resurrectionist parade, ma'am,' the rickshaw driver said, pointing towards the road ahead where a solid wall of bodies was marching in formation, droning some tuneless phrase over and over again. I couldn't make out the words, but it had to be the same kind of crap the Resurrectionists at Gran's funeral had spouted.

'Guardians!' I said, unthinkingly grabbing the Mantis's arm.

'They're not Guardians, Leletia,' she said. 'They wear the

robes as a tribute.' And looking closer I could see she was right. Two robed figures were cutting their way through the crowd, thrusting pamphlets into the hands of passers-by, and as I watched one of them pushed back his hood to scratch his thatch of brown hair.

A woman with wide staring eyes and a lumpy rash across one cheek ran up to the side of the rickshaw and shoved a piece of paper into my hand. 'Take this, sisi!' she said, and before I could react, she melted back into the throng of bodies.

The Mantis sighed. 'Why on earth do they have to do this at this time of the day?'

I looked at her in surprise. 'Huh? But you ... you're a believer.'

The Mantis shot me a shrewd look. 'Take the market road,' she snapped to the rickshaw driver, who nodded, jumped up on the balls of her feet and pulled us through a series of darkened alleyways, strung with sodden washing and full of the reek of unwashed bodies.

While the Mantis carried on barking instructions to the driver, I opened up the pamphlet. The ink was smeared where stray droplets of rain had dampened it, but it was still readable. Beneath a crap ink drawing of a large-headed child gazing up at an oval sun were the words:

> *Do you remember the terrible days of hijackings? Murder? Domestic violence? Robbery? Et cetera? Yes? Then join us in celebrating our Saviours Who Have Set Us Free. Become ReBorn with a view to a Glorious ReAnimation. New Greenmarket Square, Saturday, 12 July, Year 10.*

I scrunched it up and shoved it into the bottom of my backpack. Then, all too soon, we turned a corner and I caught a glimpse of my new school for the first time.

My first thought was: *Oh crap*. It looked like the photos I'd seen of the prisons they'd had before the War. It was ringed by a low spiked fence, and the bland brick buildings behind it couldn't have been more different from my old school, which was basically just a rondavel with a cosy thatched roof. Even from outside the gate I could smell the telltale reek of newly laid concrete. The sign on the gate read *Malema High: 'A breath of fresh air'*.

'Here we are,' the Mantis said. 'Remember, try to fit in, Leletia.'

But, as I was about to find out, that was *way* easier said than done.

'What did you say your name was?' The woman in the reception office looked me up and down disapprovingly, taking in my shorn hair and of course the boots, which I'd quickly put on when the Mantis was out of sight.

'Lele ... Leletia,' I said again.

It was gloomy inside the brick office, the windows too small to let in adequate light. She flicked irritably through the papers on her desk. 'And you're really Cleo Mbane's stepdaughter?'

'I told you that already.'

I could tell by the way her nose wrinkled up slightly, as if she'd smelled something putrid, that she was finding it hard to believe me. I'd taken an instant dislike to her – when she'd bent down to collect a form from behind the desk, I'd caught sight of a large bony Resurrectionist amulet under her blouse – and it was obviously more than mutual. She was all angles and hard edges, as if she'd been welded together, and she reeked of the grease she'd used to slick back her hair.

'I'm Comrade Pelosi. If you have any problems, you can come and see me.'

Not bloody likely.

'Let's get you to class,' she said. 'You'll be just in time for morning thanks.'

'For morning what?'

She pretended not to hear me and led me outside.

'You must feel very privileged coming to a school such as this after your time in the Agriculturals,' she said in her superior tone. 'We're very proud of our beautiful school.'

'Yeah,' I said. 'I can see why.'

She glanced at me suspiciously, as if she'd detected the sarcastic undertone in my voice, but I smiled innocently back at her.

Comrade Pelosi led me past a bare area dominated by a rusty sculpture of a sun with dull metal rays poking out of its centre and towards a squat barn-like structure with a domed roof. It instantly reminded me of the shed where we used to keep the sheep in the winter.

'All your classes will be in here.'

My stomach flip-flopped, and taking a deep, calming breath, I followed her inside.

The room was as gloomy as the reception area – the only lighting coming from oil lamps that were placed on each desk – and although there had to be thirty or so students in the room, it was almost eerily silent. Everyone had their heads bent, their hands clasped on the desks in front of them.

A freakishly tall man stood at the front of the classroom, his eyes closed and his arms raised above his head. He was almost as skinny as the Mantis, and his long hair was scraped back so tightly his brow looked as if it took up two thirds of his face. He immediately made me think of the huge rain spiders we'd sometimes find on the walls of Gran's cottage.

His eyes snapped open. 'So we give thanks to the Guardians for the air that we breathe, the food that we eat and the safe environment in which we flourish,' he said.

A low murmuring started to hum in the background. Comrade Pelosi, or Acid Face as I had decided to dub her, cleared her throat.

'Comrade,' she said. 'Sawubona. New pupil for you.' Then she stalked out, leaving me stranded at the side of the classroom.

'Please come to the front,' the teacher said.

Squirming with self-consciousness, I walked stiffly towards him. My boots clunked over the concrete floor, and a couple of girls in the front row sniggered. The words *Give thanks for each new day* were written on the blackboard, but the rest of the dusty brick walls were bare. There were no windows, and despite the size of the room I began to feel claustrophobic.

'Welcome,' the teacher said, his flat black eyes boring into my skull. 'I am Comrade Xhati. Please, tell us a bit about yourself.'

Crap. I really *really* didn't want to stand in front of all these strangers and talk about myself. I turned to face the class, heart hammering in my chest, everyone's eyes focused on me. The girl directly opposite me smothered a yawn and flicked her hair over her shoulder. It was intricately plaited and fell almost to her waist. The Mantis was right. I was one of the only students with cropped hair. My first day, and already I stood out like a sore thumb.

'My name's Lele ...' My voice cracked, and I had to clear my throat and start again. Someone giggled. 'My name's Lele. I live with my dad and stepmother and ...' What else was there to say?

'Thank you, Lele. And why are you joining us halfway through the year?'

'Um ... I've just moved here. My grandmother ...' I could feel tears starting to build up, and I swallowed. 'She died recently – we lived with her out in the Agriculturals – and so my brother and I were sent here to stay with my dad.'

The door at the back of the room opened, and a tall guy with a hectic mass of dreadlocks entered, letting the door slam behind him with a crash.

Comrade Xhati sighed and narrowed his eyes. 'I hope you have a good excuse, Thabo.'

The latecomer held up a piece of paper. It was impossible to tell for sure from where I was standing, but it looked like one of the pamphlets the Resurrectionists in the parade had been handing out. 'Sorry, Comrade Xhati,' he said. 'Got caught up. The cause, you know.'

Comrade Xhati nodded, but he didn't look entirely convinced. 'I see. Well, take your seat.'

The girl with the plaits whispered something to her neighbour and squirmed around in her seat to stare at the late arrival. She gave him a small flirty wave, but I couldn't see if he responded or not.

'I'm sorry for your loss,' Comrade Xhati said, reaching over and touching my hand lightly. His fingers were icy. 'But you must think of your grandmother as being in a better place.' He paused as if waiting for me to agree with him. I didn't. 'Do you have an exercise book? Something with which to write?'

I nodded, not trusting myself to speak again.

'Good,' he said. 'You'll find a seat near the back.'

The desks all looked fully occupied, but then I spied a space at the rear of the classroom that was hidden in its own pool of darkness, its lamp unlit.

I dropped my head and retraced my steps, a flurry of whispers tracking me as I walked to the back of the room:

'Are those army boots she's wearing?'

'What a freak.'

'Check out her hair!'

Careful not to catch anyone's eye, I slunk into my chair.

Comrade Xhati asked a question about the life cycle of an aphid, and the students all started writing industriously. Bending down to my bag, I pulled out my sketchbook. On the first page my best friend Thandwisa had written: *Don't let them grind you down. We love you and will miss you stacks, so don't forget us. XXXX.* Thanks to the tears welling in my eyes, the writing was blurry, but I knew the message off by heart.

Now all I had to do was to figure out how to light the lamp. I tried to attract the attention of the guy next to me, a gangly kid with taped-together glasses and furious acne, as he scrawled something on a sheet of rough paper, but he appeared to be ignoring me deliberately.

Now the tears were really building up.

'Is there a problem, Lele?' Comrade Xhati called from the front of the class.

'I'm fine,' I said as a tear escaped and crept down my cheek. I wiped it off with the back of my hand, but I could feel others waiting to take its place. I wished I could tell everyone that I wasn't crying because of them, but instead I looked down at my desk and watched as a second tear plopped down onto its varnished surfaced. I smudged it away with my finger. Another one fell onto Thand's message, but I didn't try and brush that away. Instead I watched as the R and I in 'grind' swelled and bled on the page.

I almost jumped out of my skin when I felt a tap on the back of my shoulder. It was Dreadlock Guy – Thabo, the teacher had called him. 'Here,' he whispered, handing me a box of matches. I smiled gratefully and took them out of his hand. 'First days suck,' he said.

'You got that right,' I replied, hastily wiping my wet cheeks, and hoping he wouldn't think I was lame for crying.

The first match died, but the second caught and the lamp in front of me flickered and glowed. Someone had etched *Everything's better with zombies – NOT* into the wood of my desk, and this made me smile.

I passed the matches back to Thabo. 'Thanks.'

'No worries,' he said, smiling lopsidedly at me and winking. He was cute. Very cute. High cheekbones, dark eyes, awesome hair. He was wearing an old army greatcoat over a washed-out T-shirt, but he somehow made the outfit look cool. I could feel blood rushing into my cheeks.

He leaned back in his chair, and I turned to face the front. Somehow the fact that the lamp was lit on my desk made me feel better – more connected to everyone – and the tears finally dried up.

While the other students scratched away with their pencils, I glanced around me. With the exception of Zit Face next to me, none of them wore the regulation uniform. Most appeared to be wearing denim or canvas jackets that could only have come from before the War. A couple of the girls had brightly coloured plastic beads around their necks, and some even had sparkly clips and slides stuck into their hair. I'd never seen anything like it. And there I was in my itchy grey tunic, with my agricultural enclave anti-lice haircut and my mother's boots. I couldn't have stood out more if I'd tried.

Not knowing what else to do, I flipped to one of the few free pages in my battered sketchbook and started drawing. Sometimes I do this without actually knowing what the sketch will eventually be, and this time, as I shaded and cross-hatched lines over the page, a face began to emerge. It looked just like the Rotter I'd spied outside the gate: large, fathomless eye sockets, a dark space where the nose should be and the curve of a skinless jaw. Looking up I saw Zit Face watching me, an expression of disgust on his face.

'We'll continue after break,' Comrade Xhati said. There was the clatter of chairs being pushed back, and everyone started streaming out of the door. Zit Face pushed past me, knocking his bag against my chair. He didn't apologise.

I hung back before following them out into the rain, down a narrow corridor and into a wide concreted rec area covered with a stretched tarpaulin and dotted with wooden tables and benches. Cliques of students of all ages were already gathered around the tables in the centre. I looked around for Thabo – the only person so far who'd seemed human – but couldn't see him anywhere.

I hesitated, not sure which table to head for. A couple of girls were pointedly staring at my boots, so I made an issue of glaring at them and headed for an empty bench in a corner, away from the main throng of students. The rain was beating a tattoo on the canvas above me, and a fine mist blew through the edge of the covering, but I didn't care about getting damp. I was just grateful not to be the centre of attention. Sitting down, I pulled out the roti Dad had made for me that morning. I wasn't in the slightest bit hungry, but I picked at it for something to do while I checked out the kids around me.

For Rotter-lovers, they really knew how to dress, and now that I could see them in the daylight it was clear that everyone was wearing at least something – even if it was just an accessory – from before the War. My eye kept being drawn to one guy in particular. He wore bright blue jeans that weren't even slightly faded and he'd pinned guineafowl feathers to the lapel of his denim jacket. His straightened black hair was tied into three bunches at the back of his head, and he was surrounded by a group of girls. Every time one of them spoke, they glanced at him as if seeking approval.

I had no idea how I was going to get through the day. Everyone seemed to know everyone else, and they all wore those vile Resurrectionist amulets. The cult hadn't really caught on in the Agriculturals, and I tried to imagine what Thands or my other friends would say if they could have seen me surrounded by a group of Rotter-lovers.

'Hey,' a voice said.

I looked up. Two girls stood in front of me. I recognised one of them – the girl with the plaits. Now that I was close to her I could see that her hair wasn't actually real; the plaits looked plasticky and synthetic. The other girl was about my height, short and stocky, her mouth full of large square teeth. 'I'm Summer,' Plastic Hair said. 'And this is Nyameka.'

'Hi,' I said, barely able to drag my eyes away from their clothes. Summer's jacket was a soft, pale pink satin, the stitching intricate and neat. Nyameka was wearing gorgeous, rubbery, slipper-like shoes. 'I'm Lele.'

'So, like, you just moved here, right?' Summer said.

'Looks that way,' I replied, trying to smile.

'And, is it better than your old school?'

'No.'

The two of them giggled. 'Seriously? But aren't you from the Agriculturals?'

'Yeah.'

'What's it like out there? Do you really all live in huts and stuff?'

I couldn't believe what I was hearing. 'No!'

'But you don't have, like, running water and toilets, right?'

'Of course there's running water! It's not that different from here.'

They seemed to find this hilarious.

Finally Summer managed to control herself and sat down next to me on the bench. Too close if you ask me; she reeked of garlic. 'Now, Lebo –'

'Lele.'

'Right.' (Giggle.) 'Sorry.' (Giggle.) 'You know the Lottery Ball's, like, at the end of term?'

I almost dropped my roti on the floor. I couldn't believe Summer had just mentioned the Lottery so casually. Fortunately she didn't pick up on my shock.

'And I'd really *really* appreciate it if you'd vote for me to be Queen,' she continued, handing me a pamphlet. There was a crap sketch of a sun scrawled on it, and at the bottom the words *Vote Summer for Queen!*

'Great slogan,' I said.

'What?'

'Never mind.' Detecting sarcasm clearly wasn't one of her strong points.

'All you have to do is sign your name at the bottom and post it in the ballot box in Comrade Pelosi's office.'

'So what do you win if you're Queen?'

They giggled again, which was really starting to annoy me. 'You don't actually *win* anything,' Summer said. 'It's, like, a total honour to be named Queen.'

'Why?'

'Because everyone says that then you have a better chance of getting picked.'

'You're not serious,' I said.

'What do you mean?'

She looked genuinely confused. I couldn't get my head around it. When we'd first got wind of the Lottery several years earlier, no one in the Agriculturals had taken it seriously. Most of us had assumed that it was just a crazy rumour. But what I really couldn't understand was why Summer would want to win what for all she knew was basically a death sentence (or worse). I mean, at that stage no one knew for sure what happened to those who 'won' the Lottery. Just that, for some reason, the Guardians prized teenage bodies so highly that they were willing to trade water, paper, food, building materials and even electricity for their yearly supply. I remember thinking: Was she seriously that brainwashed?

I decided it was probably best to keep my opinions to myself. I was already enough of an outsider as it was. And this was, after all, a radical Resurrectionist school. 'Where did you get your clothes?' I asked instead.

'You like?' Summer said with a flick of her hair.

'Yeah. They're cool. Is your jacket from before the War?'

Summer and Nyameka shared a look. 'Well, *ja*. Obviously.'

'So is there a shop or somewhere where they sell this stuff?'

'You really don't know?'

'I wouldn't ask if I did.'

'Well, see, if you want something you have to order it from Thabo.'

'The guy with the dreads?'

'Ja.'

They giggled again.

'So where does he get the stuff from?'

'It's a secret. He's totally connected, though.'

'Totally connected to who?'

'I don't know, but, like, if you want stuff from him it costs the *earth*.'

Nyameka stared at my hair and curled her lip, obviously thinking this would be out of my reach.

'So?' Summer said, leaning into me and totally invading my personal space. 'What do you say? Will you vote for me?'

'I'll consider it,' I said.

'Cool! What are you wearing to the Ball, by the way?'

'I'm not sure I'm going.'

They both looked appalled. ''Scuse me?' Nyameka spoke for the first time. 'Everyone at the school has to go. It's compulsory.'

'Yeah. But I'm not eligible for the Lottery.'

'Huh?'

It wasn't as if I could keep it a secret forever. 'My brother was taken.'

Nyameka looked confused. 'Taken? What do you mean?'

'He was taken by the Guardians.'

Their faces lit up. '*Seriaas?*' Nyameka asked. 'Wow! When?'

'At the beginning of the War.'

'No ways!' Summer said. 'Tell us all.' She edged even closer.

'Nothing to tell.'

'Is he like one of those kids they brought back all, you know ...'

'All what?'

'I mean, isn't he, like, retarded or freaky or something? No offence.'

'I'm really not comfortable talking about this,' I said, handing the flier back to Summer. 'Give this to someone else.'

'Chill out,' Nyameka said. 'Just because you can't win, doesn't mean that you can't vote.'

I shrugged.

Summer stood up and the two of them drifted away, heading towards the guy with the feathers. They whispered something to him, and he looked over at me, a sneer on his face. For a second our eyes met, then he turned back to the other two and said something that made Summer collapse with mirth.

I dumped the remains of the roti in the bin, appetite now completely squashed, and pulled out my sketchbook. I spent the rest of break and the whole of the afternoon adding Summer and Nyameka to the drawing of the Rotter. Not very nice of me, I know.

5

And things didn't improve.

I spent the first week stuck in my own little bubble. Not even Zit Face, the weirdo who sat next to me (who was clearly also an outsider), seemed to want anything to do with me. The mornings were the worst. I don't think I'd ever felt as alienated as I did during morning prayers. While everyone else droned away, I kept my neck bent, eyes fixed on the *Everything's better with zombies – NOT* scrawl on my desk. Everyone knew everyone else, and from what I could make out, they spent most break times gossiping about what they'd be wearing to the Lottery Ball. I was trying to build up the courage to approach Thabo, but he was more often absent than not, and even when he was at school he always seemed to be surrounded by an impenetrable posse of giggling girls.

The only person who'd spoken to me was Zyed, the guy with

the feathers, and that hadn't exactly gone well. He'd stopped at my desk one day, just before break, Summer and Nyameka hovering behind him.

'Hi,' he said. 'I'm Zyed.'

I didn't reply. I hadn't forgotten the look of contempt he'd given me on that first day.

'So,' he said. 'I was wondering. Why don't you wear the sign?'

'The what?'

Summer and Nyameka giggled. 'I can't believe she just said that!' Nyameka whispered.

Zyed touched the amulet around his neck. It looked more expensive than the others I'd seen; smaller, more intricate. 'This.'

'Not my scene,' I said, willing him away.

'What do you mean? You're not a believer?'

I shrugged, not keen to get into this particular conversation.

'I heard you're Cleo Mbane's stepkid, that right?' he asked.

'So?'

'So how come you look like you do?'

'Excuse me?'

'The hair. Can't you afford shampoo? Short hair is so ... *rural*.'

Summer and Nyameka were almost doubled over with glee at this stage.

Anger surged through me, and I clenched my fists under the desk. 'I like it like this,' I said.

'Oh, *ja*? How come?'

'I've got better things to do than spend hours messing with my hair, like some people.' I stared at his own intricate hairstyle, got to my feet and pushed past him and his adoring audience.

I pretended not to hear the words, 'Sheesh, maybe that's what you call Farm Girl chic,' that followed me out.

So school was pretty much a waking nightmare, and, apart from Jobe, home wasn't much better. So much so that I'd taken to walking home instead of going by rickshaw, dragging my feet to make the journey last as long as possible, ignoring the jeers from the market traders and hawkers. I was getting to know the sector of the city where we lived quite well now, but it didn't make me loathe it any less. I spent most of my time in my room, sketching and daydreaming, doing my best to keep a low profile and avoid one of the Mantis's lectures. She'd finally accepted that I wasn't going to be thanking the Guardians every time I sat down to eat, but the atmosphere at the dinner table wasn't exactly a bundle of laughs. And my loathing wasn't just restricted to the Mantis. Dad agreed with everything the Mantis said, as if he was some kind of wimpy non-person. I remember wondering if maybe the Mantis fed on his soul every night, sucking out his life like a vampire. Or if maybe he'd lost his guts when he'd lost his arm.

Worst of all I was no closer to coming up with a plan to get Jobe and myself out of the city enclave. For a day or so, especially after my run-in with Zyed, I even considered dropping out of school and joining the breeders. But I seriously couldn't imagine myself pushing out babies for the rest of my life.

But at least, I thought, I was flying under the radar.

I couldn't have been more wrong.

6

I arrived one morning to find the classroom buzzing with excitement. I'd tried to dawdle on my way to school and miss the prayers, but it looked as if the ritual had been abandoned. Even Comrade Xhati was distracted: he was busy cleaning the board at the front of the room and didn't even sigh with irritation when I came in late.

'What's going on?' I asked Zit Face.

'There's going to be an announcement.'

'About what?'

He opened his mouth to answer, but then Acid Face Pelosi and a tall man I hadn't seen before strode into the room. The man was dressed in a spotless black suit, and even in the poor light his shoes shone. Acid Face Pelosi was reverentially carrying a large book bound in black material, a smug smile almost cutting her face in half. As they made their way to the front to join Comrade Xhati, Thabo slid into the classroom. As he collapsed into his chair I turned my head to smile at him: he hadn't been in class for days and I'd missed him. He winked back at me and my stomach flipped.

'Attention everyone!' Acid Face Pelosi said, her voice ringing around the room. 'We have a very important visitor. Please welcome Comrade Nkosi, the embassy's new CEO. He has an announcement for you.'

She smiled at the newcomer and he stepped forward, clearing his throat as he did so and gazing unhurriedly around the room. 'Thank you, Comrade Pelosi, for that warm welcome,' he finally said. 'How wonderful to see so many young and eager faces in front of me.' Confidence blasted out of his every pore, and he spoke slowly, in the manner of someone who was used to being listened to. Every eye was fixed on him, and I'd never heard the classroom so quiet – even during morning prayers. 'Now, I'm sure most of you can guess why I'm here, and I'm not going to keep you in suspense. Thanks to the efforts of my comrades in the embassy, the Guardians have agreed to begin the transition, so that electricity can be brought to the enclave.'

There was a collective gasp, and he nodded in approval. 'Yes, my friends. And soon, every person, every household, will have access to warmth in winter, running water all year round, lighting and all the benefits a civilised society can bring.'

The excited murmuring rose again, and then stopped as Comrade Nkosi held up a hand.

'But there is a price to be paid for this, as you know.' He paused again and clasped his hands in front of him. 'It is a price that many of you, as good and true believers are happy to pay, but it is a price nonetheless. This year, brothers and sisters, there will be five Lottery winners, and three will be chosen from this school – the jewel of the enclave.'

This time the gasp was much louder. Everyone began to turn around in their seats to whisper to each other. Most looked excited, some even overjoyed. I wished I could have turned around to check out Thabo's expression, but that would have been way too obvious. Next to me, Zit Face was looking down at his desk, and his hands were shaking slightly. I tried to catch his eye, but he didn't look up.

Acid Face Pelosi clapped her hands for silence, but she was still wearing a wide grin.

'I wish you all the best of luck,' Comrade Nkosi said as the noise died away. 'And may I say, on behalf of the city and all its people, thank you.'

The room erupted into applause. I shoved my fists under the desk and squeezed them tightly as Comrade Nkosi strode towards the door on a tide of cheers and applause. I wanted to stand up and scream. I wanted to yell that what he'd just said was madness, insanity. But of course I didn't.

Acid Face Pelosi waited for the applause to die down before she clapped her own hands for attention.

'Isn't that just wonderful news?' she said. 'What an honour for the school!' She beamed at the students in the front row. 'And I have some more wonderful news for you.' She handed the book she was hefting to Comrade Xhati. 'We received this from the embassy's education department this morning. It's your new history syllabus!'

The reaction to this piece of news wasn't so jubilant. In fact, there were quite a few groans to be heard.

'Thank you, Comrade,' Comrade Xhati said. 'I'll take it from here.'

Acid Face Pelosi's nauseating grin faded, and sour-faced once again, she also made her exit.

The minute she was gone, the room erupted into a cacophony

of giggling, but Comrade Xhati wasn't having any of that. 'Silence!' he barked. 'You can discuss this wonderful news at break. Now, much as I'm sure you're all eager to explore the new history syllabus, we must complete yesterday's maths lesson.'

While he rambled on, I pulled out my sketchbook and started drawing. I was feeling antsy – my stomach a tight knot. I knew I wasn't eligible for the Lottery, but it was sickening to think that most of the students thought this was a cause for celebration. I concentrated on breathing steadily and let my pencil find its own way across the page. This time the drawing didn't morph into the face of the Rotter outside the fence, but slowly showed itself to be the Guardian's horse that had almost trampled me after the funeral.

'Hey!' Thabo whispered behind me. I jumped. I'd been lost in the drawing and my thoughts. 'Can I see?' he asked.

'See what?'

'Duh,' he said, grinning. 'What you're drawing.'

Reluctantly I passed the book back to him. He studied the sketch for what felt like way too long. I began to squirm, worried that he thought it was crap.

He finally looked up at me. 'It's amazing.' He sounded like he meant it.

'Thanks,' I said.

'You're really talented.'

I shrugged. 'Not really. I just enjoy it.'

'Wish I could do something like that.'

'Thabo!' Comrade Xhati's voice blasted our way. 'Do you have a problem with Lele?'

'No problem,' Thabo said. 'No problem at all, actually.'

Giggles erupted around us again and I felt my face growing hot.

'So you won't mind sharing what you were saying to her with the rest of the class, then, will you?'

'I do mind,' Thabo said. 'It was a private conversation.'

There was a gasp of shock and I had to bite down on my bottom lip to stop myself from grinning.

Comrade Xhati flinched, and a flinty edge entered his voice. 'I see. I wasn't aware that private conversations were part of the school curriculum. I was under the impression that this was a maths lesson.'

Thabo shrugged. 'That's your problem,' he muttered.

'What was that?' Comrade Xhati said.

'Nothing,' Thabo replied.

'And I suppose you were far too involved in your private conversation to tell me the answer to the maths question I just asked?'

By now almost everyone had turned around in their chairs, craning their necks in Thabo's direction.

Thabo sat back in his chair, stretched his arms behind his head and yawned.

'I'm waiting,' Comrade Xhati snapped.

Thabo grinned his lopsided grin, and let the seconds stretch on. 'Seven to the power of ten,' he said.

Comrade Xhati blinked. 'What?'

'Seven to the power of ten. That's the answer to your last question.'

I couldn't help but smile, but no one else dared to react. For a second Comrade Xhati seemed to focus his fierce black eyes on me, but then he turned back to the blackboard and began to wipe it furiously.

'That is correct,' he eventually said, his back still to the class.

Comrade Xhati seemed to take far longer than was necessary to clean the board. Finally, he cleared his throat, grabbed the black book that Acid Face Pelosi had been carrying and held it up. 'Who would like to read the introduction out to the class?'

I ducked my head and flipped to the last clean page of my sketchbook as a flurry of hands shot into the air.

'Lele!' Comrade Xhati called. 'We haven't heard much from you in class. Why don't you come forward?'

My heart sank. Zit Face and the kids sitting nearest to me all turned around in their chairs and stared at me as I closed my sketchbook and got to my feet. As I clumped my way down to the front of the class, Zyed whispered something to Summer and they both sniggered.

Comrade Xhati handed the book to me. It was way heavier than I was expecting, and I almost dropped it. The fabric that bound it was slippery and padded, as if the book was coated in flesh.

'Where shall I start?' I asked.

'The introduction please, Lele.'

The book's pages were thicker than normal paper, and the ink looked globular and almost wet.

I flipped through it. On the first page there was a pen and ink sketch of a group of people encircling a sun with jagged rays poking out from it. The caption below the drawing read *The Dawning of a New Age*. The next page was filled with a grainy photograph of a distraught teenager carrying a blood-caked child wearing a school uniform in his arms. The photo looked familiar, but I couldn't remember where I'd seen it before. I scanned the print beneath it:

> *The terrible death of Hector Peterson during the height of apartheid. Sights such as this were a daily occurrence in the 'bad old days', when violence, destruction, injustice and cruelty ravaged the land. The aim of this New History is to ensure that we learn from our mistakes.*

'We're waiting, Lele,' Comrade Xhati said.

I took a deep breath and started reading: 'Is there another country in the world with such a shameful History as South Africa? The authors of this book believe that there is not. Before the War, South Africa was a mess of violence, extreme poverty, HIV infection, incest, child abuse, terrorism and murder.'

I scanned the rest of the paragraph, barely believing what I was reading.

'Lele! Read *aloud*, please,' Comrade Xhati snapped.

My arms were beginning to ache from the weight of the book, but that was nothing compared to the unease I was feeling. However, I didn't have much choice but to continue: 'Fortunately, salvation was at hand. When the Reanimates rose, and started adding other saved souls to their flock, the Guardians who came among us decreed that the remaining chosen would be taken care of, all the better to look forward to their reward in Heaven on Earth. This is a True History of our glorious new beginning, as we look back at the past injustices rife in a society fragmented and torn, and consider how fortunate we as a United Race have been to be allowed to flourish under the watchful eyes of our Fathers and Mothers, the Guardians. How can we compare Life before our Salvation ...' My voice trailed away. I didn't remember much about the War and its immediate aftermath, but I did know that it wasn't a great big mash-up of love, happiness and rainbows.

'Lele?' Comrade Xhati said. 'Is there a problem? Please, read on.'

'I can't.'

He blinked. 'What do you mean, you can't? Do you feel unwell?'

'No ... it's just ...' The sniggering had stopped and I could feel the weight of everyone's eyes on me. 'Um, Comrade. This is a rewriting of history.'

'This is your government set book, Lele.'

'But Comrade Xhati – seriously – even I know this isn't … right.'

'I see.' He smiled at me, although his eyes were cold. 'Would you like to tell us *your* version of history, then?'

'Not really,' I said, and the room erupted into laughter.

'Silence!' Comrade Xhati roared. The giggles trailed away. 'Please, Lele. We're all waiting.' The hard edge was back in his voice.

Zyed was staring at me, toying with one of the feathers on his jacket. He looked like he was enjoying himself.

I'd made a terrible mistake, but there was no going back. 'I don't know where to start,' I said.

'Well, Lele, I think you should start with your version of why the War started in the first place.'

'But Comrade Xhati, no one really knows why the dead –'

'Do your best, Lele.'

'Well … something – some kind of parasite or whatever – came from the sky or from an asteroid or whatever –'

Someone in the classroom snorted.

'Silence!' Comrade Xhati snapped.

'– and it wormed its way into the bodies of the dead, bringing them back to life. It happened slowly at first, but the more people died, the more bodies there were, until eventually the dead began to show themselves and started attacking us. Then the Guardians came, and they kept the Rotters away while –'

'We don't use that term here, Lele,' Comrade Xhati said.

'Huh?'

'Rotters. We don't use that pejorative term.'

'Okay. Sorry. Well, the Guardians came and they kept the … Reanimates in check while the enclaves were built.'

'I see. And why do you think this happened, Lele?' Comrade Xhati's voice was soft and he even sounded mildly interested, but his eyes were still cold.

'No one really knows for sure, do they? I mean, it could be like, aliens, or some sort of virus, or ... I don't know. No one knows.'

'Aliens,' Comrade Xhati said, shaking his head in disbelief. 'But surely, Lele, you do agree that life is better for all of us in Cape Town now that the Guardians watch over us? Now that we have been given a fresh start, a clean slate as it were?'

'No!'

The room erupted again as everyone started whispering to each other at once. This time Comrade Xhati didn't tell them to keep quiet.

'Thank you, Lele,' he said. 'You can sit down now.'

He didn't speak again until I reached my seat. No one was sniggering now and no one caught my eye, not even Thabo.

'So,' Comrade Xhati said, voice ringing around the classroom. 'Does anyone else agree with Lele's interpretation?'

No one spoke up.

Zit Face nudged me and pushed his exercise book towards me. Across it he'd written *BAD MOVE* in large looping letters.

7

I don't remember much about the rest of the afternoon. After break, Summer carried on reading from the history book, but I tuned out. I didn't even feel like sketching, and I passed the time reading and re-reading the slogan scored into my desk.

Everything's better with zombies – NOT
Everything's better with zombies – NOT
Everything's better with zombies – NOT
Everything's better with zombies – NOT

I'd screwed up big time – and I knew it.

The hours dragged on and on until, finally, the torturous afternoon limped to an end. I gathered my stuff together as fast as possible, but Comrade Xhati wasn't going to let me off that easily. 'Lele?' he called as I swung my bag onto my shoulder. 'Could you stay behind for a few minutes?'

My heart plummeted.

'Just agree with him,' someone whispered in my ear.

I turned around. Thabo was leaning so close to me that I could feel his breath on my cheek. 'Trust me,' he said. 'Just play their game.' Then he stood up and left the classroom without looking back.

Zyed and Summer stalked past me, smirking, but I ignored them.

'Lele,' Comrade Xhati said, approaching my desk as the classroom emptied out. 'I don't think I have to tell you that I'm very disappointed in you.'

I opened my mouth to tell him to stick it, but then I remembered Thabo's advice. 'I'm sorry,' I said.

He wasn't expecting that, and his expression softened slightly. He sat down on the edge of Zit Face's desk. 'I understand that you've been to one of those,' he waved his hand vaguely in the air around his head, 'rural schools. That you lived your formative years out in the Agriculturals, is that correct?'

I nodded.

'And no doubt that's where you formed your ... views on the Guardians?'

I nodded again.

'You see, you might not remember much about life before the War. But those of my generation do. Life was hard back then – the poor ravaged by drugs and HIV, the rich living empty worthless lives fuelled by nothing but lust for material possessions. The government riddled with corruption and greed. It was no way to live. The coming of the Reanimates changed all that.' His spiel had a practised ring to it. 'Don't you see that things are so much better now that we have the chance to start over?'

I wanted to say: *Sure. Trapped in a muddy, stinking prison, surrounded by a sea of dead people and ruled by a bunch of hysterical nutters, that's so much better than before. Not.* But of course I didn't say that. 'You're right, Comrade Xhati,' I lied. 'It does make much more sense.'

But he wasn't that stupid. 'You're not just spinning me a line, are you, Lele?'

Time to backtrack. 'It's just ... the way you've explained it. It does make sense. I probably feel – felt – the way I do about the Guardians because of my brother.'

'Your brother?'

'He was one of the children taken by the Guardians during the War. And when he returned ... What they did to him ... Well, he wasn't the same. He'd changed.' I considered trying to cry, but decided against it. I didn't want to overdo it.

'Ah. I see.' Comrade Xhati stood up, and I breathed a secret sigh of relief. He leaned towards me and put a hand on my shoulder. 'I didn't know.'

I nodded, wanting nothing more than to shrug his hand away. I bit the inside of my cheek to stop myself from saying anything stupid.

'Your parents are Resurrectionists, of course.'

I nodded, still not trusting myself to speak.

'You must honour them, Lele. Follow their lead. Leave your old beliefs behind and embrace the new. It's easier this way. More fulfilling.' He finally took his hand from my shoulder. 'Are we clear on this?' he asked.

'Oh, yes,' I said. 'Crystal clear.'

'Good.' He nodded, turned, and then hesitated. He held my gaze for several seconds, his stare so intense that I started to sweat. 'Look, Lele. You must understand, I am not a stupid man. Much as I am grateful to be part of our new beginning, sometimes I find myself missing things from before.'

So he *was* human after all. 'What things?' I asked.

He smiled sadly and shrugged. 'It doesn't matter.'

I'd really like to know.'

'Books, mostly. You know that before the War I was a professor of literature?'

'No. I didn't know.'

'Yes. Poetry was my specialty.' He shook his head and straightened his back. 'But that is not important. You will try to honour your parents' beliefs?'

I nodded.

'Good! Then, you may go.'

I was almost out of there before he spoke again. 'Oh, and Lele!' he called. 'Choose your friends wisely.'

Of course, later on, I found out exactly what he meant by that.

When I arrived home, brain buzzing with the day's events, Dad was on his way out of the house. It was strange to see him without the Mantis hovering behind him.

'Lele.' He nodded at me as if we were just acquaintances instead of father and daughter. 'School okay?'

I shrugged. 'Dad, can I ask you a question?'

'Sure.'

'Do you really believe life is better now?'

'What do you mean?'

'Was life really so bad before the Rotters came?'

He shrugged. 'There were problems, yes. Violence, of course. HIV. Unemployment. Drugs. Poverty.'

He sounded like one of the crap pamphlets the Resurrectionists handed out at their rallies. 'So you're saying that you really believe we're better off? I mean, even though we can't leave the enclave, and with the Lottery and everything?'

He plucked at the empty arm of his jacket. 'In some ways, yes.'

'But how can you say that after Mom ... And after what the Guardians did to Jobe!'

He sighed. 'There is always a price to pay, Lele.'

'What kind of answer is that?'

'I have to go,' he said.

'Where to?'

'I'm on fence patrol tonight.'

I shivered. News of the city's Rotter break-in four years earlier had reached the Agriculturals, and the thought of it had given me nightmares ever since. A pack of Rotters had slipped through a hole in the fence at the far reaches of the city and gone on a killing spree before the Guardians finally showed up and stopped them.

'Checking to see the Rotters don't break in?' I said.

Dad sighed. 'Don't let your mother hear you calling them that, Lele.'

'She's not my mother.'

He sighed again. 'I must go. I'm going to be late.'

I watched him walk away, shoulders hunched like a far older man, before heading for my room.

Jobe and Chinwag were already snoozing on my bed, curled up together, Jobe's hand lightly clasping the kitten's front paw. Carefully, so as not to wake them, I got down on my hands and knees and rummaged under the bed for Gran's old leather suitcase. It was filled with the stuff she'd managed to salvage during the War. Unzipping it, I lifted out the dress that was folded on top – the one Mom had worn when she and Dad had gone to their Matric dance a million years earlier. It was made of shiny emerald green material that caught the light and seemed to shimmer like a reflection on water. It was no longer wearable, the fabric had given way to time in places, but it still smelled very faintly of perfume and smoke – my mother's scent. That was all I had of her. No memories; I couldn't remember her at all, not even a little bit. I didn't even have a photograph of her as they'd all been destroyed in the fire that had ravaged the city.

I dug out my old history book, and climbed onto the bed next to Jobe. He muttered something in his sleep, but I couldn't make out the words clearly. Then he snuggled closer to Chinwag, and his eyelids flickered as if he was dreaming.

I paged through to my favourite section – the first-person anecdotes. The first one was the story of Jacob White, the guy who had worked in the city morgue. He'd been one of the first to discover the reanimated corpses. No one had believed Jacob at first, thought he was on drugs and seeing things, and he'd only managed to get away at the last minute, climbing through the narrow window in the morgue toilets after being trapped in a stall for hours. Next there was the account of a rich businesswoman who'd evaded the dead for two weeks, sealed in the living room of her Camps Bay mansion, living off tins of asparagus and packets of cashew nuts, the reanimated corpses of her chauffeur and housekeeper moaning at her from outside the locked door. Some were too awful to read again, like the eyewitness account of someone who had seen a group of religious fanatics rushing out to greet the dead, convinced that this was the coming of the Rapture, only to be turned into more walking corpses. Or the stories of the mass suicides that had taken place in the wealthy suburbs and the unstoppable fires that had raged through Langa and Gugulethu, destroying the dead and living alike.

I flipped through to my favourite story.

Name: Levi Sole
Occupation: Schoolchild
Age: 14
Nationality: Malawian
NOTE: *Levi was questioned three months after he and his father were relocated to the Cape Town city enclave. His story begins after they were rescued from the informal settlement fires that raged through the city two days after the dead started rising.*

After the fire started, we escaped to the big soccer stadium. All around us the city burned; even the mountain was on fire. The smoke was so thick in the air that many of us were struggling to breathe. And the air was hot, like it was the middle of summer. But the heavy smoke meant that we did not have to see the horrible things on the roads. I mean, I was trying to be brave. I was too old to be scared, but I was glad for the smoke. Already I had seen my neighbour struck down, her stomach spilling from between her fingers, and then, as she stood up again, her eyes rolled back in her head as if she was mad. And with her guts outside her body, she walked away. Impossible things were happening.

When we arrived at the stadium my father and I spent many hours looking around for my brother, but he had been taken away on one of the other buses, and we could not find him.

We never found him.

There were so many of us! Most, like me, came from Khayelitsha; others from all over Cape Town. There were white people, black people, coloured people, refugees like us from Zimbabwe, the DRC and Malawi, rich tourists who had come out here for the World Cup soccer, old people, children, babies (some without mothers), sick people and the dying. We stayed there for three weeks, fighting off the Dead Ones who managed to break in. Many of us died. But the Dead Ones weren't our only problem. We had very little food and water, and the smell of the toilets was terrible. It was bad, and many got sick. And then, just when we thought we would starve to death, just when some were saying that they would kill themselves, the first of the Guardians came to us. We didn't know what to think of them at first. Whether to trust them or not. We knew, in our hearts, that they were not people like us, but they did not try to kill us like the Dead Ones. They wore robes like priests and did not speak to us. But they brought us food. There were many fights at first over the food, but those who caused trouble were taken away quickly. At first people called them the Shepherds, as they would guard us from the Dead Ones, as if we were sheep. But then people started to call them the Guardians.

Then we were moved out of the city, and the stadium was destroyed. Some were taken far away, to the agricultural enclaves, but me and my father, we were brought to what was to become the city enclave. At first we did not recognise where we were. The ground was black and burned, the buildings and many of the trees were gone. Then we realised! We were back in Khayelitsha! The first thing we did was try to find our old house, but nothing was the same.

At first life was like being back in the refugee camps, like the one my father and I came to when we left Malawi for the first time, and where we were sent for a short time in Messina. We all had to camp together in these very large army tents and those who were not injured were sent to work. I was sent to work building the fence – which was small at first, not like it is today. After all this time, I do not know if the fence was created to keep us in, or to keep the dead out. But either way, I was helping to build a prison, of that I am sure.

Some say it is aliens that made the dead wake up. Or maybe it was an angry god or demons. Just like some say that it is God who sent the Guardians to save us. Like I have said, I have seen many terrible things during this time and life will never be as it was. You see –

My door creaked open, and I quickly shoved the book under my pillow.

'Are you awake, Leletia?' The Mantis entered the room.

'Yeah,' I said.

'Were you reading something?' she asked. She never missed a trick.

'Just history homework,' I said.

'I see. And why would you want to hide that?'

Crap. I had to think fast. 'I thought you'd be angry if you saw I was still awake?'

'But it's still early. And you didn't eat supper.'

'Not hungry.'

'Everything okay at school?'

'Fine.'

She was looking slightly antsy about something, which wasn't like her at all. 'The embassy is showing a film tomorrow evening,' she said. 'I thought it would be nice if all of us went together.'

What she meant was that it would look weird if I didn't show my face – I knew she wanted everyone to think we were some sort of happy family.

'Okay,' I said. The thought of seeing a movie again was too much of a temptation to resist.

'Wonderful!' she smiled at me. She didn't look like such a bitch when she smiled.

'Is that it?' I asked.

'Leletia, it would mean so much to your father if we could just get along.'

'Okay,' I said, remembering Thabo's advice from earlier in the day to 'play their game'. 'That's fine by me.'

The look of shocked surprise on her face almost made the lie worth it. But now there was something else on my mind. The thought of Thabo had made my stomach do that swooping thing. I remembered the feel of his breath on my cheek and his cute lopsided grin. And sometimes, I wasn't absolutely sure, but sometimes I thought I could sense him looking at me.

'Cleo? Can I ask you a question?'

'Sure.'

This was embarrassing. 'How do you know if someone likes you?'

'What do you mean, Lele? You mean, like a boy?'

'Or a girl.'

She started slightly, but her smile didn't slip. 'I think the question you should ask yourself is if *you* like ... this person,' she said. She touched the area just below her ribs. 'You feel it here. Your stomach dances, and if it lasts for more than a week, then you could have something special.'

'Okaaaay,' I said. 'But what if he – or she – likes you. How can you tell?'

'You can see it in their eyes. They flicker. Like a light going on.' The Mantis's voice had become almost dreamy, and for a couple of seconds I thought I could actually see what it was Dad saw in her.

'Is that how you felt when you met Dad?' I asked.

'Yes,' she said simply.

'Thanks,' I said, faking a yawn. There was no way we were going to get all pally-pally suddenly. She could forget that idea. 'I should get some sleep.'

'Sure,' she said. 'Good night, Leletia – Lele.'

She crept out, closing the door softly behind her. As soon

as she was gone I pulled the book out from underneath the pillow and turned back to the page I had been reading. One day, I thought, I'd like to meet the guy who wrote this story. Go up to him and say, thanks. Thanks for being honest and not messing with the truth.

9

I had a lot to think about on the walk to school the next day, although if I'm honest I mostly thought about Thabo. I tried to convince myself that there was no way he'd ever look at me in that way, not when he could have his pick of the girls in class, but there was still a tiny kernel of hope that refused to die.

I was so lost in my daydreams that I almost walked straight past the crowd that had gathered around the gate. Acid Face Pelosi and several of the older students were speaking in low voices, tutting and shaking their heads. Then I saw it.

The words *ANZ: Red not Dead* had been spray-painted over the Malema High sign, the red letters completely obscuring the *breath of fresh air* motto.

Acid Face Pelosi caught sight of me. 'Don't dawdle, Leletia. Get inside!'

I secretly gave her the finger as she turned her back on me.

Once inside, I headed towards the sun sculpture. I could make out a thatch of dreadlocks above the heads of the students crowded around it. Thabo would know what was going on. But, as usual, he was surrounded by a bunch of girls, and I couldn't summon up the nerve to approach him.

I wandered over to Zit Face instead. 'What's happening?' I asked him.

He shrugged and pushed his glasses up his nose. 'What do you think? The ANZ are up to their old tricks again.'

I nodded as if I knew what he was talking about, but at that stage I hadn't even heard of the ANZ, let alone any of the tricks they got up to.

Acid Face Pelosi and Comrade Xhati strode towards us, serious expressions on their faces. 'School will begin ten minutes later today,' Acid Face Pelosi said. 'There will be no morning prayers.'

I couldn't stop the smile that spread across my face and Acid Face Pelosi scowled. 'No need to look so pleased with yourself, Leletia,' she snapped as the two of them stalked off towards the office.

'Farm Girl probably did it,' a familiar voice said behind me.

I whirled around. 'What was that?' I asked Zyed. 'What did you just call me?'

'Farm Girl,' Zyed said. 'Baaaaa.'

But I wasn't going to let Zyed get away with dissing me again. 'Get lost, Zyed. Go and pluck some feathers or something.'

Zyed smiled at me. A nasty, cold smile. 'At least I don't look as if I just fell off a vegetable wagon.'

'No. You look like you just lost a fight with a flock of guineafowl.'

Several of the kids around us laughed, and Zyed's smile slipped from his face. 'Why don't you go back to where you came from, Farm Girl?'

'Farm Girl? Is that the best you can do? That's really original.'

Zyed whispered something to Nyameka and Summer, who responded with their usual giggling fit.

'Oh, I see how it is,' I said, aware that part of me was now actually enjoying this. My heart was thumping in my chest, but it wasn't an unpleasant feeling. 'You don't have the guts to say what you've got to say to my face.'

My voice was getting louder and I began to realise that the pack of kids around us had stopped chattering and laughing.

'Why would I bother wasting my breath on someone like you?' Zyed said.

'You tell me, Zyed. You're the one that seems to have a problem with me. What did I ever do to you?'

He shook his head in disgust. 'You're not even a believer,' he said. 'You don't belong here.'

'I don't *want* to belong here,' I said. 'You call me Farm Girl, but you lot are the sheep.' I jumped in again before Zyed had a chance to speak. 'And in this school, I see that even the bitches run in packs. All three of them.'

He flinched. 'What that supposed to mean?'

'You know what I mean, Zyed.'

Summer and Nyameka looked slightly confused – my crack had obviously gone right over their heads – but Zyed knew what I meant. The thing was, I'd already sussed him out. It wasn't the feathers. It wasn't the hair. It was the way his eyes followed Thabo whenever he was around. That's the thing about being an outsider: you notice things others don't see.

It didn't take him long to regain his composure, though. He flicked his hair and smiled that cruel smile. 'You really want to know what I was saying about you?'

'If you've got the guts to repeat it.'

'I was just saying, it must run in the family.'

'What are you talking about?'

'Do I need to spell it out for you, Farm Girl? I heard your brother's one of those freaky reject kids. Being a retard must be in the genes.'

The bolt of fury that jolted through me almost took my breath away; the mention of Jobe tipping me over the edge. Before I was even aware of what I was doing, I'd grabbed Zyed by the lapels of his jacket, and shoved him back against the sculpture. He was taller than me, but he was no match for the rage that surged through my veins. 'You are so going to regret saying that,' I yelled at him.

I raised my fist, planning to punch Zyed on the nose, but someone caught hold of my arm, and I felt myself being dragged backwards. 'You don't want to do that,' a voice hissed in my ear. I struggled free and swung around. It was Thabo.

Zyed was smoothing the front of his jacket, and I felt a surge of triumph at his shocked expression. Summer and Nyameka looked equally traumatised.

'Come on!' Thabo said, grabbing my arm and pulling me towards the gate.

'Huh?'

'We're getting out of here.'

He dropped my arm and strode off. Zyed shot me a hate-filled glance as he and his clan started heading towards the office.

Thabo paused and turned around. 'Well?' he said. 'You coming or not?'

This time I didn't hesitate.

10

'Where are we going?' I asked Thabo, struggling to keep up with his long strides.

'Away from this place.'

'Won't we get into trouble?'

'Yeah,' he said with a grin. 'By the way, nice moves back there, Ninja Girl. You're way stronger than you look.'

'What's a ninja?' I asked.

He chuckled. 'You got anything to eat?'

'Yeah,' I dug in my bag and handed him a roti.

'Thanks, hey!' he said, ripping into it. 'This is good. Your mom make it?'

'My mom's dead.'

'Snap.'

He ducked behind a stall selling Resurrectionist amulets and I followed him through a narrow covered alleyway that reeked of drains and stale cooking. It led straight into a partially tarred square, ringed with half-constructed buildings. A couple of workmen glanced at us curiously, but most of them ignored us.

'Down here,' Thabo said, leading me down another foul-smelling alleyway.

We emerged into a familiar thoroughfare, one of the busy market streets I'd explored on one of my journeys home. The market was doing a roaring trade, but then the crowd cleared and I caught sight of two robed Resurrectionists handing out pamphlets.

Thabo grinned at me. 'Watch this.'

He raced up behind one of the Resurrectionists and pulled the hood down off his head, revealing long hair and a bright pink face. 'Hey!' the Resurrectionist shouted.

Thabo grabbed his pamphlets, threw them up into the air and, with another cheeky glance at me, set off running. Hardly able to believe what I'd just seen I raced after him.

He ducked into a narrow street and I hared after him. But I couldn't see him anywhere. He'd disappeared.

'Lele! Over here!'

I caught sight of his head poking out from behind a wooden dumpster. He was sitting in the shadowy space behind it.

I crawled in and sat down next to him. 'Phew,' I said. 'It stinks here.'

'You'll get used to it. At least it's out of the rain.'

He was right; the dumpster's open lid, which was resting against the wall, formed a makeshift roof.

'Did you see those Resurrectionists' faces?' he asked. 'Dumb-asses.'

'But ... I thought you were a believer?' I pointed to the amulet around his neck.

'I told you, Lele. Got to play their game.'

'And how much trouble will we be in? At school, I mean.'

'Don't worry about it.'

'But Zyed –'

'Don't worry about him. There's no way he'll want to rehash that fight.' He looked at me meaningfully. 'But you shouldn't have said that, Lele. Implied that ...'

'That he liked boys? So what? What's the big deal?'

'It is a big deal. Don't you know that the Resurrectionists are against same-sex relationships?'

'But why?'

'Think about it. They need us to breed, right? Keep the Guardians happy.'

My heart sank. Zyed was a vicious little snipe, no doubt, but I was suddenly overwhelmed with mortification.

'Don't beat yourself up,' Thabo said. 'He gave as good as he got.' He leaned back against the wall, putting his legs up against the side of the dumpster. 'So, you're from the Agriculturals?'

'Yeah.'

'So you've been outside the enclave?'

'I guess.'

His eyes lit up with excitement. 'Through the Deadlands. Wow! I've never been outside. What was it like?'

'I didn't see anything.'

'You must have seen something. Like, are the Deadlands totally overgrown now? You see any buildings?'

'Seriously, Thabo. They brought us here at night, and the wagon had high wooden sides. You know, to stop the Rotters ...'

I'd tried to push the memory of that journey out of my mind. Jobe, Chinwag and I squashed in with the other travellers in the pitch dark, trying not to think about Gran's body stored on the roof with the others sent back to the city for 'burial'. The wagon shook and jolted along for hours – the moans of the Rotters keeping us company; the occasional terrifying thunk as something large hurled itself against the slatted wooded sides. Everyone praying that the wood wouldn't splinter; that one of us wouldn't be snatched outside before the anonymous Guardians ferrying us had a chance to intervene. I shuddered at the thought.

'You cold?' Thabo asked.

'I'm fine. So, Thabo, if you're not a Resurrectionist, what are you doing at the school?'

'The guy who adopted me after my folks died sent me here. Thought it would straighten me out. He works at the embassy.'

'So does my stepmother!'

'Seriously? So how come you look like you do?' Heat rushed to my cheeks. 'Sorry, I didn't mean –'

'It's fine. I haven't had time to conform yet,' I said, looking down at my boots to hide my hot face.

Out of the corner of my eye, I checked out his clothes. He was wearing a pair of spotless black jeans and a pair of Converse trainers that looked barely broken in.

'Thabo, Summer said that you were the person to talk to about getting clothes and stuff, you know, from before the War?'

'Ah.' He gave me that lopsided grin again.

'So where do you get the stuff from?'

He tapped the side of his nose. 'My little secret.'

'Oh, come on, who am I going to tell?'

He shrugged. 'It's not that hectic a secret anyway.'

'So? Go on, then.'

'The black market, of course. Out in New Arrivals.'

'Where's that?'

'You don't know New Arrivals? On the other side of the enclave? Back behind the factories? Sheesh, it's not as if you could miss it ... You really are from the Agriculturals, aren't you?' I bristled at this, but did my best to hide it. 'It's where they made the first settlement. Most of the workers live there.'

'Right. But won't you get into trouble selling the stuff?'

He shrugged. 'The Resurrectionists turn a blind eye to it, Lele. After all, where do you think they get their fancy clothes?'

He leaned towards me suddenly, and for a second I thought he was about to kiss me. My heart leapt into my throat and I found myself blushing again. But he was reaching across me to grab my bag.

'Hey! What are you ...?'

He rummaged in it and pulled out my sketchbook.

'No ways!' I said, trying to snatch it out his hand.

'Let me see, come on, it's only fair,' he said, holding it above his head, out of my reach. 'I told you about my sideline.'

'Okay,' I said, pretending to be annoyed. I watched his face as he flicked through the drawings, pausing to snort at one of the Rotters attacking Summer and Nyameka.

'Wow, Lele, these are amazing! Really! That's what you want to be? An artist?'

I shrugged. 'Not many trade credits in art.'

He pulled a pamphlet out of his pocket and smoothed out its wrinkles. It showed the same terrible drawing of the child with the huge head, staring up at the sun. 'I don't know. You seen this? Looks like it was drawn by a three-year-old.' He scrumpled it up and lobbed it up into the dumpster. 'You could do way better than that.'

'And you? What do you want to be?' I asked. 'You going to work at the embassy?'

'No ways! I have my own plans.'

'Well? What are they?'

He looked at me sideways. 'Can I trust you?'

I nodded.

'I want to join the Mall Rats.' He sat back to check out my reaction.

'The what rats?'

I waited for him to make fun of me again, but he just shrugged. 'Most people think they're just some kind of rumour.'

'So what are they?'

'They're amazing. They, like, go outside the enclave, scavenging for stuff from before the War. Can you imagine? I mean, Lele, they go out into the old city!'

'There's nothing left of the city.'

'There must be.' He gave me a look. 'Where do you think the clothes come from?'

'So you've seen them?'

'No. But my contact in New Arrivals has.'

'But how do they get through the Deadlands? What about the Rotters?' The image of the rotten thing scrabbling towards me after the funeral popped into my head. And that was just one of the thousands out there.

He shrugged. 'They're like this awesome band of hard-core War veterans. You have to train for years before they'll accept you.'

'And are they part of the ANC?'

He snorted with laughter. 'A, N, Z, Lele. Zee, not Cee. You do know what it stands for, right?'

'Um . . .'

'Sheesh, girl. Anti-Zombians, of course. You know, the Resurrectionists being the Zombians – zombie lovers. Duh.'

'Okay, okay, you don't have to rub it in. But what do they *do*?'

'They're the only ones who spoke out when the Resurrectionists stopped being some weird cult and started gaining power. They're underground now, of course.' I was doing my best to follow this, and he chuckled again. 'You really don't 'know anything, do you?'

'Maybe not. But I know enough to know that I've got to get out of this place.'

And then it all spilled out. About how I needed to get away; about how my plan was to find a way to get back to the Agriculturals. Things were a lot better at home, but still, I hadn't dumped the idea. And if the Mall Rats could leave the enclave, so could I.

'You'll get there,' Thabo said. 'I dunno how, but I just have a feeling you will.'

I smiled at him, and he held my gaze for a couple of seconds.

'Hey!' he said, getting to his feet. 'You want to have some fun?'

'Sure. Where are we going?'

He held out a hand and hauled me to my feet. 'You'll see.'

11

'What are we doing here?'

We were right in front of the embassy's high metal fence. Half of the huge building was obscured by scaffolding, the workers scurrying above us as they constructed yet another floor.

'Forget hospitals, right?' Thabo spat, looking up at the building that towered over its squat brick neighbours. 'Forget new housing. Long as the politicians and their priest lackeys have their fancy offices. Forget what the people need.'

We walked straight past the ornate front gate, where several men in Resurrectionist robes were standing with their arms folded, hard eyes scanning the busy thoroughfare.

I hoped the Mantis wasn't looking out of one of the barred windows that loomed above us. I pulled my hood over my head just in case.

I followed Thabo to the building's edge, where he ducked

into an alleyway that ran parallel to it. Large dumpster-style bins flanked the narrow space.

'You've really got a thing about garbage, haven't you?'

'That's why I like you, Lele,' he said.

'Ha ha,' I replied, but at least he'd said he liked me – even if it *was* in connection with garbage. 'What are we doing here?'

'This is where the embassy dumps its rubbish, right?'

'So?'

'So, I need you to keep a lookout.'

He dug in his bag and took out a spray-can. The tip of it was stained bright red.

'The sign at school – that was you? Are you part of the ANZ?'

'Not yet,' he said.

He shook the can and started spraying one of the dumpsters with the words *Everything's better with zombies – NOT.*

'It was you as well! That message on my desk.'

'Guilty as charged,' Thabo said with his lopsided grin. Across the side of another one he wrote *ANZ – Be a Red NOT a Dead-Head.*

He handed the can to me. 'You do one.'

'Me? But I don't know what to write!'

'Use your imagination.'

The spray-can was difficult to use at first, and on my first try the paint just spluttered out, running down the side of the can in a trickle, but it wasn't long before I started to get the hang of it. I chose the dumpster in the middle, drew a cartoon version of a Rotter, put a cross through its head, and, as an afterthought, wrote *Mall Rats Rule!*

Utterly lame, I know, but Thabo looked impressed.

'Hey!' A male voice called from the far end of the alley. 'What are you kids doing back there?'

'Okay,' Thabo said. 'Here's the part where we run.'

12

The Mantis was sitting at the kitchen table when I arrived home – back as rigid as a broomstick, face a solid block of stone. The peace-making vibe of the night before was clearly a thing of the past.

'I can explain!' I said before she had a chance to speak. Although I actually didn't have a clue how I was going to explain why I'd spent the day defacing the embassy after almost punching one of my classmates.

'Explain what?' the Mantis snapped. Her eyes dropped to my boots. 'I really hope you didn't wear those to school, Leletia.'

'I changed into them on the way home,' I lied, relieved. 'What's up?'

'You're late!'

'Huh?'

'For the movie at the embassy! Go and get changed, and be

quick about it!'

I raced into my room and pulled on the first clothes at hand. I was still on a high from my day with Thabo, and right then not even the Mantis could dampen my spirits.

'Couldn't you have made more of an effort?' the Mantis grumbled when I came downstairs. She was dressed in her fine woollen suit, topped off with an anorak she proudly said was made of polyester. I shrugged. I was comfortable in my threadbare jeans, Mom's boots and Dad's old army coat.

The Mantis decided that rather than cramming into a rickshaw, we'd walk to the embassy, so the four of us set off together. Despite myself I was excited. I hadn't seen a film since before the War, and could barely remember what watching one had felt like. It was something the townies took for granted, and I was pretty sure that the kids at Malema High deliberately tried to copy the accents and phrases they'd seen in the films.

There was a festive atmosphere in the streets that night. The Mantis eventually stopped scowling and Dad even offered to carry Jobe when he became too heavy for me. Of course, the monthly movies were not for everyone. Sure, there were crowds of poorer citizens bunched around the gates, hoping for a glimpse of the film flickering on the white wall of the embassy, but these outings were for the rich: the embassy workers, the high priests and politicians, and the wealthy store owners and their families.

'Dad,' I said as we queued to get in. 'You know anything about the Mall Rats?'

'Where did you hear that name, Lele?'

'A friend mentioned them.'

'Don't let Cleo hear you talking like that.'

'But who are they?'

'They're no one,' Dad said. 'Just fairy stories, that's all.'

'But –'

'Ssssh.'

The Mantis waved her tickets at the robed Resurrectionist stationed outside, and we were ushered through the metal gates and into a large courtyard where several rows of folding chairs were laid out. The place was packed, and we had to push our way through the crowd to find our seats. As soon as I sat down, Jobe climbed onto my lap, popped his thumb into his mouth and leaned his head on my shoulder.

The rain looked as if it was going to stay away, but most people had come prepared for the worst, bundled up in raincoats and clutching sheets of plastic to cover their heads if necessary. Pretty much everyone was wearing something from before the War, and I didn't know where to look first. There was a woman a few seats away from us dressed in a bright red silk jacket covered with embroidery. Judging from her expensive outfit and the ginormous amulet around her neck, I assumed she must be one of the high priests, and I recognised the fellow next to her. It was Rickety Legs – the Resurrectionist from Gran's funeral. I looked around for my classmates (okay, I looked around for Thabo, mostly), but the crowd was too dense, and the lighting was too subdued to make out any other familiar faces.

Finally an expectant hush fell, and then the generator roared to life. An image flickered on to the wall in front of us, and everyone started cheering and clapping. I didn't know it then, but the only films the Resurrectionists allowed were violent gangster films or slasher horrors. They wanted to remind us how violent life was back then, before the War, and the movie that evening – *Jerusalema* – was no exception. Still, I was fascinated by how life was *before*: cars, bars, restaurants, men in suits, the thump of music, everyone smoking and chatting and shooting each other. The lives the movie portrayed were so different to mine that it was almost like watching an alien race on screen. But, strangely, few people actually seemed to be watching it. They moved around, swapping seats and chatting to acquaintances, shouting over the soundtrack.

'Ah, Cleo, sawubona,' a deep voice boomed from behind us. 'So nice that you and your family could come this evening.'

I craned my neck around to see who had spoken. It was Comrade Nkosi, the guy who'd come to school to break the news about the Lottery quota.

The Mantis got to her feet and smiled nervously. I'd never seen her so ill-at-ease, and I watched with interest.

'Comrade Nkosi,' the Mantis said. 'How are you? You remember my husband?'

'Ah, yes,' the man said. 'Of course.' He reached down and he and Dad shook hands awkwardly.

'Are you enjoying the movie?' The Mantis asked him, but he ignored the question and instead stared down at me and Jobe, his eyes resting on Jobe's face for several seconds, before scanning mine.

'And this must be Leletia,' he said. 'You will know my son from school, of course.'

'I do?' I asked.

'Now where is he? I'm sure he will want to say hello to a school friend.' He scanned the crowd. 'Zyed!' he shouted, gesturing towards the end of the row in front of us.

My heart plummeted as Zyed stood up and sulkily pushed his way towards us. His jacket was adorned with more feathers than usual, and his hair had been scraped into a topknot.

'Look what he does to his clothes,' Comrade Nkosi said to the Mantis, a half-smile on his lips. But the smile didn't reach his eyes. 'Ah! Zyed,' Comrade Nkosi said when his son finally joined us. 'You know Leletia, of course.'

Zyed glared at me.

'Zyed!' Comrade Nkosi snapped, and I saw his hand twitch as if he was restraining himself from striking his son. 'Where are your manners?'

Zyed muttered a sulky hello to me, the Mantis and Dad.

Comrade Nkosi fixed his eyes on me. 'Leletia, you must be very excited about the Lottery Ball.'

I shrugged, and it was the Mantis's turn to glare at me.

Comrade Nkosi suddenly clicked his fingers. 'I have the most marvellous idea! Leletia, do you have an escort for the dance?'

I was caught off guard. 'Um ... no, I –'

'Then you must go with Zyed!'

'No!' Zyed and I spoke simultaneously, and I'm sure his look of horror was mirrored on my face.

'Zyed!' Comrade Nkosi said. 'I cannot believe that you would think of turning down such a beautiful girl!'

'But I've already got a date!' Zyed said.

'It's final, Zyed,' his father said. 'Leletia is new at Malema High, and she has no one else to go with. I'm sure your other date will understand.'

Zyed glared at me as if it was my fault that his father had come up with this horrible idea. 'Yes, sir,' he mumbled before slinking off.

'Teenagers,' Comrade Nkosi rolled his eyes. 'I must apologise for my son's bad manners.'

'It's no problem,' the Mantis said with a tinkly laugh I'd never heard her use before.

Comrade Nkosi made as if to turn away, but then he clicked his fingers as something else occurred to him. 'Cleo. About your other child,' his eyes slipped to Jobe again, and his mouth twitched slightly in distaste. 'I'm afraid there are no places available in the immediate vicinity for him, but there is somewhere else that might take him.'

I couldn't believe what I was hearing. 'What?'

The Mantis gripped my arm tightly. 'We'll talk when we get home,' she hissed in my ear.

Comrade Nkosi appeared to be oblivious to the look of shock on my face. 'Mandela House is not in the best area of town, but, as institutions go, I think you'll find it adequate,' he carried on. 'As soon as the paperwork is finalised, I'll let you know.'

'Thank you, Comrade,' the Mantis said, her fingernails now digging painfully into my skin to silence me.

13

'Well?' I said. 'What the hell was he talking about?'

Dad and the Mantis had insisted that Jobe was put to bed before we discussed the meaning behind Comrade Nkosi's words, and the wait had almost killed me. We sat around the kitchen table, Dad nursing a mug of tea; the Mantis sitting erect, hands folded in front of her. I don't think I've ever hated someone as much as I hated her right then.

Dad cleared his throat. 'Your mother and I feel –'

'My mother's dead.'

The Mantis didn't change her expression, but Dad flinched slightly. 'Must you always be so difficult, Lele?' he sighed.

The Mantis spoke up. 'We've decided that it would be best if Jobe went to a ... place where children like him can get proper care.'

'You can't do that!'

Dad held up his hand. 'Just listen, Lele –'

'But why?'

'He'll be with others of his kind.'

'He's not a *kind*. He's my brother!'

'Yes, but let's face it. He is ... different.'

'That's not his fault!'

'I know that, Lele,' Dad said.

'I'll look after him. I promise I will!'

'You don't have the time. You have to go to school.'

'No, I don't. I'll become a worker, a rickshaw driver, a builder – I don't care!'

Dad sighed again. 'Lele, your moth ... Cleo and I are working very hard to try to improve the conditions in the city,' he said. 'You know this. It won't be long before everyone will have access to electricity and –'

'What's that got to do with Jobe?'

'I'm not going to be around all the time,' Dad said. 'We can't leave him on his own.'

'Well, hire someone to look after him then!' The tears were pouring down my face, but I let them fall.

'We can't afford that sort of expense.'

'But you can afford to send him to ... Mandela House, or whatever that place is called!'

'Look, it's not going to happen straight away. But we need you to come to terms with the idea.'

'Yeah, right. That's total kak! If Comrade Nkosi hadn't said anything you wouldn't even have told me!'

Now even the Mantis began to look uncomfortable. I pushed my chair back so violently that it crashed to the floor. 'I hate you!' I said, staring straight at the Mantis. 'This is all down to you!'

'Lele!' Dad said. 'That's enough!'

'You didn't want us here!' I carried on. 'You want Dad all to yourself! You're nothing but a cruel, evil *bitch*!'

Dad got to his feet. 'Leletia! That's enough! How *dare* you talk to your mother that way!'

'She's not my bloody mother! And I wish you weren't my father!'

Dad flinched again at that, but neither he nor the Mantis replied. The long silence was only broken by the sound of the kitchen door creaking open.

'Gogo?' Jobe said, peering in at us from behind the door, the expression in his eyes making him look about a hundred years old.

'You can't take him!' I said, scooping up Chinwag who had made her way under the table, and moving to grab Jobe's hand. 'I won't let you!'

Right then I knew I had to come up with a plan. And I had to do it fast.

14

I practically ran to school that morning. I needed to talk to someone, and who else was there but Thabo? As soon as I slipped through the gate I caught sight of him lounging against the sun sculpture, chatting to a plump girl with light brown, frizzy hair. For once I didn't hang back. 'Thabo,' I said, striding straight up to him. 'I really need to talk to you.'

The girl looked at me curiously, but not unkindly, and with a small wave and a 'catch you later' to Thabo she wandered towards the classroom. He watched her go, and I couldn't help but feel a small twinge of jealousy as he did so. Finally he gave me his full attention. 'Let's get out of here,' he said. 'I've also got some news.'

We headed to the dumpster alley, neither of us speaking, although it was clear from the speed Thabo was walking and the way he kept clenching and unclenching his fists that he was also bursting with news.

'You first,' I said as soon as we were hunkered down behind the dumpster, although I was dying to let all my anguish out.

'I went to a meeting last night, Lele.'

'What meeting?'

'An ANZ gathering. At New Arrivals. It was amazing. You should have heard them speak. There was this one guy – Michael. What he said made so much sense. If we don't make a stand now the Resurrectionists will end up ruling the enclave with an iron fist. They –'

'But they do rule the enclave.'

'Exactly! But it's only going to get worse. Last year three teenagers were given to the Guardians; this year it's five. What's next? All of us? And why don't we know what happens to them? It has to be stopped!'

Thabo was right, but I couldn't think about it then. All I could think about was getting Jobe out of the city, away from Mandela House, but I let him speak; he was so fired up by what he'd heard that the excitement was practically crackling out of him.

'Sorry,' he said, finally. 'I've been talking for ages. Your turn.'

I started at the beginning. I told him how Jobe had changed after the Guardians had brought him back with the rest of the children they'd taken, about how awful it was to see him stay the same size, the same age, while I grew up. My brother's growth stunted; his thoughts trapped inside his head. I finished with the Mantis and Dad's plans to dump him in Mandela House.

'I've always been there for him, Thabo. I can't let them take him away from me now.'

'But how can you stop them?'

'I need to find a way to get back to the Agriculturals. It's different there, freer. I've got friends there. I can make a life for us.'

'What as? A farmer? A field worker?'

I bristled. 'There's more to life there than just farming, Thabo.'

'But to hire someone to take you through the Deadlands, Lele – that's impossible. And even if you did find someone willing to risk it, it would probably cost a fortune.'

'What about the Mall Rats?'

'What about them?'

'You said they go outside the enclave.'

His eyes slid to the left. 'Forget the Mall Rats, Lele,' he said.

'What? Why are you saying that now?'

'I've got an idea,' he said, brushing my questions away.

He dug in his backpack and pulled out a piece of paper. There was a poorly executed pen-and-ink drawing of a Rotter's head with a cross scored through it, and the words *Make a stand, save our future, ANZ.*

'What's this?'

'We need to increase our membership ...' (Thabo's use of the word 'we' didn't escape me.) 'We're distributing pamphlets, spreading the word. You think you could do better than this?'

It wouldn't be difficult. The sketch was on a par with the large-headed kid and sun emblem the Resurrectionists used.

I shrugged. 'I guess.'

'If you help the ANZ, maybe they'll help you,' he said.

'Really? You think they would?'

'Why not? It's worth a shot, isn't it?' He nudged me. 'And, oh yeah,' he said, with his lopsided grin. 'What's this I hear about you and Zyed going to the dance?'

I mumbled something, but I couldn't think straight. My mind was racing. All I could think was that this could be my way out of the city.

Thabo picked up on my distractedness. 'Look, don't worry,'

he said. 'I'm sure your brother will be fine whatever happens. You'll deal with it; you're strong.'

I looked up at him. 'You don't get it, Thabo. He's not just my brother. He's my twin.'

15

I spent the whole weekend working on the ANZ pamphlet design, barely leaving my room. Late on Sunday evening there was a knock at the door. I shoved the sketchbook under my pillow as Dad and the Mantis poked their heads into my room.

'We've got a surprise for you, Lele,' Dad said.

'Oh yeah? What? You going to send me off to a special home as well?'

The Mantis ignored this, and stepped forward. 'Ta-da!' she said, pulling something out from behind her back.

It was hideous. Truly hideous. I don't want you to think that I was ungrateful, but just ... *wow*! The dress the Mantis was holding was so pink it hurt my eyes, and it was covered in ruffles and ribbons and shiny flecks of lace.

'What the hell is that?'

'Your dress. For the dance,' the Mantis said, her smile

slipping a little.

'You have got to be joking.'

'Of course we're not joking!'

I opened my mouth to speak again, but Dad held up his hand. 'Come on, Lele. You've been holed up in here for far too long. Let's get some fresh air.'

'But –'

'No arguments.'

We walked through the streets in silence at first, Dad seemingly picking our direction at random.

'You shouldn't give her such a hard time, Lele.'

'She hates me!'

'No, she doesn't.'

'Dad, seriously, how can you say otherwise?'

We headed towards the embassy road. Two robed Resurrectionists were scrubbing at the front gate, but I could still see the outline of yet more ANZ graffiti. I hid the smile behind my hand. Thabo – or another member – was getting bolder.

'She's doing her best, Lele,' Dad said. 'You have to give her a chance.'

'Whatever,' I mumbled under my breath. 'Maybe I'd give her more of a chance if she wasn't so keen on getting shot of my brother.'

'We've discussed this, Lele. The subject is closed.'

Another group of robed Resurrectionists passed by, making no move to step out of our way. One of them nodded approvingly at the amulet that hung over Dad's jacket.

'Why did you become a Resurrectionist, Dad?' I asked. 'I

mean, you fought in the War, so why have you joined up with the enemy? You don't really believe in all that crap, do you?'

He sighed. 'Lele, not this again.'

'But if we all stuck together, we could get out of here.'

'There's nothing we can do to stop the Rotters. There are too many, you know that.'

'But we could at least try.'

'The Guardians will eventually free us,' Dad said, spouting the party line.

'Will they?' I asked. 'Or are they just using us? Why else would they have the Lottery?'

'They have sworn that all will be revealed soon.'

'And you believe them? It's been ten years, Dad.'

Dad sighed again. 'You don't know what it was like, Lele. The War was ... hard on everyone. If it wasn't for the Guardians, we'd all be out there.' He waved a hand in the direction of the fence, and, as if on cue, the Rotters' moans drifted towards us.

'At least the ANZ is doing something,' I said.

Dad looked around nervously. 'Lele! Don't speak that way, even as a joke.'

I began to notice that the streets around us were clearing, passers-by scuttling away down alleyways, their heads bent. The hawkers and workmen had moved as far away from the centre of the road as possible, and were all standing with their backs to it.

'What's going on?' I asked Dad.

'Guardians,' he replied simply, pulling me up against a stall.

'Real ones? In the city? I thought they never came to the city? I mean, except for funerals.' And as far as I knew the food they collected from the Agriculturals was dropped off at the gates to the enclave.

'Of course they come into the city occasionally, Lele. They

have to negotiate with the embassy.'

I hadn't considered this before. 'Does the Man – does Cleo speak with them?'

He shook his head.

'But does she know what they are? *Does* she?'

Before he could answer there was the clip-clop of horses' hooves as a huge wagon appeared in the street, heading in our direction. It was drawn by two more enormous black horses and the Guardian driving it was flicking the reins and urging the animals on. The horses looked as terrified as the one I'd seen on the day of Gran's funeral. They tossed their heads and lifted their feet high. Then I heard something else.

The faint sound of screaming.

The wagon drew alongside us. It was painted black and had high slatted wooden sides. I caught a glimpse of an eye peering through a crevice in the wood, and it seemed to stare straight at me. And then I realised: The screams were coming from inside the wagon.

'Don't look, Lele,' Dad said.

The wagon passed, carrying on up the street, and as it did so the hawkers and street workers raised their heads and went on with what they had been doing as if nothing had happened.

'There were people in there. What *was* it, Dad? Where were they going?'

'They're being taken outside the fence.'

'Huh?'

'The embassy likes to call it "relocating".' Despite what he'd been saying earlier there a was a trace of bitterness in his voice.

'Dad, I really don't know what you're talking about. Who were those people in there?'

'Criminals. People guilty of petty theft, violence, insurgency. People the embassy feels are … troublesome.'

'But who judges that?'

'They do of course.'

'But ... but how can people just let them do that?'

'The people voted them into power, Lele. They had the majority.'

'But the people in there – they're still alive!'

'Not for long,' Dad murmured.

'Dad! You have to do something!'

He took my arm firmly. 'I can't.'

'But we have to!'

'Let's get back,' he said, withdrawing inside himself again.

For the rest of the night, all I could think about was the Rotter I'd seen outside the fence on the day of Gran's funeral. I tried not to imagine the fate of the criminals, but the images wouldn't quit.

16

'Lele! This is amazing!'

Thabo and I were sitting in the deserted rec area, the rest of the students busily clearing and decorating the classroom for the Lottery dance. Thabo flicked through the ANZ sketches I'd spent the whole weekend working on, pausing at a sketch of a blank-faced Guardian towering over the city enclave, the people below attached to puppet strings that disappeared into the Guardian's sleeves.

'Nah,' I said. 'It's just okay.' But I knew it was the best thing I'd ever done.

He nudged me. 'It's awesome. Michael will love it.' He ran his fingers through his dreads. 'I'm going to join them, Lele.'

'The ANZ?'

'Yeah, I'm going to quit school and join them.'

'But isn't that dangerous?' I told him about the relocation

wagon I'd seen the night before.

He nodded and his eyes glittered with fury. 'I know. You see? That's just the start. What will they do next? Arrest everyone who doesn't worship the Guardians? Relocate everyone who refuses to swallow the party line?'

'Hey, guys ...' I looked up. Summer and Nyameka were standing in front of us. 'Hi Thabo,' they said, and giggled.

'What do you want?' I snapped. 'Zyed let you off the leash, has he?'

'That's what we wanted to talk to you about,' Summer said. 'So, like, Zyed said that his father's making him take you to the Ball.'

'Yeah, well, tell him not to hold his breath,' I muttered.

'What do you mean?' Summer said.

'I mean I might not be going.'

'*Seriaas*? Oh, cool! Well, if you're not going for sure can you, like, let me know?'

'Yeah, yeah, whatever. Now, if you don't mind, this is a private conversation.'

'Sorry.' (Giggle.) 'Later.' (Giggle.) And with that they turned back towards the classroom.

Thabo seemed to have calmed down, the anger no longer flashing in his eyes. 'You've got to go, Lele,' he said to me.

'Why?'

'You can't let him win.'

'Win what? It's not a competition. Besides, you should see the dress my stepmother's got me for the dance.'

'Gross?'

'So far beyond gross it's not even funny. Looks like a bunch of Rotters threw up on it.'

'Can Rotters throw up?'

'Who knows? Anyway, if they did it would be an improvement.'

'But how about if you had something cool to wear?'

'You mean an outfit that wouldn't make me a laughing stock?'

'Yeah.'

I shrugged. 'That isn't going to happen.'

He grinned at me again. 'Come on.'

'Where to this time?'

I followed him out of the school gate, assuming that we were heading for our usual skive spot, but this time he hailed a passing rickshaw. He climbed in and grabbed my hand to haul me up next to him.

'Seriously, where are we going?'

'You'll see.'

The rickshaw driver set off at a cracking pace.

'So, who are you going to the Ball with?' I asked, trying to keep my voice steady. After all, he could have his pick.

He smiled at me. 'I'm going with you, of course.'

17

'Welcome to New Arrivals, Lele!'

At first sight it seemed to be a chaotic mishmash of corrugated-iron shacks, dilapidated caravans, army tents and bumpy, muddy lanes. The neighbourhood we lived in seemed orderly in comparison, and I had no clue how Thabo could find his way though the labyrinthine byways and narrow, claustrophobic alleyways; it was so huge it was almost like an enclave within an enclave. Despite the rain, there were barefoot children and adults everywhere, and a raggedy group of kids, who couldn't have been more than five or six years old, skipped behind us for half a kilometre or so as we wormed our way deeper into the sprawling mess.

Thabo finally told the rickshaw driver to stop outside a rickety two-storey building, painted bright pink and adorned with multicoloured flags and a crude painting of a bright blue eye. It was surrounded by drab army tents and an elderly guy sitting outside one of them eyed us suspiciously. Thabo stalked up to the front of the pink house, reached past a metal security gate and knocked three times on the door's wooden slats.

The door opened a crack, closed again, and then was opened all the way by a burly man dressed in army fatigues. Thabo murmured something to him and the guy stood back to let us in.

Inside, the place was gloomy and reeked of smoke and something medicinal that I suspected might be home-brewed alcohol. The room we were in was bare except for three battered armchairs covered in faded floral fabric, and a poster of a man wearing a beret stuck up on the far wall.

A curtain rustled as a hugely fat woman manoeuvred her way into the room. She smiled when she saw Thabo.

'Hola, Thabo,' she said breathily, the sweat standing out on her forehead. 'Kunjani?'

'Ngikhona,' Thabo replied as she waddled towards him and trapped him in a bear hug, 'wena unjani?'

They chatted for a few minutes in Xhosa. I could make out maybe one word in four, but I couldn't grasp the gist of what they were saying.

The burly guy looked me up and down, his eyes lingering on me long enough to make me uncomfortable. 'How you *doing*, girl?' he said to me.

'Leave it, Armand, she's young enough to be your daughter,' the woman snapped at him, breaking off her conversation with Thabo.

'Can't blame a guy for trying, *non*?'

The woman clucked her tongue at him 'Sies.'

'This is Lungi,' Thabo said, turning to me. 'Lungi, meet Lele.'

The woman gave me a small, tight smile.

'Lungi's your fairy godmother,' Thabo said, nudging her.

'Eish, Thabo, you're full of rubbish,' Lungi said, but nonetheless she grinned at him flirtatiously before turning to lead us through an arched doorway and into a makeshift kitchen. There was a huge metal pot of some kind of stew bubbling on the stove. It smelled spicy and delicious and . . . different.

'I don't have much stuff at the moment,' Lungi said. 'But let me see . . .'

Her eyes scanned my body for several seconds, making me feel self-conscious, before she sank to her knees and rolled up the threadbare rug that covered part of the floor, revealing a trapdoor. She heaved the door open and reached down into the space below it, hauling out a large drawstring bag. When she dug in the bag and started pulling out clothes I could barely believe what I was seeing: jeans, T-shirts and dresses spilled out all around us. They were all from before the War, all looked to be brand new, and some even had labels attached to them.

'Wow!' I said. 'Where did you get all this stuff from?' I glanced at Thabo. 'The Mall Rats?'

Lungi shot me a sharp glance. 'Ask me no questions, sister, and I'll tell you no lies. Now, I know I have something here . . .' She rooted in the bottom of the bag and pulled out a swatch of material. It was dark green silk – almost the exact shade of Mom's Matric dance dress. She shook it out and handed it to me. 'This dress should fit. Yes! It will be perfect.'

The dress felt almost weightless, and the slippery fabric seemed to whisper across my fingers. I held it up to myself doubtfully. It didn't appear to have any straps, and was simply but elegantly styled. It looked way too small and insubstantial, as if it would barely cover my thighs, but there were no two ways about it: it was beautiful.

'How much?' Thabo asked.

'For you, Thabo? It is nothing.' Lungi looked at me closely. 'But I want it back, nè? I can get a good price for this. No making it dirty or getting up to mischief in it, okay?' She threw back her head and laughed, showing off a mouth full of gold teeth.

Thabo grinned at me. 'What you waiting for, Lele?'

'Go on, sisi,' Lungi said, pointing to the corner of the room, where a grubby shower curtain hung in front of a tiny changing area that was dominated by a cracked full-length mirror. 'Try it on.'

As soon as I was behind the curtain I started to get changed. Dumping my school uniform on the floor, I pulled the dress over my thighs and up over my torso, struggling to zip it up at the back. I turned around and checked out my reflection. Unbelievable! I looked like a totally different person. The dress clung to my body, fitting so perfectly that its glittery fabric almost appeared to be painted on to my skin. I didn't look like me. I looked like someone sophisticated, glamorous; even my too-short haircut seemed to suit the dress. But what if this was all in my imagination? What if I actually looked horrible? Or stupid?

'Let's see!' Lungi called to me.

I pushed my way out from behind the curtain and stood shyly in front of them.

Thabo was looking at me strangely, almost as if he was seeing me for the first time. Lungi checked out his expression and chuckled.

'Well?' I said. 'Is it okay?'

Lungi snorted. 'Okay? Hayibo, sister. I tell you something, you watch yourself. You are going to cause some trouble tonight!'

She didn't know the half of it.

18

'Leletia!' The Mantis's eyes were bulging so far out of their sockets they were in danger of plopping onto the kitchen floor. 'Where did you get that dress?'

'A friend gave it to me,' I said. Well, it was true, wasn't it?

'But it looks brand new!'

'So?'

'What about the other one? It cost me a fortune in trade credits!'

For once Dad stood up for me. 'Just let her wear what she likes, Cleo,' he said.

'But –'

'You look beautiful, Lele,' he said. 'You really do.'

I gave him a small, grateful smile. But the Mantis hadn't finished. I tuned her out and concentrated on settling Jobe for the night. He'd been acting strange all evening – clinging to my legs and whimpering under his breath. I was almost grateful when Zyed showed up.

I had to admit he looked good. For once the feathers were absent, and his tailored black suit must have cost an arm and a leg. I wondered if Thabo and Lungi had also kitted him out for the evening, or if there were a whole series of suppliers. He did a double take when he saw the dress, but did his best to hide his shock. Smiling politely at Dad and the Mantis, he turned on the charm, but as soon as we were outside, his face shut down.

'Look, Zyed,' I said, climbing into the rickshaw he'd hired for my night. 'I don't want to do this either, 'kay? So let's just get it over with.'

'Fine,' he snapped.

We sat in silence as the driver pulled us out into the thoroughfare. But I hadn't forgotten about what I'd said to him. Guilt made me speak again. 'You worried about the Lottery?' I asked.

'No,' he said

'Because the chances of you getting picked ... They're not that great.'

'You really think my father would allow me to get chosen?' he said scornfully, staring out into the city. 'When we get there, you're on your own. Don't talk to me, don't look at me; as far as I'm concerned you don't exist.'

'Ditto,' I snapped. If he didn't want to make an effort then there was no way I was going to.

But even with the world's most miserable date at my side, I still couldn't help but feel my excitement building. Thabo would be there. And the way he'd looked at me when I'd tried on the dress – I was sure it meant something.

The rickshaw had barely come to a stop before Zyed pushed past me, leapt down and stalked through the gates. I climbed down with difficulty. Lungi had loaned me a pair of red high-heeled shoes that clashed with the dress, but went better with it than my boots. I did my best, trying not to break an ankle as I skittered through the deserted courtyard and onwards to the classroom. The place looked even uglier at night, the rays of the crappy sun statue spreading shadowy fingers across the desolate concrete.

I stood outside the door, listening to the beat of the band inside the classroom, then I took a deep breath and walked in.

I managed to time my entrance with the end of one of the band's songs, and, caught by a sudden gust of wind, the door slammed behind me. Heads turned. Eyes stared. Pretty much everyone was dressed in clothes from before the War, but in comparison to mine, most of their outfits looked shabby and old. A flurry of excited whispering followed me as I did my best to walk across the room without tripping over my feet.

The crowd parted and Thabo walked towards me. He looked fantastic. He was wearing a long leather coat, a gleaming white T-shirt, black jeans and boots.

'You're late,' he said.

'I know.'

'But you're worth waiting for. You scrub up well.'

'So do you.'

'Huh? What do you mean?' he said with his trademark grin. 'I always look this good.'

He held out his arm. I linked mine through his, and we walked slowly towards the stage area, the crowd parting in front of us.

'Would you like to dance?' Thabo asked, looking deep into my eyes.

'Yes,' I said. 'I'd like that very much.'

And then, just like in all the best fairy stories, he took my hand and led me to the centre of the room, and everyone gasped and couldn't believe how beautiful I was and how handsome he looked and even Zyed couldn't help but smile at us, and then, one by one, everyone in the room began to clap slowly as Thabo and I glided across the dance floor.

Right now you're either about to throw up or you're thinking: Ahhh, how sweet. What a *perfect* ending.

But this isn't the end. And of course it didn't happen like that at all.

Quite the opposite, in fact.

This is the part where it gets *really* hectic.

Part Two

1

My head was pounding ... I kept as still as I could for several seconds, breathing in deeply. My mouth tasted weird and metallic, the saliva gummy on my tongue. Gradually, I began to realise that I was lying on a dusty wooden surface, and wherever the hell I was, it was dark, and the floor seemed to be rocking from side to side. It smelled strongly of sweat, rotten vegetables and mouldy wood. I finally managed to lift my head and pulled myself onto my hands and knees. For a horrible second I was hit with a wave of dizziness, and I was sure I was going to be sick. My stomach lurched and then, as fast as the feeling had come upon me, the nausea was gone.

I tried to sit up, and finally managed it on my third attempt. As the rest of my senses kicked in, I could hear the clip-clop of horses' hooves in the background, and there was another sound – hitching gasps as if someone close by was sobbing.

'Hello?' I called. My voice sounded groggy, almost as if it was arriving from far away. Had I fallen? I ran a hand over my scalp, but I couldn't feel any damage.

'She's awake!'

The voice sounded vaguely familiar.

'Who's that?' I said, struggling to place it. Then it started coming back: what had *actually* happened at the dance.

And, suddenly, I knew exactly where I was.

Zyed and I had arrived at the school just like I described, but when I'd walked into the classroom, Thabo wasn't waiting for me. In fact, I couldn't see him anywhere, and although several students glanced at me curiously, nearly everyone's attention was focused on the stage – the packed room humming with excitement.

Acid Face Pelosi was standing in the middle of the stage, basking in the attention – her bright pink dress fitting her body like a sausage skin; her Resurrectionist amulet swinging in front of her bony chest. Comrade Xhati and Comrade Nkosi stood to her left, and behind them a grim-faced nurse with swollen ankles and two burly men dressed in Resurrectionist robes stood rigidly to attention.

As I pushed my way through the crowd, searching for any sign of Thabo, Comrade Nkosi glanced at his watch, murmured something in Comrade Xhati's ear, and with a nod in Acid Face Pelosi's direction, stepped off the stage and disappeared into the crowd.

Acid Face Pelosi clapped her hands and started saying something, but I didn't bother listening, and besides, I only had eyes for Thabo – I'd caught sight of him at the far side of the room. I started edging my way towards him, waving to grab his attention until he finally saw me and shot me a grin and a thumbs-up.

I'd opened my mouth to tell him to join me, when his smile instantly snapped off.

I looked behind me, trying to figure out what could be wrong. 'What?' I mouthed at him.

And then it dawned that he wasn't the only one who was looking at me as if I'd just sprouted another head.

'Leletia de la Fontein!' Acid Face Pelosi called. 'Come up to the stage, please.'

I looked up at her. 'Huh? Why?' The room was now silent, and my words rang out clearly.

She smiled at me coldly. 'You have been picked.'

I gazed at her stupidly. 'Picked? For what?'

'You've won the Lottery, of course!'

I felt my mouth dropping open. I suppose I must have looked ridiculous, but my image was the last thing on my mind right then. I struggled to find my voice. 'But ... but that's impossible!'

'Come on, Leletia!' Her smile was fading fast.

'But I can't be chosen!' I stammered.

'I'm afraid that is not so,' Acid Face said.

'My brother – I'm not eligible! I told you this! Comrade Xhati, tell them! Please!'

'It is an honour, Leletia,' Acid Face Pelosi said cheerfully, grinning down at me as if she were giving me good news instead of basically handing down a death sentence. I didn't like that smile. Not one bit. It was the kind of patronising smile you give to someone who's delusional. I looked around for Comrade Nkosi – who I suspected was the only one with the power to stop this insanity – but he was nowhere to be seen.

I think it was then that I knew I wasn't going to talk my way out of this. I knew I had to flee, right that second. But thanks to the shock and the part of me that didn't believe it was actually happening, I hadn't noticed that the two burly men had left the stage and skirted around behind me. In the split second I decided to make a run for it my arms were grabbed from behind and I was propelled forward.

'Thabo!' I yelled. 'Help!'

He'd been standing, frozen, staring at me, but as soon as he saw the two men in Resurrectionist robes grab me, he leapt into action and started fighting his way towards me. I tried to struggle, and even managed to wriggle free, but then one of the men forced my arm up behind my back, and the pain that shot through my shoulder took my breath away. If I fought much harder I'd be in danger of breaking my arm. 'No!' I screamed as they hauled me up onto the stage.

'Let her go!' Thabo yelled as he forced his way to the front of the stage, but when he tried to climb up, one of the men kicked him in the chest, sending him flying backwards.

Acid Face Pelosi glanced at the nurse and gave her a small nod. She started walking towards me. I tried to back away, but the man still held me firmly. When the nurse was close enough, I lashed out with my foot and landed a vicious kick in her stomach. She doubled over, staggering, but it wasn't going to be that easy. Grimacing in pain, she stood up and shot me a cold, professional smile. It was then that I realised she was holding a syringe in her right hand.

'It's okay,' the nurse murmured as she jabbed the needle into my arm. 'Your reaction is quite normal.'

'Wait!' Acid Face Pelosi said. 'I think we should –'

Then everything went dark.

2

My eyes were starting to adjust to the gloom, and I could make out the four shapes of the other Lottery winners. I knew that two of them must be from Malema High, but it was too dark to make out any familiar faces. All I knew for sure was that we were in the back of a high covered wagon, and judging by the way it rocked and shook, we were travelling over rough terrain.

'That was quite a performance you put on at the dance,' the same voice said. 'The nurse had to leave the room after she injected you.'

I tried to make out his features, finally recognising the outline of a pair of taped-together glasses. It was Zit Face.

'You sit next to me in class,' I said.

'Well, duh.'

'I don't even know your name,' I said. I didn't bother to sound apologetic; it wasn't like he'd never been nice to me.

'Paul.'

'What did they give me?' I asked him.

'Who knows? Some kind of sedative, I guess. You went out like a light.'

'Didn't they give it to you, too?'

'I didn't fight,' he said.

'Why not?'

He paused. 'I knew it was going to happen,' he said in a small, tired voice. 'I had a feeling. You can't stop them.'

'This can't be happening,' I groaned. 'I'm not supposed to be here.'

'Get used to it,' he said, but not unkindly. 'We're screwed and there's nothing we can do about it.'

'How long have we been in here?' I asked.

'Couple of hours. We're in one of the relocation wagons, I think.'

The sound of sobbing was intensifying.

'Who's that crying?' I asked.

'That's one of the guys from one of the other Resurrectionist schools. Hasn't stopped once.'

'Who else is here?'

'Another chick I don't know.' Paul gestured over to where a small figure was curled in a ball in the corner of the wagon. 'She hasn't moved or spoken. And Lucille de Beer. She also goes to Malema High.'

The name wasn't familiar.

'Do not fear!' a girl's voice cried. 'We are the chosen ones.'

'Excuse me?' I said.

'That's Lucille,' Paul explained. 'She's totally lost it.'

'I have not!' Lucille whined. 'We should be looking forward to our rebirth as part of Heaven on –'

'Oh, shut up!' I snapped. The last thing I needed right then was an earful of Resurrectionist crap.

'You can't talk to me like that!' Lucille cried. 'Who do you think you are?'

'Someone who's getting out of here,' I snapped. And, suddenly, saying it out loud made it seem possible.

Using the side of the wagon as support, I pulled myself to my feet.

'You really think we can escape?' Paul asked. 'How? I've tried the back flap and it's totally secure.'

'I'm working on it,' I said.

'Embrace the future!' Lucille began again. 'You don't understand that –'

'No, *you* don't understand that if you don't shut up, I'll be shutting your mouth for you!' I yelled, the fear and shock melding into fury.

Lucille let out a squeak, but stayed quiet, which was all I wanted.

'Jislaaik, Lele,' Paul said. 'Way to go.'

I was beginning to like Paul, and I remember thinking that perhaps my first impression of him had been wrong. But, right then, the past didn't matter. All that mattered was getting out of the wagon. I had to think. There was definitely light coming from somewhere, which was a start. I glanced up at the roof. There it was – a faint glimmer of moonlight slanting through a rip in the tarpaulin.

'Has anyone got any matches?'

'Here,' Paul thrust a box into my hand. I shook it. There weren't many left, but they would have to do. 'You going to start a fire?'

I considered it. It wasn't such a bad idea. But then I decided against it. It was too risky. We might only have one shot at this, and I didn't want to risk burning us all to death. I lit one of the matches and held it above my head. The rip was about the size of a man's hand.

'You haven't got a knife by any chance have you, Paul?' I asked.

'I wish,' he said.

I'd lost one of my shoes, but I was sure I could use the metal heel of the other one to punch holes in the fabric and maybe make enough of a gap to squeeze through. It was worth a shot. The match burned down, singeing my fingers. Swearing under my breath, I lit another.

The first hurdle was going to be getting up there. The roof was more than a metre above my head. I needed to stand on something, but apart from my fellow Lottery winners, the wagon was empty. I assessed everyone. The sobbing boy was clearly the tallest.

'Hey! You!' I said to him. 'What's your name?'

'J-J-Jamale,' he stuttered.

'Okay, Jamale,' I said. 'I need you to stand up.'

'Why?'

'I need you to help me. Please. Just do it. I'm going to get us out of here.'

'Huh? Really?'

'Yeah,' I said.

He struggled to his feet and I lit another match so that I could get a better look at him. I felt a pang of pity for him – the front of his trousers was stained a darker colour, where he'd obviously lost control of his bladder, and waves of nervous sweat blasted off his body – but I could see from his height that if I sat on his shoulders I could easily reach the roof.

'Listen, Jamale, I'm going to try to break open the tarpaulin so that we can sneak out. But I'll need to balance on your shoulders. You cool with that?'

He nodded.

'Okay. Shuffle over here.'

I positioned him underneath the spot in the roof, and handed my shoe to Paul.

'Pass this to me when I ask for it, okay?' I said to him.

'You want me to go?' he asked.

'I'm lighter.'

'No!' Lucille screamed. 'You can't!'

'Lucille,' I snapped. 'If you want to stay here and let the Guardians do ... whatever to you, then fine. But if you interfere with me, then they won't get a chance. Got it?'

'But –'

'I said, *have you got it?*' I knew I sounded like I was turning into some kind of hard-core bitch, but someone had to do something. 'Keep an eye on her,' I said to Paul.

I was glad it was dark, as I had to shuck the dress up to my hips to climb onto Jamale's shoulders. He staggered slightly as the wagon rocked beneath us, and for a second I was sure I was going to lose my balance, but then he steadied himself.

'Okay, Paul,' I said. 'Pass me the shoe.'

My arms were killing me by the time I'd widened the gap. It was slow work, and I fought for every inch.

'Hold still, Jamale,' I said.

He grunted something. Using the edges of the tear in the tarpaulin to steady myself, I stood on his shoulders. My head poked through the top, and I dragged in a lungful of clean night air. Wriggling as best I could, I forced my shoulders through and used my arms to leverage the rest of my body up and out onto the roof.

But I hadn't thought it through properly.

One minute I was catching my breath, enjoying the chill of the night air on my skin, the next I was flying through the air, swept off the roof by a tree branch that had sprung out of nowhere. I felt myself falling, and then the air whooshed out of me as I landed on my back, my head smacking the ground, my arm a bright burst of pain as it slammed against a rock with a sickening crack.

And for the second time that night, everything went black.

This time when I came to it was daylight, and judging by the haze in the air it was some time early in the morning. I had no clue how long I'd been out, but I couldn't see any sign of the wagon; the pathway it had taken snaked out of sight behind a copse of Port Jacksons.

I stretched my limbs one by one to make sure none of them were broken, then wiggled the fingers of the arm that had hit the rock. Apart from a couple of bruises, everything seemed fine.

One thing was for sure: I'd been incredibly lucky, and I was filled with a surge of triumph.

I'd escaped! I'd made it!

I was outside!

Then it really hit me.

I was outside, all right.

I was outside *in the Deadlands*.

I hadn't even considered this when I'd climbed on to the roof, and clearly this hadn't occurred to Paul, either. I hadn't thought that by escaping from the wagon I'd actually be exchanging one unknown horror for something possibly far, far worse.

Scrambling to my feet, I realised that I could hear moaning in the distance. I had no idea how far away the Rotters were, or what the hell I'd do if there were any in the area, but I was about to find out.

My only option was to climb a tree and scope out where to go.

I chose a large pine, and got moving.

The branches ripped into Lungi's dress as I climbed higher and higher, my hands sticky with tree sap, but I pushed on, ignoring the rough feel of the bark as it grazed my skin. Then something caught my eye, something white, which was totally unexpected. As far as I knew there weren't any white buildings in the enclave; everything was either grey brick or mud-spattered brown.

I edged along a branch, really taking a chance now, the bough lurching dangerously. There was no doubt about it, the flash of white looked as if it was part of a wall of some description. And there was something peeking over the top of it, something metallic that glinted in the sun. The sight of it nudged at my memory.

Then I had it.

I was looking at the distant shape of a roller coaster.

I began to wonder if I'd hit my head harder than I thought, and I was actually in the middle of some hyper-realistic dream.

After the roller-coaster sighting, I'd scrambled down from the tree as fast as I could, and ditched the path for what was clearly a grassed-over highway, stumbling past the shells of cars hidden under shrouds of foliage and fynbos. I didn't care that I was headed away from the enclave, Table Mountain behind me in the far distance. I didn't care that I could hear the plaintive moan of what had to be a huge group of Rotters. All I could think was: This can't be! This is *impossible*!

I was right outside a shopping mall, the multilayered parking lot around it still housing the remains of several cars. Nature was making its mark on the exterior – the Port Jacksons extended right up to the mall's walls, and ropey creeper strands had long ago forced their fingers into the brickwork – but I could still make out the Ster Kinekor and Woolworths signs, and a faded billboard with the words *Ratanga Junction: Under twelves ride free!* emblazoned across it. I'd recognised the looping skeleton of the Cobra thrill ride that formed part of the massive mall complex instantly, a long-forgotten memory sparking into life at the sight of it. Years earlier Jobe and I had spent hours begging Dad to take us there, but we'd never made it. The closest we'd ever come was driving past it on the way to visit Gran.

And here it was. Intact.

I walked past more car-shaped humps and overturned shopping trolleys, entranced by the remains of the dried-up canals that snaked past the buildings. I skirted past a long-dead café, the chairs overturned and riddled with rust, the tiled floor now home to thigh-high grass. A family of cats mewled and scampered out of a dilapidated kombi, and above my head, a cloud of Egyptian geese dipped and whirled.

Obviously, my brain was bursting with questions: Why hadn't I known about this before? Was this why the Guardians only let us travel at night? And why, out of all the buildings in Cape Town, had they left these standing?

And most importantly: What the hell was I going to do next?

But the choice was taken away from me.

The parking lot may have looked abandoned, but it wasn't.

The Rotters' moans were getting louder and louder, and I caught a glimpse of movement in the dark depths. They were shambling around the cars, and I suspected that if I didn't get it together, they'd be on me in a matter of minutes. I had no way of knowing if the others' disinterest had been a fluke. I only had one option. I had to head inside the mall and figure out what to do next.

I sprinted up a ramp, leaping over the mangled corpse of a shopping trolley, and headed towards the glass doors in front of me.

I pushed against them, but they didn't give.

Then I noticed the metal door handle. What an idiot! I grabbed it with both hands, turned it, and headed straight into heaven.

5

Or hell, depending on your point of view.

The first thing that hit me was the piped music. It took me right back to before the War, although I didn't recognise the tune. It was some woman singing breathily about another chick called Amy, over a beat like a juddering pulse.

There was another sound I couldn't place at first – a low humming. Then I figured out what it was: electricity. It had been so many years since I'd heard it, I'd forgotten how loud it actually was.

I moved forwards, staring at the marble pillars, the giant pots spewing fronds of plastic greenery and the huge, gleaming picture windows, behind which rows of beautiful, immobile people glared back at me.

The outside may have been taken over by nature but the interior was untouched.

I don't know how long I stood there, taking in the shining floors, the double row of whirring escalators, the painted eyes of the mannequins. Everything was pristine. As if the War and the Great Fire had never happened. As if my biggest problem right then was what flavour of ice cream to buy, or which book to choose with my birthday money. It was only the lack of customers that spoiled the illusion, though the doors to the clothing stores nearest to me were all open, as if they were waiting for shoppers to start milling through them.

I was alone in an immaculate, fully stocked shopping mall.

So I did the only thing I could have done right then.

I went shopping.

6

I know what you're thinking: I must have lost my mind, right? That maybe the smack on the head really *had* scrambled my brains. But be honest, would you have done any different? It had been ten years since I'd seen anything like this and I couldn't resist.

I chose the first shop at random, some sort of clothing store, and walked numbly over to a rack of clothes. I grabbed a pair of jeans and pulled them on under Lungi's dress. They were a size too big, but I picked out a black silk tie decorated with dinosaur skulls and used it as a belt. Then I ripped off the dress completely and exchanged it for a tight black T-shirt with the words *Team Jacob* on it, and flicked through a rack of leather jackets until I found one that looked to be my size. The clothes felt soft and comfortable and unbelievably delicious next to my skin. Next: shoes. I dug through boxes of fur-lined boots, trying on several pairs until I found ones that fitted snugly. I bounced up and down on their springy soles. I felt like I could walk forever in them.

Finally, I gazed at my reflection in the mirrors that lined the store walls. A stranger stared back at me – a stylish stranger in a kick-arse leather jacket and boots to die for. I'd forgotten all about the enclave, the Lottery and the Rotters outside in the Deadlands. Bizarrely, at that second all I could think was: If only Thabo could see me now.

And this was only *one* of the shops in the mall.

Grabbing a backpack from a shelf, I slung it over my shoulder and left the clothing store. Outside, I walked past shops frozen in time: a store selling intricate carpets and ridiculous bendy chairs; another one that seemed to sell nothing but twisted silver forks and decorative cutlery. It was totally bewildering, and I didn't know where to start. I slipped into a Body Shop and grabbed the first things I saw – scented shampoos and bars of colourful soap – greedily shoving them into my bag, before pausing for several seconds to take in the clean perfumey smell of the shop.

Heading for the escalators, I cruised up to the next level and chose an aisle at random. The place was huge: it was on two levels, with double-barrelled corridors that looped around, running parallel to each other, the rows of shops stretching off as far as the eye could see.

I darted in and out of every shop I passed, and within ten minutes the backpack was stuffed full. I'd picked out another pair of jeans, a short dress made of glittery material, and three pairs of Converse sneakers in different colours. Then something struck me. There had to be a bookshop! I quickened my pace, passing a shop bulging with ball gowns, and another furniture store – the televisions in the window showing nothing but static – but at the end of the aisle, I caught a whiff of delicious perfume. Unable to resist, I followed the scent through a set of gleaming glass doors and found myself in a sprawling store that seemed to sell everything: shampoo, make-up, wheelchairs and bottles of herbal medicine. But it wasn't long before the heady scent of perfume started to make me feel a bit nauseous, and I wandered out into the main walkway again.

By now I had forgotten all about my decision to search for a bookstore and when I spied the open doors of a huge department store I wandered inside and began flicking automatically through a rack of silky T-shirts. But I was beginning to flag. There was just too *much*. Too much to think about. Too much to see, to smell, to digest. The mannequins seemed to be staring at me with their dead painted eyes – and the hair on the back of my neck started to prickle. I suddenly had the feeling that I was being watched, and I didn't think it was just because the mannequins were giving me the creeps.

I think it was at that moment that I started coming to my senses.

What the hell did I think I was doing?

Who was running this place? Why hadn't it been destroyed along with the rest of the city?

What if it was a trap?

I knew I had to get out of the store, out of the mall, and as far away from it as possible. And I had to do it right that second.

But by then it was too late.

7

The muzak suddenly cut out and was replaced with a tremendous roaring noise that seemed to make the air around me throb. The sound was ear-shattering, and I clamped my hands over my head and threw myself down on to the carpet, almost sending a mannequin toppling as I banged heavily against its legs. Then, as quickly as it had started, the sound cut out.

My ears buzzed, and I realised I'd been holding my breath. I stayed where I was for a few seconds before finally shuffling forwards. Nothing. Whatever it was had gone. I started to get to my feet, but before I was even, halfway up, I felt a hand clamp down over my mouth. I didn't have a chance to struggle – the next thing I knew I was being dragged into a curtained-off changing room.

I twisted to get away, but whoever was holding me was incredibly strong. In desperation, I bit into the hand clamped over my mouth, and, suddenly, I was free. But even as I turned to run my legs were swept out from underneath me, and I landed with a thump on my back, staring up at a dark-haired guy who was looking at me with a combination of fury and exasperation.

Moving faster than I thought possible, he dropped to a crouch and clamped his hand over my mouth again.

For a couple of seconds I just stared up at him. Using his free hand, he brushed his floppy black hair out of his eyes and leaned closer to me. 'Shhhh!' he hissed into my ear. 'Keep still.'

I tried to speak, but my words were muffled against his palm.

'Just be quiet!' he whispered. 'You have to trust me.'

He had to be joking. Why would I trust someone who'd just knocked me to the floor and had his hand over my mouth? I struggled again, trying to lash out at him with my legs.

'Do you want to die?' he hissed in my ear. I stared straight into his eyes. They were different colours: one was dark brown, one greenish grey.

I shook my head.

'Good. Keep very quiet. Don't even breathe. Okay?'

For the first time it really hit home that I was out of the enclave and none of the normal rules applied. Anything could happen to me. Anything at all.

Several seconds later I heard the same roar I'd heard earlier, but this time it faded in seconds. The dark-haired guy didn't move a muscle until the sound had totally disappeared. Then he removed his hand from my mouth and shook it. I could make out teeth marks in his palm where I'd bitten him, but I hadn't broken the skin.

I sat up and glared at him, not sure whether to be furious or terrified. 'What the hell is going on?' I said.

'We have to get out of here,' he replied. 'And we have to get out of here fast.'

'Why?'

'Questions later,' he snapped.

He held out his hand to help me up, but I ignored it. He was dressed in scuffed black jeans, a leather jacket and a plain grey T-shirt – and under normal circumstances I would have said he was cute. Or he would have been if he wasn't staring at me as if I was a piece of crap he'd found on his shoe. It was then that I noticed that he had something strapped to his back. When I realised that it was a large curved panga, I wasn't sure whether to scream or laugh out loud.

'Are you going to kill me?' I said, struggling to my feet under my own steam.

'Don't be stupid!' he snorted, shouldering a huge rucksack. 'I just saved your life. Now, let's go!'

He grabbed my arm and almost effortlessly propelled me towards the exit. I shrugged myself out of his grip. 'I can walk by myself.'

Then I remembered something. I scooted away from him and raced back to retrieve my backpack. He shook his head again and rolled his eyes at me. 'Follow me,' he said. 'And keep close.'

He paused at the shop's exit and looked in both directions before setting off. Taking a left, he bounded down corridor and onto the escalators, taking the stairs two at a time, the heavy leather boots he was wearing somehow barely making a sound. He didn't run, but he was way taller than me – Thabo's height at least – and I had to take two strides to every one of his.

At the bottom of the escalator he put his fingers to his lips and gestured towards the end of the hallway. I stopped dead, heart leaping into my mouth. I couldn't believe what I was seeing. A bunch of Rotters were industriously slopping water over the shop windows, pausing every now and again to dunk their sponges into the buckets at their feet.

'We're going to have to go past them,' he whispered. 'You going to be cool with that?'

I shrugged, not willing to let my fear show. What if they *could* actually see me this time? But the guy didn't seem that concerned about their presence, which helped.

I kept close to his side as we made our way past them, but they didn't even turn in our direction; they just carried on sloshing water across a shopfront as if we didn't exist. Clearly the guy was as invisible to them as I was.

I followed him down a side aisle and down towards a revolving glass door. I could see the blue glimmer of the sky beyond it, and I quickened my pace.

We pushed through and out into the fresh air.

Grumpy Panga Guy strode down a weed- and bramble-infested ramp that had once ferried cars into the multi-storey lot, and we crossed what was clearly a grassed-over highway as we made our way towards the theme park's walls, the concrete at our feet lumpy with fig tree roots. There was someone leaning against the wall directly in front of us. At first, with the afternoon sun blinding me, I only saw whoever it was in silhouette – a tall chunky figure with spikes sticking up from its head. But as we got closer I could tell it was a girl; the crazy spikes were backcombed hanks of hair. She was dressed in a similar fashion to the guy: black jeans, heavy lace-up boots, cropped leather jacket and a bag as large and bulky as his lay at her feet. Thin chains were laced around her hands and forearms and she was wearing mirrored shades, so I couldn't read her expression. Like Grumpy Panga Guy, she seemed to be about my age, maybe a few years older.

'Took your time,' she said to him. She didn't seem to show any surprise at the sight of me.

'Tell me about it,' he said. 'You won't believe what this chick has just done.'

'Hey!' I snapped. 'My name's Lele, not "this chick" and will someone please tell me what the *hell* is going on?'

'I'll tell you what's going on, Zombie Bait,' the girl said, her voice slightly accented – Malawian, Batswana, maybe. 'Ash here just saved your arse.'

'Ash?' I said to him. 'Is that really your name?'

He nodded curtly.

'And you are?' I said to the girl.

'Saint,' she said with a curl of her lip.

'What?'

'Lost your hearing as well as your sense of self-preservation?'

'No need to be such a bitch,' I said. 'I was only asking.' I thought of adding that at least my name wasn't as lame and clearly made-up as theirs, but something made me keep quiet. 'Where are you from?' I asked her.

'Later,' the girl said. 'We have to get out of here. It's going to get dark fairly soon.'

'Where to?' I said.

Again the girl stared at me as if I was mad. 'Back to the enclave of course. Where else? The nail salon?'

'Hey!' I snapped, 'I didn't ask to be –'

'Shut up!' the girl hissed as a low moaning sound drifted towards us. Ash and Saint flattened themselves against the wall, and motioned for me to do the same. The moaning grew louder, and several seconds later a crowd of Rotters came casually wandering out of the entrace to the theme park as if they'd spent the day riding the roller coaster.

Saint crept forward and checked them out. ''S'cool,' she said, relaxing. 'They're way past their sell-by date.'

This was getting weirder by the second. 'So they can't sense you either?' I asked.

'Course not. We wouldn't last five minutes, otherwise.'

'But why can't they?'

'Don't you ever stop asking questions?' she said.

'I need to know!'

She sighed. 'Look, we don't know for sure. Some of us just have that ... ability.'

That was when the full horror of it struck me. 'Oh, no!' I said. 'The others – the others in the wagon! We have to help them!'

'There's nothing you can do about that now,' the guy – Ash – said. 'Get over it.'

I glared at him, then turned back to Saint. 'What will happen to them?'

'Sweetheart,' Saint said. 'Your guess is as good as mine.'

Without checking to see if I was going to follow them, they started walking off along the grassed-over highway, heading in the direction of the mountain. I hesitated for a second and then jogged after them. My mind was racing, question after question forming on my lips, and I wasn't going to let the only people who could answer them get too far away.

As we skirted around the remains of a bus that was lying on its side, I paused and looked back towards the mall. It rose above the jungle of overgrown weeds like a ginormous white ship.

I turned back to Ash and Saint, but they'd gone. Where they'd been a moment earlier, there was only fynbos and high grass. 'Hey!' I shouted.

Racing around a sprawling myrtle thicket, I caught sight of them. They were deep in conversation and I increased my pace so that I could eavesdrop.

'You get them?' Saint asked Ash.

'Yeah. Weighs a ton, though.' He shrugged his shoulder

under the backpack.

'Tough! You should have done the underwear run. Nice and light!'

'Lucky you. Want to swap?'

'As if! You should have left the books to Ginger. He loves that sparkly vampire crap. It's your tough luck that Hester needed him back early.'

'Yeah. But he did it last time. Besides, it gives me a chance to beef up my muscles.'

Saint snorted. 'Like you need it.'

It didn't take me long to figure out what they were talking about. Their rucksacks were obviously stuffed full of goods from the mall.

'You're Mall Rats!' I said, remembering Lungi's stash back at the shack in New Arrivals. I'd never considered when Thabo had told me about them that there would be a *real* mall involved.

'Give the girl a prize,' Saint said, without turning around.

'How far is the mall from the enclave?' I asked.

'Not too far. Maybe ten kilometres.'

'How are we going to get back in?'

'Relax, Zombie Bait,' Saint said. 'It's under control.'

Ash said something under his breath to her and she laughed. The irritation I was feeling was beginning to turn into something like hate for him. I hung back as they walked on, chatting. They were obviously close, and they joshed each other like Jobe and I used to do in the old days. At one stage Saint nudged his shoulder hard enough to make him stumble, and he retaliated by pretending to try and trip her up.

It hadn't taken nature long to take over Cape Town. Ten years. Impossible to imagine that what we were walking down was once a six-lane highway. In places the Port Jacksons, pines and keurboom trees were so high that I couldn't see anything but bush and sky in front of me, and sometimes duikers and other small buck darted and skipped around us, more curious than afraid. Every so often we'd come across a group of feral cats, but they also fled as we stomped through their territory. Ash and Saint took a right into the bushes, weaving around the trees and junked cars effortlessly as if they knew exactly where they were going, and I realised that they were following a path. It wasn't easy to see at first, but after a while my eyes became accustomed to searching out the shortened grass and flattened patches. We skirted the crumpled remains of a squatter camp, stepping over rusted corrugated iron, and entered a grassy clearing.

'Smoke break,' Ash said, dumping his rucksack on the ground. 'My shoulders are killing me.' He sat down on the ground and leaned back against a rock.

Saint shook her head. 'As if smoking will help,' she grumbled, but she shrugged off her own rucksack all the same and sat down next to him.

Ash pulled a box of cigarettes out of his jacket pocket and lit up, inhaling deeply. He grimaced. 'Stale,' he said.

'Those coffin nails will kill you, Ash. And if Hester finds out you've started again, then lung cancer will be the least of your worries.'

He grinned for the first time. 'She won't find out, though, will she?' He glanced at me. 'What you staring at?' he asked.

'Nothing much,' I fired back, and Saint laughed.

'Sit,' she said to me, and I did so gratefully. My leg muscles, which were already aching from the trudge through the mall, were now on fire. I followed their example and leaned against my own bag. I watched as Saint rummaged in her rucksack, pulling out a small plastic packet. 'Catch!' she said to me, chucking the packet my way.

I reached out and caught it just in time.

'Nice reflexes,' she said. 'You see that, Ash?'

He just grunted.

I shook the packet. 'What's this?'

'Sour worms,' she said.

For a second I thought I must have misheard her. 'What?'

'Sweets.'

'Oh, wow! Thanks!' I ripped into the bag. I couldn't remember the last time I'd had any real sugar. She wasn't kidding about the sour part, but I relished the burst of sweetness on my tongue.

'No problem,' she said, leaning back and closing her eyes. The bushes behind us started to rustle and I glanced around, expecting to see another duiker.

'Ash!' Saint hissed.

She stood up and for a second I thought she was staring straight at me, a look of pure hatred in her eyes. Ash followed her example, whipping the panga out from behind his back, the metal hissing as it slid out of its holder.

'What's going on –' I started to say, not sure if I should start running or not.

'Shhh!' Saint hissed, holding up her hand.

A low moan filled the air, and Ash and Saint stood back to back, faces grim, eyes searching the bush around us. Saint pulled two spiked metal balls out of her bag and attached them to the ends of the chains around her wrists.

'You ready?' Saint asked under her breath, so softly that I had to strain to hear her.

'Always,' Ash said, his mouth drawn in a tense line.

'Keep down!' Saint said to me.

The bushes shook again and, then, with a crash of breaking branches, several figures burst into the clearing.

At first I assumed they were normal people like us – their

clothes were relatively neat – and it was only when I saw their faces that I realised what they were. Their eyes were rolled back in their heads, and their skin was the grey of the newly dead, as if all the blood in their bodies had been drained away. One of them threw back its head and howled, a horrible keening sound, more human than the moans I was used to hearing.

The Rotters moved as one, racing towards us so swiftly that their limbs almost seemed to blur. Saint flicked her wrists, the chains around her arms whipping outwards. She started to spin them in an arc in front of her, then she twisted and flicked them towards the nearest Rotter and they coiled around its neck. Ash stepped forward and, faster than I could really take in, lopped the thing's head from its body. Saint threw her arms out in a graceful motion, and this time the chains on either wrist simultaneously caught two of the Rotters around their necks. She pulled them together, and Ash smoothly ducked underneath the chains, whirled around and sliced off their heads. This time, the cut was so cleanly done that the heads remained where they were, only falling bloodlessly from their bodies as Saint released the chains. It was incredible to watch. Horrible, yet surreally beautiful, like watching an intricately choreographed dance.

They dispatched the last one almost effortlessly, and this time, its head tumbled from its body and bounced towards me, ending up only a few feet from where I was still sitting.

I couldn't take my eyes off it. I know it sounds sick, and you're probably thinking that I should have been puking in shock or something, but it wasn't like that. I knew it wasn't human, you see. There was no blood, and at first, I just gazed at the head, transfixed. Thin white curling tendrils, that reminded me of incredibly fine tree roots, were emerging from the stump of the neck. They seemed to stretch towards me, and I found myself leaning forward to touch them.

'No!' Ash yelled, glaring at me and kicking the head away. 'Don't touch them!' He shook his head at me, and stalked back to his rucksack.

Saint wrapped her chains back around her arms, securing them at her wrists, then walked over to me. 'What is that stuff?' I asked her, noticing that the same tendrils were emerging from the heads and necks of the other bodies. 'That white stuff?'

'Don't you know?'

'No.'

'But you were around during the War, weren't you?'

'Yeah, but ...'

'Don't they teach kids anything these days? We call it spaghetti,' she said with a grin. 'That's what reanimates the bodies. It grows inside them. You know, like, in their veins.'

I shuddered. 'Like some sort of ... parasite?'

She shrugged. 'I guess. Gross, right?'

'Yeah,' I said. Although, to be honest, there was something almost beautiful about the way the tendrils had curled and spread out. 'Are they dangerous?'

She snorted. 'Dangerous? You hear this chick, Ash?'

He was wiping down the blade of his panga and just grunted as if what I'd said was beneath his contempt.

Still shaking her head in disbelief, Saint walked back over to Ash and the two of them started piling the bodies at the edge of the clearing. I didn't offer to help. It wasn't my fault I didn't know what was going on, and I'd had enough of being treated like an idiot. They were whispering and laughing together as they went about their grisly work, and at that second, I don't think I'd ever felt so left out, not even during my first days at Malema High.

It was then that I saw it – the flash of a red jacket in the bush behind them.

'Look out!' I yelled.

With no conscious knowledge that I was reacting within a split-second of shouting my warning, I reached behind me, grabbed a rock and threw it as hard as I could. I watched it fly through the air and hit the emerging Rotter right between its eyes. It staggered back, giving Saint just enough time to lash out with her chains, and for Ash pull a vicious-looking army knife out of his boot.

Ash and Saint stood back to back for several more seconds, their eyes searching the bush.

'That was close!' Saint said, shooting me a small grateful smile.

Ash wiped his knife on his jacket and walked over to me. 'You okay?' he asked me.

'Shouldn't I be asking you that?' I said.

'Good aim,' he said. 'Thanks.'

'No problem,' I said casually, as if throwing rocks at dead people was what I did every day. But I realised then that I'd overlooked something vitally important.

'They could see us!' I said.

'Yeah,' Ash said, pulling out his box of cigarettes and lighting up. He offered the box to me, but I shook my head. 'Fresh ones can.'

'Fresh ones?'

'The newly reanimated. It takes about a week for their senses to dull. We call them Hatchlings. Normally you don't see a bunch together like that. The embassy must have just relocated a group of them.' He swore under his breath.

I thought back to the relocation wagon Dad and I had seen. Was this how the screaming people locked in the wagon had ended up? I shuddered.

'So the longer they've been ... infected ... the less they can sense you?' I said.

He nodded, squinting as the smoke from his cigarette curled up into his eyes. 'Yeah. Except you've really got to watch the ones who were alive when they were turned.' He gestured towards the pile of bodies. 'Like this lot. When they change, they're fast.'

My head was swimming. 'So you mean ... when I was in the mall, I could have bumped into a bunch like this?'

Saint wandered over and dug in her rucksack. 'Yeah,' she said. 'Unlikely, though. There aren't that many.'

'Why not?'

She sighed. 'Think about it. Except for Lottery day and the re-locations, the only time the Guardians get fresh corpses is when someone dies. And that doesn't happen every day.'

'Still,' I said. 'I suppose I *was* lucky.'

'Or you've got a guardian angel,' she said.

'Or a Saint,' Ash said with a grin, and for a second our eyes locked. Then he looked away and his face became inscrutable again. Still, I was glad to see he did have a sense of humour, however lame.

'Where did you learn to fight like that?' I asked.

'You'll find out,' Ash replied. 'Maybe.'

'What do you mean?' I said. 'Can't you just give me a straight answer for once?'

'Enough questions,' Saint said, rubbing her shoulder as if she'd strained it. 'We have to move on.'

There was a faint blush of colour in the sky, and I knew that it would be fully dark in half an hour or so, but I wasn't going anywhere until I had all the answers I needed. I wasn't going to let them ignore me again or treat me like a three-year-old.

'No!' I said. 'I need to know now.'

Ash also got to his feet and stubbed out his cigarette. 'Tough,' he said, turning his back on me. 'We have to get going.'

I couldn't hold in the resentment any longer. 'Hey!' I said, almost yelling. 'You don't have to speak to me like that! I saved your life just now!' I jabbed him in the back with my index finger.

He whirled around. 'If I hadn't got you out of the mall in time,' he said, staring down at me, 'you wouldn't have been *able* to save me.' He was so close that I could smell the cigarette smoke on his breath.

Then he shoved past me, shouldering his rucksack as he went.

'Hey!' I said, my voice trembling with anger. I could feel furious tears building up. 'Hey!'

'Just leave it,' Saint said, grabbing my shoulder.

'Screw you!' I shouted. The tears were seconds from falling and I knew that I'd rather die than let these two see me crying, even if they were just tears of rage and frustration. Throwing my backpack onto my back, I stalked off into the bushes, not caring where I was heading.

'Hey! Wait up! It isn't safe!' Saint called, but I could hear a trace of amusement in her voice, which fuelled my anger even more. She didn't think I'd actually have the guts to go it alone, and I was determined to prove her and her stuck-up boyfriend wrong.

'Leave me alone!'

The path dipped and curved though fairly dense bush, and I increased my pace when I heard the scramble of footsteps behind me.

'Lele!' Saint called. 'Don't be stupid!'

Slipping behind the trunk of a huge dead tree, I held my breath and waited until I could hear that she was inches away from where I was hiding. Then, throwing my entire weight behind it, I swung my rucksack as hard as I could. It slammed into Saint's stomach, the weight of the shoes and clothes and soaps and shampoos enough to send her flying.

I heard her gasp and call out for Ash, but I wasn't going to hang around. I dumped the bag and sprinted away, legs pumping as if my life depended on it, dodging around tree stumps and leaping over branches. The blood roared in my ears, but I kept on going until I found myself at the foot of a steep embankment. Without looking back, I pulled myself upwards, using tree roots to steady myself.

I heard shouting behind me, but I couldn't risk hesitating, not for a second. 'Lele!' Ash shouted. 'Don't! You're going the wrong way!'

I peered behind me. He was at the base of the embankment, Saint behind him. She was slightly out of breath, but otherwise didn't seem too hassled.

'Come back!' he called again. 'It's dangerous!'

But I was nearly at the top. Ignoring my burning lungs, I urged myself up to the top of the rise, and pushed through the clump of Port Jacksons that sprouted along the top of it.

I stopped dead, a scream stuck in my throat.

I'd stumbled right into the middle of a mass of Rotters who were shambling along the top of the embankment. There were literally hundreds of them, and the old-book smell of them was intense. Most seemed to be in the last stages of deterioration, and they bumped and stumbled against each other in silence; the only sound was the hiss of the long grass brushing against their bodies, the silence making the sight of them even more disturbing. Several were nothing more than loosely knitted-together skeletons, and I could see the ropey white tendrils of spaghetti stuff snaking around their bare bones.

I started to back away, but then the crowd parted and I caught a glimpse of the enclave fence in the distance.

I had a choice to make: Make my way through the Rotters and leg it towards the enclave, or go back and join Saint and Ash and carry on being patronised.

It wasn't a difficult decision, but I'd be lying if I said it wasn't nerve-racking. I had to skip and dodge past tight knots of stumbling Rotters. I kept my eyes fixed on the ground wherever possible to avoid looking at them. Because, let's face it, Gran was out there somewhere, her body infested with that weird white stuff, a reanimated facsimile of someone I'd once loved with all my heart.

And I knew that if I saw her I'd lose it for good.

I slipped between two particularly skeletal specimens and breathed a sigh of relief. The edge of the embankment was less than five metres away. But I wasn't looking where I was going, and I stumbled over something hidden in the grass. I reached out reflexively and my hands brushed the back of a Rotter dressed in a rough tweed suit. It whirled around with the speed of a cobra, and I literally had to leap out of the way to avoid it touching me, skimming my palms on the rough ground as I caught my weight. Despite the attack I'd witnessed back in the clearing, I'd become used to their shambling gait and I'd been lulled into thinking that they were harmless. It shook its head from side to side as if it was trying to see out of the empty holes that had once held its eyes, and then it bent its neck right back and let out a totally inhuman moan. One by one, the others around it stopped their aimless shuffling and followed suit. The sound rose higher and higher as more joined in, until it sounded like the howl of an immense wind. I could feel the hairs on my arms standing up.

Dragging my body to the side of the embankment, I slid down until the ground flattened out and I could stand easily. In front of me was a stretch of wasteland that looked as if it had once been some sort of parking lot, although the building it serviced was now nothing but rubble. I jumped over the carcass of a puff adder, and began to make my way through the labyrinth of burned-out cars, shuddering as the ghastly moan started up again behind me. It was almost as if I was hearing it deep down, in my stomach. Then, without warning, it cut out and I heard Saint and Ash calling for me.

'Lele!'

I had no shortage of places to hide. I picked a rusted kombi at random, pulled the door open and crawled inside. The seats were still fairly intact, although the upholstery had rotted through, and I crawled under the back seat, grateful for once for being so skinny and small.

The voices were getting closer and closer.

'Lele!' Ash called.

'Come on, Lele! It's not safe out here for you!' Saint joined in.

By the sound of things they were now right outside the kombi.

'You sure she came this way?' Ash asked.

'No,' Saint snapped back. 'Of course I'm not sure.'

'I was only asking, Saint.'

'Whatever.' There was a pause before Saint spoke again. 'It would take balls of steel to walk through all the zombs around here.'

'Where else could she have gone, though?'

'Dunno. I hope she's okay.'

For a second I thought about showing myself, but then I heard Ash say something that changed my mind.

'She's a bloody liability,' he snapped. 'Who does she think she is? Running off like that. Idiot!'

I bit my tongue, the anger flaring in my veins.

Now I was determined not to be found.

'We can't go back without her,' Saint said.

'We might not have a choice,' Ash replied. 'What a total pain in the arse.'

'Well, we weren't exactly nice to her.'

'So? What is this? Primary school?'

There was the sound of something thunking against the kombi – probably one of them had kicked a rock against it. The floor was dusty and covered in rat droppings, and I had to stifle a sneeze.

'Anyway,' Saint continued. 'Didn't you think she was cute?'

'Yeah right, Saint.'

'Be honest, Ash ... I saw the way you looked at her.'

I held my breath so that I could hear his answer.

'Grubby little nobody like that? You have to be joking, Saint.'

'I know you better than that, Ash.'

'She's not my type,' he snapped. 'Just leave it, will you?'

'Okay, okay.' There was a pause. 'Anyway, I thought she was cute. Sexy.'

Ash snorted. 'You would, Saint.'

'Come on, she's probably reached the fence by now. We can pick her up there. Let's just hope that she doesn't run into any Hatchlings.'

'I don't know about that. She looked like she could handle herself.'

Although I was still squirming with hatred for his stuck-up attitude, I couldn't help but feel a brief spurt of pride.

'Yeah. But there's something else. What if she gets back into the enclave before we find her?'

'How would she get back in? Impossible.'

'But what if she does?'

'What are you saying?'

'Duh, Ash. What if she talks?'

'You think she will?'

'I don't know.'

Their voices began to fade as they started to walk away. I decided to wait ten minutes or so before leaving my hiding place, but my eyes were getting heavy, and before I could stop myself, I was out like a light.

9

Something was tickling my nose. I opened my eyes and found myself gazing at an enormous rat. I tried to keep as still as possible while it sniffed around me, trying not to flinch as its rubbery tail brushed against my cheek, but it took every ounce of self-control I had. With an angry squeak it finally decided to skitter away.

Had I *really* won the Lottery?

Had I *really* been inside a shopping mall?

I glanced down at my unfamiliar clothes. It certainly looked that way.

And had I *really* met the Mall Rats?

I remember thinking: What would Thabo say? He'd described them as hard-core War veterans, not stuck-up teenagers with attitude problems and stupid nicknames.

Of course, right then it hadn't occurred to me that the

chances weren't great that I'd ever see him again.

Fresh early morning light was streaming into the kombi, dust motes dancing in the air. I sneezed and started to drag my aching limbs out of the rusted interior.

Outside, I stretched and looked around for any sign of Saint and Ash, but I wasn't too concerned. I'd slept right through the night – my new clothes keeping out the worst of the cold – and I was fairly sure they would be long gone. I glanced back towards the highway, but the shambling crowd of Rotters had also disappeared. In fact, the only movement came from a mole snake, which slid out of the bushes in front of me, heading towards a patch of sunlight.

In the bright morning light, the enclave fence looked far closer than it had the night before, and I got moving. My mouth still tasted bitter and gummy – I was desperate for a drink of water – and my stomach growled, adding to the discomfort, but hunger and thirst I could deal with.

It took me less than half an hour to reach the fence, but that, as it turned out, was the easy part. There was no way I was going to be able to climb over the top of it; it loomed above me, twelve feet of welded metal, ancient car parts, bricks and wood. Like the fences that ringed the Agricultural settlements, it was impenetrable. Years of labour had gone into its construction, teams of workers slaving around the clock to extend the enclave's boundary metre by metre, endlessly patching over any potentially vulnerable sections. I tried to peek through a crack in one of the slats, but I couldn't see anything except for a brownish blur that could have been anything. I had a vague idea of maybe alerting one of the fence crews that patrolled the enclave's borders day and night, but there was no way I'd be able to get their attention, even if they happened to be right on the other side of where I was standing. I needed to find a gate.

I carried on, keeping as close to the fence as I could. A small dog padded behind me part of the way, but when I stopped and held out my hand to it, it ran away, tail between its legs. I drank from a brackish puddle, splashing muddy water over my face. My stomach grumbled again, but there was nothing I could do about that.

At first my senses were on high alert, but this close to the fence there didn't seem to be any Rotters – their moans sounded miles away – and for once the day was still and clear, so I was fairly sure I'd hear anyone or anything approaching. There was the occasional sound of something largish crashing through the undergrowth, but I convinced myself that it was probably only a buck.

I sat down for a break, my back against the fence, and it was then that I heard the jangle and creak of an approaching wagon.

It sounded as if it was fairly close, but I couldn't see any sign of it. Trying to keep as quiet as possible I jogged through the myrtle bushes, soon coming across a grass track that appeared to run parallel to the fence. A few metres in front of me a wagon was bumping along. It was moving quickly, the huge black horse pulling it picking its feet up in a trot.

Using the trees around me for cover, I followed. I had some half-formed idea of sneaking onto the back of it, in the hope that maybe it was heading into the enclave – even though the track was now moving further away from the fence. I ran to catch up with it as it rumbled over a steep rise. It was heading down towards a large white hill of some sort. Catching my breath, I crept forward until, gradually, I began to realise what it was I was looking at.

I had to clamp my hands over my mouth to stifle the scream.

It wasn't a hill, after all. It was a graveyard.

10

To describe what I was seeing as 'grotesque' or 'horrific' would be a serious understatement. The hillock was a huge sprawling pile of bones and skulls. Thousands upon thousands of them. And it appeared to be moving.

Filled with a horrible fascination, I edged closer, making sure that I kept out of sight. I could make out a few tufts of rotten material stuck in amongst the bones, and as I made my way down the slope I realised why I'd thought the pile was moving. Slippery tendrils of white stuff – what Saint had called spaghetti – were snaking in and around the skulls and body parts.

Sick with disgust, I hid behind a scrubby thorn tree, watching as the wagon finally came to a halt and a Guardian climbed down from it. It glided around to the back, hauled out a shrouded corpse and flung it carelessly onto the pile. Then, mission complete, the Guardian climbed back on to the wagon and wheeled the horse around in a sharp turn. Seconds later, the cart was rumbling back the way it had come, passing so close to where I was hiding that I could have easily jumped on to the back of it. But I didn't. I stayed where I was. Transfixed.

As soon as the Guardian had thrown the corpse on to the pile, the tendrils of spaghetti stuff had seemed to shiver as if they'd been hit by a gust of wind. Then, in a sinuous waving movement, they slid towards the body, sneaking under the shroud – the covering drifting away as if pulled by invisible hands.

Of course, I was being completely stupid. There was no way now that I'd be able to catch up with the wagon, and I'd been so riveted by the bone mountain that I'd completely forgotten what Ash had said about the newly reanimated.

Until, that was, the corpse sat up and stared straight at me.

For a weird stomach-clenching second we both held our positions, and then it scrambled on to its hands and knees and started scuttling in my direction, snuffing at the air like some sort of hideous animal.

I raced back towards the fence, not daring to look behind me, rocketing back up the rise, and throwing myself through the tangle of bushes. I could hear it crashing after me, sounding closer and closer, and I expected to feel its hand grabbing at my back at any second.

I tried to leap over a tree trunk that blocked my path, but only succeeded in catching the edge of my boot on it. The trip sent me flying into a pile of squishy dead leaves. Rolling onto my back, I readied myself to kick my legs out at the approaching Rotter, when an ear-splitting roar cut through the air, followed by a shout that sounded like: 'Time to paaaaaarty!'

I looked up and stared into the eyes of a giant.

Well, he wasn't exactly a giant, but he was the tallest guy I'd ever seen. His head seemed to be nothing but a bright orange halo of hair, and one of his arms was encased in a thick leather glove that was attached to a huge chainsaw.

As the Rotter burst through the bushes, the giant revved the chainsaw, stepped forward and swung the machine in an arc as if it weighed absolutely nothing. The Rotter's head went flying over me, but it had all happened so quickly that its body carried on moving forward for several steps before crumpling into a heap.

The giant revved the chainsaw again and then it cut out. The silence was almost shocking after the incredible noise. 'Awright, mate?' he said.

I nodded. I think that my mouth was probably hanging open at this point. 'Thanks,' I said when I could speak. 'You saved my life.'

'No worries.'

Looking up at him I realised that he actually wasn't that much older than me. And he was wearing the same sort of outfit as Saint and Ash – black trousers and a dusty army greatcoat, the sleeves of which didn't actually reach his wrists.

'Who are you?'

He laughed. 'I'm Ginger, innit,' he said, and I found myself smiling back at him. I couldn't help it. 'So you're the chick who outsmarted Ash and Saint, yeah?'

'You know Ash and Saint?'

'Yeah! Course I do, mate.' He crossed the fingers on his free hand. 'We're like that!'

'Where are they?'

'Back home. I'll tell you something, though; they're going mental. How'd you manage to lose them, anyway?'

I couldn't place his accent and I had to concentrate to make out what he was saying – the words seemed to run into each other.

'Where are you from?'

'Same place as you, mate. Where else?'

'But your voice ...'

'Think I speak funny, do you?' he said with another grin.

'Well ... kind of.'

'Oh yeah, that. Was out here when it all kicked off, innit.'

'Out here?'

'Yeah. During the War. Me and the family come out here to watch the World Cup, you know, the soccer. And then it all went pear-shaped and I got stuck out here.'

'From where?'

'The UK.'

'England?'

'Yeah, course. London.'

'I'm sorry,' I said. I didn't know what else to say, and I knew I sounded hopelessly pathetic. Still, at least he'd managed to hang on to his accent.

'Come on,' he said, holding out the hand that didn't have the metal blade attached to it. I grabbed it – it felt like holding a side of ham – and he hauled me up with no effort. Even on tiptoe I barely reached his shoulder.

'Where to?'

'To see Hester, of course, where else? ' He nodded back towards the bone mountain. 'You really don't want to hang around there.'

'What is that?'

''S'where the Guardians dump the used-up zombs. Got to put them somewhere, I s'pose.'

I shuddered.

'Yeah, I know,' he said. 'Not even the vultures want to touch it. Kind of like recycling, though, when you think about it, innit?'

'I guess –'

'Oh, wait!'

He dug in his backpack and handed me a tin, the label faded and spattered with rust.

'What's this?'

'Coke. Bit past its sell-by date, but I don't think it can rot, if you know what I'm saying.'

I cracked the tab and swallowed it in one long draught, not caring that it ran over my chin. It was warm, but the blast of pure sweetness was wonderful. I gulped it down, burping loudly as I swallowed the last drop.

'Nice one!' Ginger said.

'So who's Hester?' I asked.

'Hester's, like, the coolest person in the world. You know that movie, *Wanted*? You know, like, the character that Angelina Jolie plays? Well, Hester is, like, totally *way* cooler than that.'

'I have no clue what you're talking about, Ginger.'

'Okay, well you know the dead cool rat guy who trains the Ninja Turtles –'

'The *what*?'

'You seriously don't know what I'm on about?'

'Seriously,' I said.

'Come on. It's a long walk. Save your breath. I'll fill you in.'

He wasn't lying. Turned out that I needed every ounce of energy to make it. Not that I could have got a word in edgeways if I'd wanted to. For the rest of the walk Ginger described every scene in the film and the TV series he'd mentioned in minute detail, even putting on the voices of the characters.

11

I was about to admit I couldn't walk any further, when Ginger stopped and sank to his knees in front of a squat thorn bush.

'Check this out,' he said, lifting it up by its roots to reveal a wooden trapdoor underneath. He grabbed the metal ring handle, and hefted it upwards. 'Ladies first,' he said with another infectious grin.

I peered down into a gloomy space, a rope ladder stretching into the dark beneath. 'Where does it go?' I asked. Although it was obvious: it snaked underneath the enclave fence.

'Home, course. Cool, innit? Like James Bond.'

It didn't even occur to me that I might be walking into a trap. There was just something so trustworthy about Ginger – something so reassuring and safe.

Climbing down, I found myself in a low tunnel. The walls were solid earth, propped up with metal and wooden struts, and

I tried not to think about the weight of the city on top of me. I could just about stand upright, but Ginger had to bend almost double. There was a faint rumbling sound in the background.

'What's that noise?'

'The generator, of course.'

'Generator? You mean you have electricity?'

'Well, duh. Of course. How else would I watch my DVDs?'

'Oh.' I nodded as if what he'd said made perfect sense.

Halfway along two tunnels split off in opposite directions and in the dim light I could make out several doors cut into the earthen walls. 'Where do these tunnels go?' I asked.

'Dorms. Where we sleep, you know.'

'You live down here?'

'Duh,' he said.

Ginger edged past me as the tunnel curved sharply to the left, ending at a small wooden door. He pulled it open and I followed him through into a huge, bare room that was so brightly lit I had to blink several times before my eyes adjusted to the light. The walls were lined with pangas and several gleaming swords, and in the corner of the room stood a roughly carved man-shaped block of wood. There was a tang of sweat in the air.

'This is the training room,' Ginger said.

'Training for what?' I was beginning to sound like an echo.

'What do you think? Got to keep in shape. Otherwise them Hatchlings, well, you know.'

Yet another miniscule door was cut into the earth at the far end of the room. 'We're hoooooome!' Ginger called, opening the door and stepping back so that I could go first.

By now I was so tired and hungry and bewildered that I wasn't feeling even slightly wary.

I walked into another huge area that was furnished like a room from before the War. Squishy couches were dotted around randomly, the roughly plastered walls were painted a vivid blue and there was even a carpet on the floor. But of course I only really took all these details in later. What really held my attention right then were the three people staring at me.

Ash and Saint were leaning against the wall, arms crossed, but my eye was instantly drawn to the woman sitting on a wide padded bench in the centre of the room. She was even smaller in stature than me and her brown face was a mass of wrinkles. There was something about her – some kind of inner stillness – that instantly reminded me of Gran. I know that sounds like wish-fulfilment, but I'm just telling you how I felt.

'Lele,' she said. 'I am so glad Ginger found you.' She heaved herself to her feet, wincing in pain. I couldn't tell how old she was, but she was obviously a War veteran – a shiny clump of scar tissue spread over her left cheek, just below her eye – and she moved slowly as if she was testing each limb to see if it would work before she put any weight on it. She took my hand in both of hers. 'I am Hester. It is wonderful to meet you.'

'You too,' I said, my manners kicking in. And it was kind of wonderful. I felt immediately at ease around her.

'And you've met Saint and Ash, of course.'

Saint didn't exactly look pleased to see me, but she gave me a small nod of acknowledgement. Without her sunglasses her eyes looked weirdly naked.

'Hi, *Saint*,' I said.

Ash ignored me completely, but two could play at that game.

'And I imagine you already know Ginger quite well by now,' Hester said with a smile.

Ginger winked at me. 'Yeah. We're old mates.'

'Now, Lele, you must be hungry and thirsty, no?'

My stomach grumbled again. 'Yes,' I said.

'Please, sit.'

She gestured towards a brightly coloured sofa, which looked like the most comfortable chair I'd ever seen. I sank into it gratefully while Hester moved towards a small kitchen area. 'Let me do it, Hester,' Saint said, but Hester waved her away with an impatient gesture. Everything seemed to be run on electricity. There was even a clanking fridge in the corner of the kitchen, and at the far end of the room I saw something I hadn't ever seen in the enclave – a television. Ginger's eyes kept flicking over towards it.

'Not now, Ginger,' Saint said.

'Yeah, awright.' He turned to me. 'Hey, tell you what, later I'll show you that film I was talking about.'

I nodded numbly.

Hester handed me a bowl of bean stew that smelled delicious, and a glass of water so cold that I could barely hold it. I gulped the water down in seconds, and dug into the stew – so hungry that I didn't feel even slightly self-conscious eating in front of everyone.

Hester waited until I'd cleaned the bowl.

'Now, Lele,' she said. 'You must have many questions. I will do my best to answer them.'

'Thank you.'

She smiled again. 'Saint tells me that you have heard of us. That you know who we are.'

'You're the Mall Rats.'

'Ja. Not my choice of name. I suppose you understand the irony? That no one suspects there's an actual mall out there?'

I nodded. 'Why wasn't it destroyed like the other buildings?'

'That, Lele, I cannot answer. It is a mystery only the Guardians have the answer to.'

'But ... who else knows it's there?'

She shrugged. 'As far as we are aware, only my team.'

'But that's impossible! Surely the embassy – the Resurrectionists – must know?'

'Not as far as we know. Besides, what does it matter if they know it exists? They cannot go there, can they?'

'Not without getting smooshed, anyway,' Ginger said. 'But you don't have that problem, eh, Lele?'

Something struck me. 'Hey! How did you know the Rotters couldn't see me, anyway?'

Hester smiled. 'Saint?'

'We followed you,' Saint said.

'When?'

'When you were in the mall. You wouldn't have made it anywhere near that far if they could sense you.'

My head was beginning to spin again. I opened my mouth to ask the next question, but Hester spoke first. 'And I suppose you have figured out why Ginger brought you to meet me.'

'Um ...'

'We would like to invite you to join us.'

'Join you? Me? Why?'

'Why do you think? You have a very special talent.'

'But ... I can't. I have to get back – get back to my brother.'

'I'm afraid that's not possible, Lele.'

I stood up. 'You'd keep me here against my will?'

'No, of course not. But you must understand: you have been out of the enclave.'

'So?'

'Think about it. Everyone thinks you have been sent out into the Deadlands. The Resurrectionists, well, if they saw you, they would take you in for questioning.'

'And we all know where that leads,' Saint said with a snort.

'I don't,' I said.

'Let's just say that once you've been taken for questioning, you're not likely to leave in a hurry.'

'I don't get it.'

Ash sighed and shook his head as if I was the stupidest person he'd ever encountered.

'Just what is your problem with me?' I snapped at him.

'Whoa! You go, girl!' Ginger said in a silly high-pitched voice. I knew he was making fun of me, but I couldn't help smiling at him.

'And we don't know what the Guardians would do if they knew about you,' Hester said.

'But they'll know I'm missing, won't they? I mean, when they look in the wagon. And who says that the others didn't escape?'

'They didn't,' Saint said. 'And as far as the Guardians are aware, you're just another Rotter by now.'

I shuddered. 'Are you guys part of the ANZ?'

'No, Lele,' Hester said with a smile.

'And you're obviously not Resurrectionists.'

'Obviously not,' Saint snapped.

'Lone wolves, that's what we are, Lele,' Ginger said. 'We run in the night, masters of our own destiny, renegades, rule-breakers –'

'Yes, thank you, Ginger,' Hester said.

'And if I join you ... what's in it for me?' I said, doing my best to sound world-weary and wise, although my heart was galloping in my chest.

'Cut of the profits,' Saint said. 'Same as everyone else.'

'How much do you make?'

'More than you've ever seen, sweetie,' she replied.

It had already occurred to me, now knowing about my special skill, that I could probably make it back to the Agriculturals without being attacked by the Rotters, although I couldn't say the same for my brother. But if I had enough trade credits, I thought, perhaps there was a chance that I'd be able to hire a cart to transport Jobe safely through the Deadlands and away from the threat of Mandela House. Or bribe someone to smuggle us into the back of a transport or mail wagon.

'Okay,' I said. 'Count me in.'

'It's not as easy as that,' Saint said.

'What do you mean?'

'If you're in, you have to be all the way in, if you know what I'm saying.' She looked over at Ash, who gave her a wink.

'You have to understand. What we are doing here – it's unorthodox,' Hester said.

'But all the kids at my school – they all wear clothes from before,' I replied.

'Yes. But no one knows exactly where the stuff comes from, do they? And we can't have a spy in our midst,' Saint said.

'I'm not a spy!'

'Lele. It is unfortunate that you ... lost Ash and Saint,' Hester gave them a look, and they shrugged uncomfortably. 'But you see there are things you have to learn before you can start earning credits. For example, you can't just walk into the mall and help yourself. There are rules you must follow.' She coughed slightly. 'Continue, please, Saint.'

'There are certain things we can't bring back. That you mustn't touch, or the Guardians ...'

'The Guardians will what?'

'We've seen them in action,' Saint said quietly. 'One of us ... she ...' Her voice faltered and she and Ash shared a glance that I couldn't read.

'So what sort of stuff can't you fetch back from the mall?'

'Like anything that could be used as a weapon. And no medical supplies.'

'Why?'

'Figure it out,' Saint said. 'It's not rocket science.'

I glared at her, but decided not to ask what the hell she was talking about in case I looked stupid. 'Okay,' I said. 'What else?'

Ginger spoke up. 'See, mate, the first rule of Mall Rats is: Never talk about Mall Rats.'

Saint groaned. 'Here we go.'

'And the second rule of Mall Rats, is: Never talk about Mall Rats.'

'I got it the first time,' I said to him.

'Like in *Fight Club*,' Ginger said proudly.

'Huh?'

'Ginger is obsessed with movies, Lele,' Hester said.

'It's true, I am.' He nodded.

'So what's the third rule?' I asked. 'Never talk about Mall Rats?'

'No,' Ash said, speaking up unexpectedly. I found myself staring into his eyes – that peculiar mix of dark brown and grey. 'The third rule is: If you ever see Ginger running, run after him as fast as you can.'

'Why?'

'Hey! Don't diss me in front of the newbie, Ash,' Ginger said, but he was smiling.

Saint punched him playfully on the shoulder, and he pretended to wince in pain before bursting into giggles again. Hester shook her head and rolled her eyes. It was clear that they all knew each other really well – as if they were part of a family – and I started to feel left out and self-conscious.

As if she'd picked up on this, Hester approached, bent down and kissed me on the cheek. 'It is settled, Lele. Welcome to the team.'

Ginger gave me a bear hug that lifted me right off my feet and Saint walked over and shook my hand briskly.

Only Ash remained where he was.

12

'Bathroom's in here,' Saint said, pointing to a low wooden door that was cut into one of the tunnel walls.

I peered in. There was a compost toilet, a sink and even a shower. I longed to wash away the dirt and dust and sweat of the last two days, but Saint was having none of it. 'Come on,' she said, leading me further down the corridor. 'You'll be sharing with me,' she added, not looking too charmed at the thought.

The room was small and the two mattresses on the floor took up most of the space. I had to admit it was cosy, though. A poster of a beautiful woman wearing skin-tight clothing and posing above the words *Tomb Raider* was the only decoration.

'Ginger gave me that,' Saint said. 'It's one of his favourite films.'

'Where does he get his movies?'

'His DVDs? The mall, of course. Where we get everything

else.' Saint pointed to a rickety cupboard in the corner. 'You can stash your stuff there.'

'I haven't got any stuff,' I said. 'I chucked it after I . . .' I let my voice trail away. I didn't want to remind her about whacking her in the stomach with my bag.

She rolled her eyes. 'Well, you'll just have to wear what you've got until we do another mall run. The last lot's all been spoken for. And my stuff will be way too big for you.'

She sat down on the mattress nearest to the wall.

'How long have you lived here?' I asked her.

She shrugged. 'Five years.'

'And Ash and Ginger?'

'Ash has been here a lot longer. Ginger about the same as me.'

Saint pulled off her leather jacket, and started unravelling the chains that criss-crossed her arms.

'Where did you get those chains?'

'They are my weapons,' she said, as if that was all I needed to know.

I flumped down on the mattress, looking up at the wooden beams that held the earth above me at bay, the events of the last twenty-four hours racing through my brain.

Then I sat up.

So much had happened that I hadn't even considered *how* I'd won the Lottery. I mean, I was supposed to be exempt. The only way I could have won was if someone had engineered it that way.

Someone had wanted me dead.

And they'd almost got their wish.

'What is it?' Saint asked.

I told her about my suspicions, but she kept her face impassive. 'I see,' she said when I'd finished my explanation.

'But don't you get it? Someone wanted me dead. Someone planned this.'

'You any idea who?'

'It has to be my stepmother.'

'Well, there is nothing you can do about that now. Get used to it.'

She was right, but there was something final in her tone I didn't like. She lay down, her back to me.

'Saint?'

'Yeah?'

'Where are you from?'

'Same place as you. From here.'

'But you're not South African.'

'No. I was born in Botswana. Gaborone.'

'So what are you doing here? I mean, how did you end up in South Africa?'

'Nosey girl, aren't you?'

'I'm interested.'

She sighed, and at first I thought she wasn't going to answer me. Then she said: 'I was in boarding school here when it happened. The War.'

'How old were you?'

'Nine.'

So she was nineteen. I wondered how old Ash was, and Ginger for that matter. 'That must have been awful for you,' I said.

'It wasn't great.'

'So, you're like Ginger,' I said.

'What do you mean?'

'No home.'

'You're wrong there, girl,' she said. 'This is my home, and it's yours too.'

I almost blurted out the whole plan right then – that as soon as I had enough credits I'd be out of there – but I clamped my mouth shut at the last moment.

'Saint?'

'What?'

'How did you become a Mall Rat?'

'Okay, that is enough,' Saint said. 'I need to sleep, and I am not here to answer your questions all night, you understand?'

'Yeah, I get it.'

I lay back, the day's events continuing to run crazily through my mind, but the mattress was far more comfortable that it looked and within minutes I was dead to the world.

13

My mind was still buzzing from everything that had happened the day before, and for a second or two after I woke up I had to struggle to remember where the hell I was.

Saint's bed was empty, and all I could hear was the rumble of the generator. Grabbing my filthy jeans and the leather jacket, I padded into the corridor and headed for the bathroom. I didn't know what the water situation was, but I decided to have a shower anyway, lathering my body with a tube of orange-scented Body Shop shower gel that felt delicious on my skin. There wasn't a mirror in the small room, but as far as I could tell, my body had far fewer bruises and abrasions than I'd been expecting.

Feeling refreshed, tingly clean and full of nervous excitement, I wandered through the training room and into the kitchen and lounge area.

Ginger, Ash and Saint were sitting at the table when I walked in, and they all immediately fell silent when they caught sight of me – no prizes for guessing the topic of their conversation.

'Good morning, Lele,' Hester said. She was stirring a pot on the stove, and she appeared to be genuinely pleased to see me.

'Awright, Lele?' Ginger said as Saint nodded to me. 'You have any cool dreams?'

'Can't remember,' I said, relaxing slightly even though Ash hadn't looked up from the book he was reading.

'Hungry, Lele?' Hester asked.

'Starving,' I said. Hester handed out bowls of mealiemeal porridge to each of us, and placed a huge jar of honey on the table. I hadn't tasted honey since I'd left the agricultural enclave and my mouth watered at the sight of it.

Ginger pushed the pot towards me with a grin. 'Like that, do you?' he said.

'My favourite,' I replied. 'Where we used to live, there was a guy who kept bees. We'd have fresh honey all summer long.'

'Nice one.' He chugged back the Coke he was drinking and crushed the can, burping noisily.

'Ginger!' Hester said.

'Sorry. Can't help it.'

'You shouldn't drink so much of that stuff.'

'Yeah,' Saint said. 'It's poison.'

'It's delicious is what it is,' he replied, winking at me.

Ash was still lost in his book. I decided that I wasn't going to sink to his level, and at least make an attempt at politeness. 'What are you reading, Ash?' I asked, trying to sound friendly and interested.

Without looking at me he held the book up so that I could read the title. *Ways of Dying*. I'd never heard of it. 'What's it about?' I said, trying again.

'Stuff,' he said, again without glancing at me.

I bit back my retort. If he wasn't going to make an effort, then neither was I. 'Are we going back to the mall today?' I asked Hester instead.

'We only go once a week, Lele,' Ginger said. 'Unless we get a special order.'

'Right. So what do you do the rest of the time?'

'We train,' Saint said.

'Train for what?' But then I remembered what Ginger had said the day before about the Hatchlings.

Saint gave me a savage grin. 'You'll see, Zombie Bait.'

Hester clucked her tongue at her. 'Be nice, Saint,' she said. 'But Lele, you must eat up. You will need your strength. You have a busy day ahead of you.'

'Doing what?'

'We're going to teach you how to handle yourself, girl,' Ginger said. 'We're going to teach you how to give the zombies a good arse-kicking.' He stood up and lashed out an arm, almost sending the honey pot flying.

Hester sighed and shook her head. 'Ginger, for that, you are to do the washing up.'

'Aw, what?'

'No arguments.'

I felt the weight of someone's eyes on me, but when I glanced at Ash, he was seemingly lost in his book again.

14

'That's for blindsiding me in the Deadlands,' Saint said.

I glared up at her, fighting to get my breath back. She'd swept my legs from underneath me and I'd fallen hard. Anger surged through me, and I leapt to my feet and rushed at her. She sidestepped gracefully, almost casually stuck out her right leg, and sent me sprawling onto my back again. This time I hit my head, and when I closed my eyes silvery stars danced in front of me.

Now I was really angry, the tears seconds away from falling.

I stood up and brushed myself down, Hester, Ginger and Ash watching from the sidelines.

'Ready to go again, Zombie Bait?' Saint asked, grinning.

Every inch of me was itching to lash out at her, but I was done. I hadn't signed up for this kind of treatment. 'Screw you!' I shouted at Saint and stalked towards the door.

'Hey! Where're you going?' Saint asked.

'I'm out of here!' I yelled back. 'You don't fight fair.'

'Hey! You think the Hatchlings fight fair, sweetheart? Well, do you?'

'But you're supposed to be training me! Not beating me up!'

'Then go,' Saint said. 'Walk away. Cry your tears like a spoilt baby.'

'That's enough, Saint,' Hester said. She walked over to me. 'Lele. You have to learn to control your anger.'

'I can't do this,' I said.

'You just going to give up, Zombie Bait?' Saint asked. 'It's an easy thing to walk away. It's the easiest thing in the world.' She shook her head in disgust and walked over to Ash and Ginger. 'Told you,' she muttered to Ash.

I ran up behind her and pushed her, the force of my fury giving me added strength. Saint stumbled forward, and I tried to lash out with my leg, but she was far too quick for me. She whirled around, grabbed my arm, forced it back and sent me spinning on to the floor again.

'That's enough, Saint!' Hester said.

Now the tears were flowing freely. With difficulty, Hester sank down on her haunches and took my hand. 'Lele,' she said, 'the anger you have, you must learn to use it, to control it. It is just as much a monster as the things we fight outside.'

'Whatever,' I muttered, wiping my cheeks.

Instead of looking annoyed at my rudeness, Hester smiled. 'You have a lot of spirit,' she said. 'You are strong. Come . . .' She held out a hand, but I remembered how she'd struggled even to walk without wincing in pain, and I didn't want to cause her any more discomfort. I got shakily to my feet without her assistance.

'Here is a trick for you,' Hester said, reaching out and wiping a stray tear from my face. 'When you feel the anger starting, try to picture something in your mind that you love or that you hold dear. Try to replace the anger with that image.'

'I'm not cut out for this, Hester,' I said.

'You think that the others are? They all had to learn, just like you.'

'Yeah, Lele,' Ginger said. 'Ash, like, totally beat the crap out for me for weeks till I got my chainsaw.'

'You think you could give it one more go?' Hester asked.

I hesitated. Saint was watching me carefully. I knew I couldn't let her win. 'Okay,' I said.

'Try and focus this time, Lele,' Hester said. 'Don't let the anger blind you.'

'And when you fall,' Ginger said, 'let your body go limp, or try and curl up into a ball.'

Saint sighed. 'This is going to be almost too easy.'

I was hit with another surge of anger, but this time I took a deep breath and thought about Jobe, concentrating on an image of him playing with Chinwag.

Saint ran at me, and I held my ground until the last moment. Then, copying her movements from before, I stepped to the side and kicked out, catching her on her thigh. I caught her unawares, but she was still too quick for me. As soon as she'd regained her balance, she hooked her right leg around mine and for the third time that morning I landed on my back. I'd forgotten to allow my body to go limp, and it hurt, but without the anger taking up most of my energy it didn't feel quite so bad.

'You okay?' Saint asked, looking down at me as if she expected me to burst into tears again.

'I'm fine,' I said, getting to my feet. 'Let's go again.'

She blinked in surprise, but then she turned and made her way back to her starting position.

This time when she ran at me I managed to leap back in time to avoid a sideswipe, but she still caught me with a follow-up kick.

'Nice try though, Lele!' Ginger said with a grin.

Saint shrugged. 'Not great. Better, though.'

I glared at her but I actually felt that I'd achieved something. And, surprisingly, the anger had abated.

'Now,' Hester said, 'we will take a breather. Lele, there are things you should know. Let's begin with the basics.'

'Can I do the zombie talk?' Ginger asked.

Hester sighed and then waved her hand in Ginger's direction. 'Go on.'

'Cool!' Ginger turned to me. 'Thing is, Lele, there's only one way to kill a zomb. It's not like in the movies, you know, where you've got to destroy the brain. That's not going to help. These ones are different – you've got to disable the spinal cord.' He touched a spot at the back of his neck.

'Why there?'

He shrugged. 'Not sure, innit. We think it's got something to do with splitting the spine, which is where the spaghetti stuff gets its energy or whatever.'

'That's a bit vague.'

'Yeah, well, I'm not a zombie scientist, mate. The best thing is to separate the head from the body. That does the trick.'

'Gross.'

'Yeah, I know, right? But before you can get them into a position to do that, you've got to fend them off. See, zombs move quickly, 'specially the newly hatched, and they're going to come at you with everything they got. Teeth, nails, arms and legs.'

'They cannot feel pain, Lele,' Hester said. 'They move extremely quickly. Far quicker than they could in real life.'

'How is that possible?' I asked, remembering the horrible speed of the Hatchlings Ash, Saint and I had encountered in the clearing.

'Think about it. Imagine if your body could no feel pain. Imagine if your nerve endings were dead and that you couldn't feel your muscles taking strain. Nothing would stop you, nè?'

'I suppose.'

'Right,' Ginger said. 'I'm going to pretend to be a zomb, 'kay?' He stuck his arms out in front of him, rolled his eyes back in his head and lurched towards me. 'Braaaaaaiiiiiiinssss,' he mumbled. 'Braaaaiiiinssss.' He looked ridiculous, and I tried not to giggle.

Saint sighed. 'That's a Hollywood zombie, Ginger. Not a Hatchling.'

'Yeah, yeah, whatever, Saint,' Ginger said, winking at me. 'Now, say I was coming for you, Lele, what part of my body would you go for?'

I stepped forward and lightly punched him in the stomach.

'No, Lele,' Hester said. 'If you find that you are without a weapon, and a Hatchling is attacking, always grab the throat. Keep the head at arm's length. You don't want the teeth anywhere near you.'

'Yeah,' Ginger said, 'if they bite you, they can infect you with that spaghetti stuff.'

'The curse of the deadly pasta,' I said before I could stop myself. And suddenly I was giggling. I couldn't help it. It just sounded so ridiculous. Ginger joined in, and even Saint and Ash cracked a smile.

'I know, I know,' Ginger said, still giggling, 'Mental, right?'

'Try again, Lele,' Hester said, smiling at me.

This time when Ginger approached, I planted my feet firmly and shot out my right arm, grasping him around the throat, and doing my best to keep him at arm's length. He stumbled backwards, and although I knew he was faking his lack of strength, I began to feel slightly more confident.

'Well done, Lele,' Hester said. 'You are a very fast learner. Now we will move on to a few basic defensive moves. Saint, Ash, demonstrate, please.'

Saint and Ash moved to the centre of the room, and I watched as they took it in turns to block punches and kicks. They both moved gracefully and smoothly, making hardly a sound.

'She's just like Lara Croft, innit?' Ginger whispered to me.

'Huh?' I said.

'Saint. She's like ... so totally cool.'

His skin was turning bright red and I hid my smile behind my hand, wondering if Saint had any idea how Ginger felt about her.

'But it is not just the Hatchlings you need to watch out for, Lele,' Hester said.

'It's not?'

'The Resurrectionists can also be tricksy,' Ginger explained. 'You run into a border patrol, you could be in hot water.'

'I don't get it? I thought the Resurrectionists wanted the stuff you collect from the mall?'

'Yes, Lele, but we cannot risk them catching us leaving the enclave,' Hester said.

'But they must know you do?'

'They do not know for sure. And think about it: someone with your skills, or Ash's, Saint's or Ginger's, would be very valuable to them.'

'Go on,' I said.

'I think you can imagine what kind of stuff they would want you to bring back into the enclave to keep any ... rebellion down, Lele.'

'You mean like weapons?'

'Yes.'

'But the Guardians banned weapons after the War, didn't they?'

'Because they did not want another uprising. But think about it. Ot would suit them to have us fighting amongst ourselves.'

'More bodies,' Ginger sniffed, 'means more Rotters.'

'The Hatchlings may be dangerous, Lele,' Hester said, 'but someone who can think and plan can be even more deadly.' She paused. 'Ash, you're up next.'

Ash approached me. 'Grab hold of the collar of my jacket with both hands,' he said to me, face expressionless.

'What?'

'Just do it,' he said.

I grabbed the lapels on his jacket. 'Now what?' I asked.

'Now, what I'm going to do is use your weight to spin you around. Watch carefully.' He crossed his arms, took hold of my wrists, and spun me around. It happened so quickly that I lost my balance, but he caught me around my waist before I fell. I could feel the blood rushing into my cheeks.

'Now you try,' he said. He gripped the front of my jacket and I grabbed his arms and tried to whirl him around. He didn't budge an inch.

'You're way too heavy!' I said.

'You must use my weight against me,' he said. 'And move faster to unbalance me. Concentrate.' He looked straight at me, and I stared into those strange eyes of his. I closed my eyes and took a deep breath, thinking about Jobe. The sooner I learned, the faster I could try and get my brother back to the Agriculturals.

He grabbed hold of my jacket, and this time I crossed my arms, grabbed his wrists and managed to swing him around –

not all the way, but it was a start.

'See?' Ginger said. 'She's, like, a natural. You're a regular Bruce Lee, Lele.'

'Who's Bruce Lee?' I asked.

Ginger shook his head slowly and grinned. 'I can see there are quite a few other things I have to teach you.'

'Later, Ginger,' Hester said. 'Let's go again.'

15

'Can I stop now?'

'Ten more minutes,' Hester said from her place on the low padded bench. 'You are doing very well, Lele.'

'Yeah, come on, mate,' Ginger said, looking up from the comic book he was reading. 'You can do it!'

I groaned. My thigh muscles were screaming, and it took all my energy not to topple over. Along with the daily fight schedule, Hester had started me on strength training, which involved me standing on one leg for minutes at a time, or crouching in a half-squat, a position that was almost unbearably painful after just seconds. It seemed like there was always something new to learn, another technique to master, fitness regime to endure or meditation to practise to help me control my anger. I now knew that striking upward with my elbow was the best way to disable an opponent, that I had to keep my elbows tight into my sides before punching anyone (or anything), and that if I was desperate, a forceful head-butt was another effective means of attack. But no matter how hard I tried, Saint and Ash always seemed to trip me up effortlessly and send me flying. It was clear I still had a long way to go.

At that stage I wasn't exactly sure how long I'd been in the Mall Rats' lair. That was the thing about living underground: without the cues of nightfall and sunrise, the days bled into each other. But despite the daily bruises, the aches and pains and endless repetitive tasks, part of me was enjoying it. It was strange how naturally fighting came to me.

Although I'd never actually seen her fight, according to Ginger, it was Hester who'd taught the Mall Rats all their moves. He'd filled me in one morning while I practised defensive blocking.

'Hester used to run her own dojo before the War,' he'd said.

'Dojo?'

'Like a fighting school. She taught summut called ninjutsu.'

'Never heard of it.'

'It's the Japanese art of killing someone, like ninjas, you know?' Right then I'd remembered Thabo calling me Ninja Girl, but it'd seemed so long ago that it was like another life. 'Ninjas are like the coolest fighters ever. Got a few movies to show you on that score,' Ginger had continued. 'But after the War she adapted it to work on the Hatchlings.'

Hanging out with Ginger made life easier. I spent the little free time I had with him, mainly watching DVDs. He had a massive collection of movies – most of which the Resurrectionists would have approved of: Violent British and American gangster films, slasher horrors, weird Japanese animation movies. He especially loved anything with zombies in it.

I stretched my back, feeling the muscles pop. Ash and Saint padded through from the training room where they'd been practising their chain/panga dance, grabbed a couple of litres of milk out of the fridge, and slumped down on the couch next to Ginger.

'So,' I said, needing something to distract me from the fact that my left leg now felt like it was on fire. 'I have a question.'

'There's a surprise,' Saint said. She was still somewhat stand-offish towards me, but had thawed slightly. Ash, on the other hand, was still barely acknowledging me (except during training, of course), and I'd become quite good at blanking him back. I still hadn't figured out why he seemed to loathe me so much, but I put it down to the day in the Deadlands when I'd managed to lose him and Saint. He was obviously someone who liked to nurse a grudge.

'What's with your names?' I said. 'I mean, no offence, Saint, but ... *Saint*? Seriously?'

'Ask Ginger,' Saint said. 'It's his fault.'

'Well?' I asked him.

'Named her after this dead cool spy series starring Roger Moore. Ever seen it?' Ginger always asked this, even though he knew there was no way I could have possibly seen a fraction (if any) of the movies and series in his collection. 'Anyway, the series is called The Saint, right? And so I thought it was funny. 'Cos, like, the Roger Moore character is like the dead opposite of Saint. He's like this debonair white guy, and like Saint is like this straight-talking black chick.'

Saint rolled her eyes. 'Hilarious,' she said.

'Yeah, but that was before I knew you properly. I would have called you a different name, otherwise,' he said, a blush of colour blooming under his freckles.

'Okay,' I said quickly, wanting to spare him any more embarrassment. 'And Ash?'

'Well,' Ginger said. 'That's from my favourite zombie movie

ever. *Evil Dead II*. Seen it?'

'No.'

'Well, see, I haven't been able to find a copy. Looked everywhere. Anyway, the main dude in that was a fella called Ash, and he has this big mega fight against these dead things that are totally evil and possessed, right?'

'Hence the title.'

'Yeah. Hence the title. Anyway, his hand gets possessed –'

'Wow, Ginger!'

'Yeah, I know. Mental, right? So, anyway, he cuts it off and attaches a chainsaw to the stump. So, like, I got the name from him, 'cos Ash is like the coolest dude in the movies, and our Ash is totally cool in real life.'

I kept my face neutral. 'And Ginger?' I asked.

'That's his real name,' Saint said.

'Yeah,' Ginger said. 'Don't think my folks had that much imagination.'

'You think?' Saint said with a grin, nudging him in the ribs.

'And I got Ripley's name from the ...' Ginger's voice trailed away, the blood rushing to his face for the second time in a matter of minutes, turning it bright pink. Next to him Ash and Saint had stiffened, and the atmosphere had suddenly become charged. 'Sorry, guys,' he said.

Of course I was dying to hear more about Ripley, who was obviously the Mall Rat Saint had mentioned on that first day, but I kept quiet.

Hester looked up. 'Lele, you have done very well. You may relax.'

'Phew!' I said, grateful to be able to stand on both feet again.

'Yeah, nice one, mate,' Ginger said. 'You almost broke Ash's record.' Ginger glanced at Ash, but his face was inscrutable.

'And I've got a treat for you, Lele,' Ginger said, holding

up one of his DVDs. '*Transformers* – crap movie, but awesome explosions.'

Saint swung her legs down from the couch to make enough room for me to sit between her and Ash. But she needn't have bothered. The second I sat down, Ash stood up and stalked out of the room. I had no way of knowing if his departure was because I had sat next to him, because Ginger had mentioned Ripley, or because he hated movies starring giant robots.

16

A few days later I woke up to find Hester alone in the kitchen. She was sitting at the table, her head in her hands, but when she heard me approach she lifted her head and attempted to smile, trying to bury the pain I knew she was feeling beneath it. Again she reminded me of Gran: Gran who had hidden her illness from me for as long as she could.

I sat down in front of her and covered one of her hands with mine. 'Hester, what's wrong with you?'

'Nothing, Lele,' she said, smile still in place.

'That's not true. I know you're sick,' I said. It had been obvious from the first time I'd seen her. The way she walked as if every joint was on fire; the dark circles under her eyes; the yellowish cast of her skin. I'd tried to ask Saint about it once or twice but she'd brushed me off. It was clearly a subject none of the Mall Rats felt comfortable discussing. 'What does the doctor say?'

'Medical attention is only for the young, Lele, you know that.'

'But you're not that old.'

She chuckled. 'Thank you for the compliment, but since the Resurrectionists took over the city those who are pregnant or still growing have priority.'

'Can't you at least get some medicine to help you?'

'You know the Guardians' views on that, Lele.'

'But what about from the mall?'

'No. We cannot risk it.'

'Have you tried, though?'

She sighed. 'I told you, we cannot risk it. The Guardians will turn a blind eye to clothes and books and soaps and shampoos. But not to medicine. Not even aspirin.'

'Why?'

'Because they need people to die, of course.'

Stupid question. But we didn't have that problem in the Agriculturals, where there was a rich knowledge of traditional medicine and we had access to any herbs we wanted or needed.

'But there must be something I can do to help,' I said, racking my brain for the names of the herbs Gran had used to dampen her own pain.

'I am fine, Lele,' Hester said, 'but thank you for your concern.' She smiled again, and this time it seemed genuine. The pain had passed.

'Where's everyone?' I asked.

'They've gone on a mall run.'

'But why couldn't I go with them?'

'You are not ready yet, Lele.'

'I *feel* ready.'

'I know. But it will still take some time. You must be patient.'

She poured me a cup of rooibos tea and I stirred in a dollop of honey. As disappointed as I was, it was pretty cool having Hester to myself.

'Hester, how did you discover the mall? How did you know it was there?'

She took a sip of her own tea, and touched the knot of scar tissue under her eye. 'A group of us discovered it at the end of the War, while the Guardians were busy herding the survivors into the enclaves. I was part of the Last Resistance.'

I'd heard about them – a small band of diehard War veterans who had fought the Rotters till the end.

'Did you know a soldier called Cleo Mbane?'

'Yes. Briefly. A brave woman.'

'She's my stepmother.'

'I see.'

'Yeah. She works for the embassy now,' I said bitterly. 'For the Resurrectionists.'

'You mustn't think too badly of her, Lele,' Hester said. 'Everyone had a choice to make. That was hers. She certainly wasn't the only one.'

I bit my tongue. Now wasn't the time to mouth off about the Mantis. Besides, I had another burning question. 'Hester, why doesn't Ash like me?'

She smiled at me. 'You mustn't take his attitude to heart.'

'It's hard not to.'

'I know. I suppose he can be stand-offish at times.'

'That's putting it mildly.'

'He is ... He's had a hard time of it. A hard life.'

I thought of saying, *Who hasn't?* but I suspected that wouldn't go down well. 'How did you meet him?'

'During the Last Resistance. He fought by my side. He saved my life.' She smiled at my shocked expression. 'The others I was with, they did not last outside. The Rotters ... Well, I'm sure you can guess what happened to them. But because Ash was able to slip through the Deadlands undetected, we managed to hide out for long enough to construct this place.' She looked around. 'Of course, at first it wasn't as comfortable as you see it today.'

'You mean Ash fought in the War?'

'Yes.'

'But he would have been a little kid!'

'Indeed. But there were many child soldiers, Lele. Most of them were not as fortunate as Ash.'

'But that still doesn't explain why he treats me like I'm dog poo.'

'Ah. Like I say, do not take it personally. Ash has a good heart, and although he tries to hide it, he feels too much. A sensitive soul. He is just checking you out in his own way.' She paused to let what she'd said sink in. 'Now, Lele, you must drink your tea and have some breakfast. We have much work to do.'

'What are we doing today?'

She smiled. 'More work on the wooden man.'

I groaned. I hated the thing. My arms and legs were sore from endlessly punching and kicking it. But it helped that I'd nicknamed it Zyed. I'd even thought about asking Ginger to fetch me some guineafowl feathers to stick on it.

'Awesometastic!' Ginger cried.

For the first time I'd managed to jump clear when Saint ran for me, dodging the follow-up kick she'd jabbed in my direction by curling myself into a defensive ball several metres away from her, well out of her reach.

'Not bad, Zombie Bait,' Saint said, holding out a hand and helping me to my feet. 'What did you think, Ash?' she asked as Ginger clapped me on the back, almost sending me flying. 'Can this chick move, or what?'

He shrugged. 'Not bad,' he said.

I pretended to stumble backwards in shock. 'Did I just hear correctly, Ginger? Did Ash just say something almost nice to me? Shouldn't we be worried? Maybe he's ill.'

Saint grinned. 'She's got you there, Ash,' she said.

'Yeah, she's got you bang to rights, mate,' Ginger added.

'Whatever,' Ash said, but for a second he caught my eye and I was sure he was doing his best not to smile.

'I think she's almost ready,' Saint said.

'Seriously?' I said, heart leaping.

'You're forgetting something, Saint,' Ash said. 'She hasn't had any special awareness training.'

'Sorry, sweetie,' Saint said, 'but Ash is right.'

I followed Ash and Saint into the lounge area, Ginger trailing behind us. 'But what's special awareness?' I said. Ash and Saint were whispering to each other, ignoring me. 'Hello?'

'I'll take her,' Ash said to Saint. 'See how she does.'

'You will?' Saint asked, looking from him to me in surprise.

'Take me where?' I asked.

'Hey,' Saint said. 'If you take her to the market, you can get the veggies.'

'That's your job,' Ash replied.

'Oh, come on, Ash. Be a pal.' She grinned at him.

He sighed. 'Okay, okay.'

'What is going *on*?' I asked.

'You're about to go on a little outing, Zombie Bait,' Saint said.

'Outside?'

'Of course!'

My life underground had been so intense and absorbing that I'd practically forgotten what the world outside looked like, but now an opportunity had presented itself I realised that I couldn't wait to feel the sun on my skin again.

Saint handed a list to Ash. 'Hester says to see if you can get some fresh spinach. And tomatoes, if they've got any.'

'No problem.'

She dug in one of the cupboards under the kitchen sink and handed me a heavy brown robe. 'Put this on.'

I held it up to my body. 'But this is a Resurrectionist robe!'

'Duh!' Ginger said. 'You can't just go out like your normal self, innit. People will think they've seen a ghost!'

'It's the one good thing the Resurrectionists have done for us. The perfect disguise,' Saint said.

'They're such dumb-asses,' Ginger added. 'Think they're Jedi or summut.'

Ash was already pulling another of the robes over his head and I tugged mine on quickly in case he changed his mind. The wool was scratchy and rough, and hung heavily on my shoulders and arms. Saint threw a lumpy Resurrectionist amulet at me. It was surprisingly weighty, and just touching it made me feel squeamish.

'Come on,' Ash said, without looking back to make sure I was going to follow.

'Don't forget the spinach!' Saint called after us.

Ash unlocked the door in the corner of the room, and I followed him down a winding tunnel, this one gloomier than the others.

'Wait here,' he said when we reached the end. 'I need to check the coast is clear.'

Climbing up a rope ladder he hefted up a trapdoor. Light filtered down from above, and I felt the pull of the fresh air.

''S'cool,' he finally said, reaching down and grabbing my hand.

18

Even though we were in a narrow alleyway, shadowed between two tumbledown shacks, the natural light stung my eyes and I had to blink several times before they adjusted. I took a deep breath of enclave air, drinking in the scents of cooking and dust, before scurrying after Ash, who was already striding towards a bustling thoroughfare. The world seemed huge and buzzing with life after the three weeks or so I'd been down in the tunnels.

'What part of the enclave are we in?' I asked him.

'New Arrivals, of course.'

A group of elderly men, who were sitting outside a mouldy army tent, drinking coffee and chatting, fell silent as we passed. One of them shook his head, leaned forward and spat in our direction.

'They don't like Resurrectionists here,' Ash said quietly to me.

'Where are we going?'

Ignoring me, Ash hailed a rickshaw driver, who looked as if he was about to pretend he hadn't seen us.

'Where to, Comrade?' the driver asked reluctantly as Ash stepped in front of him, holding up his hand imperiously.

'Sector 6.'

At first I thought I'd misheard. Sector 6 was my old district – and the longing to see Jobe was almost overwhelming. He had never been far from my thoughts, but I'd convinced myself that I was working on the plan to get us out of the city, which had helped. But now I could barely think about anything else. Not that I thought there was any hope of seeing him.

'Why are we going there?' I asked.

'Best market. Best selection of food,' Ash said.

'Did you say something, Comrade?' the rickshaw driver asked.

'Have you found your true calling?' Ash said pompously. 'Have you accepted the truth?'

He was totally convincing, and I tried not to giggle.

'Ja, Comrade, I believe I have, Comrade,' the rickshaw driver said. 'Oh, ja.'

Ash flipped back his hood, smiled at me and winked. He seemed to have lightened up a lot, and I felt my stomach lift. I didn't want to feel that way about him. He'd spent the last few weeks treating me like crap, and I wasn't going to forgive him so easily. Still, whenever his thigh jostled against mine in the cramped space, I noticed that he didn't try to move away.

We didn't speak during the half hour it took us to wend our way to Sector 6. I was too captivated by the sights, sounds and smells around me; even the low background moaning of the Rotters was a novelty after being underground for so long. But there was something else, someone else on my mind – Thabo. We were following the same route as the one we'd taken when he'd brought me to Lungi's. I wondered if he missed me, if he had, after all, left school to join the ANZ, and if he was still spray-painting slogans around the city.

As we neared Sector 6, the roads became more congested, the buildings more substantial, and more and more Resurrectionists thronged the streets. Ash signalled for the driver to stop, and we drew up outside the looming embassy building.

'Thank you,' Ash said, passing some trade credits to the driver.

'No, Comrade,' the driver said. 'That's quite fine.'

'I insist,' Ash said.

The rickshaw driver hesitated, then grabbed the money and hurried off as if he thought Ash was about to change his mind.

'Why didn't he want to take the credits?' I asked.

Ash shook his head in disgust. 'Most Resurrectionists think they can travel for free. As if it's their right.'

I didn't like the sound of that.

Following Ash towards the bustling market place, I suddenly realised that we were right outside the narrow alleyway where Thabo and I had decorated the dumpsters. I couldn't resist peering into its shadowy depths to see if any traces of our handiwork remained. The dumpsters were covered in overflowing rubbish bags, but I could see a weather-beaten poster that had been tacked up on one of the brick walls. It was a printed version of my Anti-Zombian sketch, the words *Don't be a Puppet, join the ANZ* printed below the drawing of the huge puppet-master Guardian. So they had used it after all! I almost called out to Ash to show him, but he was striding ahead, and the moment passed.

We were now right in the middle of the market, both of us being buffeted occasionally by passing shoppers. Hawkers and stall holders shouted out their wares, the largest stall of all heaving under the weight of a huge stack of vegetables that must have recently arrived from the Agriculturals.

Ash bought a selection of potatoes and tomatoes, and I picked out a thick bunch of dark green spinach, rummaging through the pile to find the freshest leaves.

'Okay,' he said. 'Time to start.'

'Start what?'

'Your training.'

'We're going to train here? Won't people stare?'

'We're not going to fight, Lele.'

'What then?'

'It is vital that you know who is around you at all times. To my left, you see that guy with the black hair?'

I turned my head and glanced at the tall guy standing next to an amulet stall. 'Yeah,' I said. 'Guy with the ponytail?'

'He's a Resurrectionist guard.'

'How do you know?'

'See the lump under his shirt? It's a cosh. He's on the lookout for suspicious behaviour.'

I didn't think anything could be more suspicious than the pair of us checking out everyone in the market place, but obviously I wasn't going to say that to Ash.

'The trick is to look around without making it obvious, and also to be aware of who is behind you at all times.' He walked on. 'Right now,' he said, 'behind us there's a large woman carrying a small child, an elderly War vet with a wooden leg and a teenager who keeps picking at his zits when he thinks no one is watching.'

I glanced around quickly, pretending that I was checking out the woollen sheets draped over a stall. Ash was right. 'How did you do that?'

'Practice,' he said. 'Let's walk on. Keep your eyes open.'

It was difficult to see a great deal out of the hood that covered my face, but I did my best to concentrate.

'Without looking around, who is to our right?'

'An old woman selling clothes pegs and a street kid with a bandaged arm.'

'Not bad!' Ash said. 'But you missed the guy handing out pamphlets behind them. Try again.'

He was relentless. The training seemed to go on for hours, the sun beating down on us, making me sweat under the heavy fabric. One thing about the Resurrectionist robes: they definitely weren't made for comfort. But although my brain was beginning to ache, I was getting better and better.

'Okay,' Ash finally said. 'Let's take a break.'

He walked up to a vendor and bought us both a paper cup of freshly squeezed orange juice.

I gulped it down gratefully. 'Thanks, Ash,' I said to him, peering at his face, half-hidden beneath the hood.

'What for?'

'For not treating me like you hate me today.'

He blinked. 'I don't hate you.'

'But you've been acting like you do.'

He ran a hand over his face. 'I'm –'

But I never got to hear the rest of his words. From somewhere behind us came an enormous banging sound, as if three huge doors had been slammed one after another – BANG! BANG! BANG! – and then a billowing cloud of damp smoke hissed towards us.

Instantly, my eyes felt like they'd been stung by a swarm of wasps. All around us people were screaming, and I felt myself being pushed roughly from behind as a tidal wave of bodies surged forward in a panicked mass. Someone elbowed me painfully in the ribs and someone else grabbed at my arm.

I tried to manoeuvre myself free, struggling and twisting, but there was nothing I could do. I was propelled along, my feet barely touching the ground.

As the smoke cleared I rubbed at my eyes, but I'd lost sight of Ash. I looked wildly around, desperately trying to catch sight of him, but my vision was still blurry, my eyes streaming. Then, as I wiped away the tears, I saw a familiar thatch of hair rising above the heads surrounding me. It was Thabo. I was sure of it. I would recognise those dreadlocks anywhere. But as he turned his head and looked at me, the crowd swept me forward again and it was all I could do to stay upright. All around me people were screaming and yelling, mothers shouting for their children, everyone stumbling into each other.

Finally, I fought my way clear of the hysteria and stumbled down a side street. My eyes were feeling slightly better, but my ears were still ringing from the incredibly loud noise, and I sat down shakily at the side of the road, trying to make sense of what had happened. Dazedly, I realised I was still clutching the bunch of spinach Ash had bought earlier, although thanks to my fight through the jostling crowd it was nothing but a mushy mass of squashed leaves and broken stalks.

Then something struck me.

I couldn't be more than a couple of streets away from my old home. From Jobe.

I stood up.

19

Pulling my hood as far as possible over my face, I crept up to the window and peered into the kitchen.

Dad and Jobe were sitting at the kitchen table, Chinwag snoozing in a small patch of sunlight next to them. Jobe was pushing one of Chinwag's jingling toys up and down on the table's surface while Dad sketched something on a piece of paper. I couldn't make out his expression, but there was part of me that wanted to believe he looked sad.

I could feel the tears beginning to start, their saltiness stinging my still-raw cheeks and eyes.

As far as my family was concerned, I was dead. I was gone.

'Lele,' a voice said behind me. I whirled around. It was Ash. His robe was filthy and ripped in places, but otherwise he looked uninjured. 'You shouldn't be here,' he said. 'It's not safe.'

'How did you know where to find me?'

Checking around to make sure no one was watching us he dropped his hood and wiped his hands over his face. 'I've done my homework. We had to know we could trust you. We needed to know as much about you as we could.'

'What do you mean, trust me?'

'To ensure that you weren't actually a spy for the Resurrectionists.'

'Of course I'm not!'

'I know that now. But you can't be here. It's far too dangerous. If your family knew you were alive ...'

'I know. But I just had to see him. My brother.'

An expression I couldn't read flashed over his face and then he nodded. 'I understand.'

'You do?'

'But you mustn't do it again. You could put all of us in danger. If the Resurrectionists find you here ...'

'I'd never tell! I'd never tell them about you!'

'Lele, you might not have a choice. Come on, Hester will be worried.'

Pulling his hood over his head, Ash took my arm. 'We will have to take another route home,' he said. 'The road ahead is blocked.'

'What happened?'

He snorted. 'Bloody ANZ. Another one of their stupid stunts.'

I thought about Thabo. 'The ANZ did this? But ... people could have been hurt.'

'People *were* hurt, Lele. Not that the ANZ care.' He sounded furious. 'And now the Resurrectionists will come down on them even harder, and make life even more difficult for all of us.'

He was right about the route. We were forced to bypass the road that led to the embassy. A line of robed Resurrectionists were standing across the thoroughfare, arms linked, several of them with curved knives and pangas stuck into the leather belts around their waists.

I wondered if the Mantis had been caught in the chaos, surprising myself at the concern I felt for her. After all, as far as I knew, she'd engineered my Lottery win.

'We have to hurry,' Ash hissed, leading me away from the roadblock. 'They will be taking everyone in for questioning soon.'

We turned a corner and I realised that we were in the road that led to the school. A knot of students was gathered in the forecourt around the sculpture, gabbling excitedly. One or two of them appeared to be crying. I caught sight of a flash of plaited hair – Summer – and I couldn't miss Zyed, dressed in his feathered jacket.

Ash grabbed my elbow and led me towards a rickshaw. 'Come on,' he said. 'We have to be quick.'

20

'No training this afternoon, Lele,' Hester said. 'I think you've earned a break.'

What I really felt like doing was holing up in my room and sketching. My emotions were all over the place and I needed to download what had happened.

Ginger looked at me eagerly. 'Tell me about the bomb. Was it a big one?'

'Ginger!' Hester snapped. 'Not now.'

For once, Ash sat down on the couch next to me and I felt as if I'd passed some kind of test. 'It wasn't a bomb, Ginger,' he said. 'It was tear gas and a couple of grenades.'

'Aw ...' Ginger looked almost disappointed.

'What's the fascination with explosives, Ginger?' I asked.

'Ginger loves anything that goes bang,' Saint answered, sitting down on the floor and stretching out her long legs.

'It's true, I do,' Ginger said.

'I will make you some of my special chicken soup,' Hester said from the kitchen.

'Oh, ace!' Ginger said. 'Thanks, Hester.'

'For Lele and Ash, Ginger,' she replied with a smile in her voice. 'They are the ones who have had a shock, not you.'

''S'all right, Ginger,' I said. 'You can share mine.'

'Thanks, Lele,' Ginger said. 'You rock.'

The soup was worth waiting for. It was even more delicious than the broth Gran used to make for Jobe and me whenever we were ill, and Hester had, in fact, made enough for everyone, including Ginger.

'Right,' Ginger said as soon as we had finished eating. 'What's it going to be? *Nightmare on Elm Street,* or *Dawn of the Dead*?'

'Do we always have to watch horror movies, Ginger?' Hester asked, settling on to her padded bench while Saint cleared the kitchen.

'They're Lele's favourites,' Ginger replied, winking at me.

'Yeah,' I said, trying not to giggle. 'I've been dying to see *Dawn of the Dead*.'

'See?' Ginger said innocently.

Saint killed the lights and the five of us made ourselves comfortable.

For the first time I really felt part of the group.

For the first time I felt like I could actually be home.

21

'*Ag.* We're out of tea,' Hester said.

The others were out in the Deadlands, and although I'd begged to be taken along, Hester had decided that I needed more training before she would allow me to go. That day she looked more fragile than usual, and I could see in her eyes that the pain was bad. I remember wishing again that Gran was around. She would have known which herbs to use to help ease the pain. But like Gran in her last days, Hester was stoically fighting her sickness as if it were her mortal enemy. Which, of course, it was.

'I'll go and get you some,' I said. If I'm honest, my motive wasn't just to help Hester; I was dying to get back out into the sunlight. I'd spent the morning beating the crap out of the wooden man and I was feeling fitter than I ever had, even in the Agriculturals (where I'd spent weeks helping Gran and the others pick the mealies or harvest the lucerne and oat hay we used to feed the cattle). A walk outside was just what I felt like.

'You know where to go?' Hester asked.

I nodded. By then I'd been to the New Arrivals market with Ginger, and although the quality of the fresh produce wasn't as good as in the posher sectors, there were things for sale there that you'd never find even in Sector 6.

'Lele,' Hester said. 'You must be careful. The Resurrectionists are on the lookout for any strange behaviour.' She paused. 'Ash told me about your brother. About you going to see him. Please, do not do anything like that again.'

'I'll stick to New Arrivals, I promise,' I said, though it would have been a lie to say that the thought hadn't crossed my mind.

'Just ask for Patricia when you reach the herbs and spices stall, and she will give you what you need,' Hester dug a silk scarf out of a pile of clothes waiting to go to Lungi and the other suppliers. 'Give her this.'

'Don't worry, Hester. It'll be cool.'

'I would go with you if I could.' She winced as she struggled to her feet and passed me one of the Resurrectionist robes.

'Do I have to?'

'Of course.'

I pulled the scratchy fabric over my head and set off.

I ignored the stares of disgust some of the older residents and market-stall holders gave me as I walked through the enclave, wishing that I didn't have to wear the robe, that I could tell them that I wasn't a believer. Some of the hawkers were even blatantly wearing signs of their own older religions – a Christian cross; a yarmulke, several women with scarves covering their hair – though most people dropped their heads and scurried past me, unwilling to be the recipient of any religious (or political) dogma.

There were a few other robed Resurrectionists about, but nowhere near as many as in the other sectors of the city. They nodded at me as they passed, and I was careful to ensure that my hood covered my head completely.

At one stage I was almost sure one of them was following me, but after ducking through a narrow alley that led off a long muddy lane of stalls and tents, I emerged into the main thoroughfare again without a robe in sight. I put my paranoia down to the glances and mutterings of disgust from the hawkers and hurried on.

Patricia eyed me suspiciously when I asked for the tea, but when I mentioned Hester's name, and showed her the scarf, her broad face broke into a smile. She rummaged in the chest hidden beneath the stall and brought out a packet of rooibos, adding a pot of honey into the bargain.

Unwilling to head straight back to the Mall Rats' lair, I rambled around for a while until I passed a familiar-looking structure. Recognising the bright pink walls of Lungi's place, I hesitated outside it. I knew that Ginger and the others regularly dropped orders off with her, but I hadn't yet been invited along.

A man with a scar that curved across his cheek opened the door. He glared at me, and I hurried away, almost banging into a robed figure as I did so.

'Greetings, Comrade,' the figure said in a deep masculine voice that sounded fake. 'Are you on your way to the March of Souls?'

'No,' I said, turning and walking away as fast as I could. But I could hear the slap of footsteps behind me. I increased my pace, now practically jogging. Then, just as I thought that I'd lost him, I felt a hand clamp down on my shoulder. The adrenalin shot through me and I acted automatically. Keeping my back to whoever it was, I reached over, grabbed his hand and bent the fingers back as far as I could. There was a muffled yelp of pain. Without easing my grip, I whirled around, readying myself to knee him in the groin.

'Lele!'

I hesitated. There was something familiar about that voice. The figure pulled back his hood, revealing a mass of dreadlocks.

It was Thabo.

Realising that I still hadn't let go of his fingers, I released my grip. He shook them briskly, eyeing me with admiration. 'Whoa, Lele, I won't be messing with you in the future,' he said.

I was still reeling from the spurt of adrenalin, and, of course, the shock and relief. I opened my mouth to speak, but he held up his hand. 'Not here,' he said, glancing around. 'Follow me. I know somewhere safe we can talk.'

Pulling his hood over his head, Thabo strode away. I had to run to catch up as he wove his way around the hawkers and street kids, ducking down alleyway after alleyway. It was clear that he was making sure that we weren't being followed and I soon realised we were actually traversing a circle.

A couple of streets down from where he'd accosted me, he pushed into a musty army tent, scrabbled out through the other side, and headed into a small wooden shack.

I hesitated.

'Come on,' he said. 'It's me. You can trust me.'

The shack was empty, and stank of rotten wood and mould. He kicked a pile of trestles away from the floor, revealing a dark hole in the ground. It looked like the Mall Rats weren't the only ones who favoured underground living. He climbed down a knotted rope and I followed.

It was pitch dark underneath the shack, and Thabo had to light a candle before firing a paraffin lamp into life. The space was tiny, the walls plastered with pictures from ancient magazines – photos of cars and motorbikes and sailboats. In amongst them I saw the sketch I'd done for the ANZ.

'You kept it!' I said.

Thabo pulled me into his arms and gave me a hug, squeezing me so tightly that my spine cracked. 'I'm so glad you're all right,' he said. He stepped back and looked me up and down. 'And you're looking really well.'

But I couldn't say the same. He looked older somehow, and there was a bruise on the side of his face.

'What happened to you?' I asked.

'It's nothing. Skirmish with the guards. No biggy.'

There wasn't enough space in the room for much furniture – just a mouldy mattress and a couple of packing crates draped with clothes. I sat down on one, and Thabo perched on the other. We were so confined our knees touched.

'Lele,' he said, 'I'm sorry about what happened at the dance. I tried to stop it.'

'I know,' I said.

I waited for him to ask me how I'd got away from the Guardians. But he didn't. After a pause, I decided to speak up. 'Don't you want to know how I got back into the enclave?' I asked.

'It's best if you don't tell me.' He rubbed his face, wincing as his hand connected with the bruise. 'As long as you are safe, that is all that matters. Are you?'

'Yes,' I said. Now that I'd thought about it, I'd figured out why it was best that I didn't tell him. Ash had made that clear after the tear gas attack at the market.

He smiled. 'You're part of the underground now, Lele.'

'Yeah,' I said, looking around the room. 'Literally, right?'

'And the less you know about me the better, and the less I know about you too.' He caught my disappointed expression and smiled. 'It doesn't mean we can't see each other.'

'So what's been going on, Thabo? Did you leave school?'

'I left after they took you. Joined the ANZ full time.'

'Thabo ... The other day. The gas ... Was that the ANZ?'

He ran his hand through his dreadlocks. 'It was a mistake,' he mumbled. 'Got out of hand.'

'A mistake?'

'Now it's my turn to keep quiet,' he said, giving me his lopsided grin. 'But it is so good to see you!'

'You too.' It was. 'Thabo ... can I ask you something? The Lottery, someone wanted me to lose it – or win it. I mean, I wasn't eligible.'

'Go on.'

'I think it might have been my stepmother.'

'But your stepmother's Cleo Mbane, right?'

'Yeah. So?'

'Look, I don't know her, Lele, but, sheesh, I've heard the stories about what she did during the War. Doesn't sound like something a War vet would do.'

'But she's a Resurrectionist!'

'Yeah. But that doesn't mean that she'd do something that evil.'

That wasn't what I was expecting to hear, and for the first time I began to doubt myself. 'So, who then? Zyed? Comrade Pelosi?' But did they hate me *that* much?

He shrugged and he rubbed his hands across his face again. 'Look, I have to go. But, listen, come and see me again soon.'

'How will I find you?'

'Do you remember how to get to Lungi's place?'

'I think I can find it again. But I don't think she'll be too pleased to see me.'

'Why not?'

'I never returned the dress.'

'Don't worry about that. Listen, you can leave a message with her. Tell her, "Everything's better with zombies – not." 'Kay? That will be the signal that you want to meet. And, if I can, I'll meet you here an hour later.'

'Deal,' I said.

'And watch your back. The Resurrectionists are out in force. And tell your friends to do the same.'

'My friends?'

'You know what I mean, Lele,' he said. He leaned forward and kissed me very gently on the lips, and then he was gone.

22

'What's up with you?' Ginger asked when I got back. 'You look different.'

'Huh?' I said. 'How?'

'I dunno,' Ginger said. 'You look all happy and glowy.'

I felt the blood rushing to my cheeks. I was sure I could feel the weight of Ash's eyes on me, but when I glanced at him he dropped his gaze as usual. 'Just the effects of the fresh air, I guess,' I said.

'Yeah?' Saint said. 'How would you feel about a bit more fresh air?'

'What do you mean?'

Ash had grabbed a robe and was slipping it over his head. 'Got to go out,' he mumbled. Saint watched him go, frowning slightly, and then turned back to me. 'Now, Lele. You need a weapon, right?'

'Yeah.'

'Think fast.' She suddenly threw an apple at my head, and without even thinking about it I plucked it out of the air.

'Cool reflexes, Lele,' Ginger said. 'Nice one.'

'I don't get it,' I said. 'I'm going to be fighting the Rotters with fruit?'

'Not quite,' she said. 'Come on. I have an idea.'

23

'Wait here,' Saint said to Ginger and me. 'I'll be right back.'

'Where are you going?' I asked.

'You'll see,' she said with a grin, slipping away between the trees, leaving Ginger and me in a small clearing. We sat down on a couple of logs, and Ginger passed me a Coke from his bag. It would have been pleasant if it wasn't for the cluster of Rotters shambling aimlessly through a small copse of wattle bushes a little way away from where we were sitting. I could detect their old-book smell above the marshy scent of the grass and arum lilies. I knew they couldn't sense us, but I still kept half an eye on them. I still hadn't forgotten that Gran was out here somewhere, but the small pack looked to be mostly male, although it was difficult to be sure as most of them were in a bad way – clothes rotted through, the flesh dried on their bones like biltong, their hairless heads looking way too large for their skeletal bodies. I couldn't understand how they even managed to stand up.

'What do the Rotters eat?' I asked Ginger.

'Braaaaiiiins,' he said, holding his arms outstretched and doing his famous zombie impression.

'No, seriously, Ginger. Do they eat animals and stuff?'

'Far as I know they don't eat anything, mate,' he said.

'So how do they exist? Where do they get their energy from?'

'Gawd knows,' he replied. 'They keep on going until they collapse, rot away completely, like. Couple of years ago, there were thousands of the buggers. Each year there's less and less.'

'So one day there might not be any left?'

'Only if the Guardians stop taking the newly dead to the bone pile, Lele,' he said. 'And that's not going to happen. Not with the Resurrectionists sucking up to them like they do.'

'So how long do they last?' I asked, still thinking about Gran.

'Depends. Some last for years. I guess it's all to do with the condition of the body before it's turned. They'll still be some knocking around here from the War. And with all them Hatchlings –'

'You mean the people that are relocated?'

'Yeah. With them, the zombs will be around for a few years yet.' He didn't look too upset about the idea.

Saint reappeared. 'Come on,' she said to me.

I followed her past the Rotters and into a small clearing. A huge fig tree loomed above us, its ropey branches extending out like giant looping snakes. In the shadowy copse behind it I could make out the shell of a light aircraft, the windows spider-webbed, the body rusted.

Saint strode up to the tree and stuck a movie poster on to the bark.

'Hey!' Ginger said. 'That's mine!'

'You've got loads of them,' Saint said. 'Besides, that movie was totally lame.'

'It's not! It's a classic.'

The poster showed two blue people with pointy ears, the words *Avatar 3D* beneath them.

'What are you doing with that?' I asked.

'You'll see.'

She handed me a flick knife, the blade sharp enough to slice the skin of my thumb with only a light touch.

'Go further back, Lele,' she said.

I took a step back.

'Further,' she called. 'Keep on going till I tell you to stop.'

I was now a good ten metres away from the tree.

'Now, throw the knife at the poster, see if you can hit one of the blue cat-people in the head'

'Not the Na'vis!' Ginger whined. 'What did they ever do to you?'

'Shhh, Ginger. Ready, Lele?'

I weighed the knife in my hand. 'Do I throw it holding the handle or the blade?'

'I dunno,' Saint said. 'Use your imagination.'

I breathed in deeply, calming myself down as Hester had taught me. I decided to go on instinct, and without even thinking about it, I grasped the knife by the blade and threw it towards the poster. It swished through the air, embedding itself dead centre, straight through one of the character's eyes. I'd done it! And more importantly, it had felt almost effortless.

'Woo-hoo!' Saint cried, looking more excited than I'd ever seen her. 'I knew it! I knew you were a natural!'

'That was cool, Lele,' Ginger said, inching the blade out of the bark. 'Can I have a go?'

'Sure,' I said.

Ginger walked over to me, and I stood back while he narrowed his eyes and leaned forward. He chucked the knife towards the tree, but it thunked off the trunk and plopped onto the ground below.

'Hard luck,' I said.

''S'cool,' he grumbled. 'Like my chainsaw better anyway.'

'Hester will be pleased,' Saint said sarcastically. To me she said: 'Hester hates him using that thing. Says it's impractical.'

'Whatever,' Ginger mumbled.

'Try again, Lele,' Saint said, folding the knife and chucking it towards me. 'Make sure it's not a fluke.'

I threw it again, this time not even hesitating. It found its mark again.

'I think,' Saint said, 'that Zombie Bait's just found her weapon.'

24

'Rise and shine, sleeping beauty.' Saint shook me awake.

'What time is it?'

'Time to get going.'

'Huh? More training?'

'Nope. We're going shopping.'

'To the market?'

'Nope.'

I sat up so quickly my head spun. 'To the mall?'

'Yebo.' She threw a pile of clothes on top of me. 'I think these are your size.'

I leapt out of bed, gathering up the clothes – a gorgeous pair of skinny black jeans, a tight black T-shirt and a hoody with a diamanté skull across the front of it. I'd been wearing everyone's cast-offs since my arrival, and I couldn't wait to try on Saint's gift. Running to the bathroom, I jumped under the shower, dried off as fast as I could and pulled on the new outfit, the crisp clothes feeling wonderful against my skin. I tucked the knife into my belt, and smoothed back my hair. It was growing longer, and soon I'd actually be able to do something with it. This was it! I was finally going on a mall run!

Ash, Ginger, Saint and Hester were all waiting for me in the kitchen. Hester put a bowl of porridge in front of me, but I didn't have a clue how I was possibly going to manage swallowing it.

As usual she read my mind. 'You must eat, Lele. You have a long walk ahead of you.'

I gulped it down, barely feeling the heat of it.

'Lele,' Saint said, handing me a piece of paper. 'Newbie list.'

I scanned it:

13 pairs XL panties
2 x 38 DD bras
5 x socks (large)
3 x packets of boys' boxer shorts (small)

'You're doing the underwear run,' Saint said with a grin. 'Nice and light.'

'Oh, good,' I said sarcastically.

'I'll swap if you like,' Ginger said.

'What are you getting?'

'Books,' he said with a sneaky grin.

'Cool!' I said, snatching the list out of his hand. I was dying to check out the bookstore.

'You do realise that you'll have to carry them back though, right?' Saint said.

'Yeah,' I said. 'I can handle it.'

She shared an eye-rolling glance with Ash, but I didn't care. I couldn't wait to get out there.

25

I know it's probably my memory playing tricks, but, looking back on it now, the day seemed absolutely perfect. The sky was a flawless blue, the air was crisp – so still, in fact, that I was sure I could hear the faint crash of the unseen ocean on the other side of the enclave – and we'd set off so early that the dew was still glistening on the leaves of the Port Jacksons, huge spider webs shining like jewelled lace in every tree. Everything felt like it was coming together and even the occasional sight of a pack of Rotters on our way to the mall couldn't dampen my spirits.

We came across a clutch of feral kittens mewling inside a nest burrowed out of an old car seat, their eyes still closed. Their mother hissed a warning at me when I got too close. Her colouring reminded me of Chinwag, and I was hit with another jolt of longing as my thoughts turned immediately to Jobe. But now that I was actually on my way to making some trade credits, my plan to return to the Agriculturals seemed to be finally within my reach.

I paused occasionally to practise throwing the knife at a tree stump or termite hill. I was improving fast; I could now hit my target from more than twelve metres away.

'You totally rock at that, Lele,' Ginger said, shaking his head in admiration.

'So, Ginger,' I said. 'What do you do with the credits you make?'

He held up the chainsaw. 'Fuel. Costs a fortune.'

'What, all of it?'

'Yeah. Have to keep the generator going as well, innit. Can't do without my movies. That would be a disaster.'

'Where do you get the fuel from?'

'Guy I know at the embassy.'

'At the embassy?'

'Don't sound so shocked, Lele,' Ginger said. 'Everyone's on the take.'

'And you guys?' I asked Ash and Saint.

'We don't do it for the money,' Saint snapped.

'Well, Ash does, don't you, mate,' Ginger said.

Saint scowled at him and once again Ginger blushed a deep red under his freckles. I wondered if maybe Ash had a girlfriend, although I didn't understand why the idea gave me a sudden flush of jealousy. He was definitely hiding something. After all, he'd slipped away on some secret errand several times in the weeks I'd been holed up in the tunnels.

We walked on in silence – pausing only once, so that Ash could have a smoke and Ginger and I could chug down a Coke – until we pushed through a grove of trees and stepped out on to the grassed-over highway, the roller coaster's arced skeleton gleaming at us over the tops of the trees in the morning sunlight.

Ash rummaged in his rucksack and handed us each a square box with an aerial attached.

'What's this?' I asked.

'A walkie-talkie. It's the only way we can keep in touch in there. But only use it when you have to.'

He briefly showed me how it worked (it was fairly straightforward), and I attached it to my belt next to my knife.

'Welcome to our world, Lele!' Ginger said.

26

I stood outside the mall, hesitating before I followed Ash and Saint inside.

'What you waiting for?' Ginger asked.

'I still can't believe it's here.'

'Tell me about it. Makes you wonder what the Guardians are up to, right?'

'Yeah.'

'Well, don't worry, mate. It'll be cool, you'll see.'

The interior was just as I remembered it, right down to the tinkly muzak.

'Lele,' Saint said, 'you know where the bookstore is?'

I shook my head. 'I'll find it, though.'

Saint and Ash shared another of their glances, and Ash sighed. 'I'll come with you,' he said.

'It's cool,' I said. 'I don't need to be babysat.'

'It's your first run. You shouldn't go alone.'

I shrugged, keeping my expression neutral. I wasn't going to argue.

'Laters, alligators,' Ginger said, heading towards the escalators.

'Ginger!' Ash called. 'No messing around. Get what's on the list, no added extras, okay?'

Ginger put on an expression of mock-hurt. 'Who, me?'

Saint shook her head, gave us a small ironic salute and stalked off on her own mission.

'Come on,' Ash said to me.

We walked in silence down the deserted aisles, making our way past an enormous food court. It was spooky weaving through the hundreds of empty tables and chairs that would probably never be filled again (at least by anyone breathing). Draped above a restaurant entrance there was a banner that read *Happy Birthday Bongani!*, and I shuddered at the thought of the horrific birthday surprise he must have had. We passed signs for the mall's cinema complex, the walls lined with posters for the films that had been showing when it all kicked off – films that Ginger would never get a chance to see.

'Here we are,' Ash said, pausing underneath the Exclusive Books sign. 'You got the list?'

I nodded absently, my eyes already greedily scanning the shelves, taking in the titles.

'Earth to Lele?'

'Sorry,' I said. 'I've got the list.'

He took it out of my hand. 'Okay. Listen up. Two Bibles, three copies of the Qur'an, four *Twilights*, the *Norton Anthology of Poetry*, *This Carting Life*, *Zoo City*, *Pride & Prejudice* and *Harry Potter and the Philosopher's Stone*. And that's just the start.'

Searching for the titles on the list was almost like a treasure hunt, and I found myself enjoying the challenge. The poetry books were easy to find, ditto the Harry Potter novel and the *Twilights*, but I struggled to track down the old-school religious books.

'And this,' Ash said, handing me a copy of *World War Z*.

'This isn't on the list.'

'It's Ginger's birthday in a couple of days,' he explained. 'And you know what he's like with Zombie stuff.'

I followed him over to the magazine aisle, where he picked up a copy of *Hello!* magazine, a picture of a probably long-dead (or living dead) celebrity posed cheerfully on the cover. 'For Saint.'

'Saint reads this kind of thing?'

'Yeah. But don't let on I told you.'

A pile of yellowing *Sunday Times* newspapers caught my eye, the words *Kick Off!* in inch-high letters across the front page of the top copy. They were dated June 2010, and I was hit again by that feeling of being in a time warp.

He grinned. 'You okay to find the rest?'

'Sure,' I said.

And with that he headed towards the back of the store, seeming to become immediately absorbed in the African literature section.

I sourced the rest of the books on the list (the *SAS Survival Guide*, a cookery book that weighed a ton and a couple of copies of *The Long Walk to Freedom*), shoved a sketchbook and a couple of biros in the rucksack, and then traipsed over to the children's section. I sat down on the carpet and pulled out copies of *The Hungry Caterpillar* and *Where the Wild Things Are* – titles that jogged something in my memory. Mom or Dad must have read them to us before life changed forever.

A grinding sound jolted me out of my daydreams.

I stood up and looked around the store, but Ash wasn't anywhere to be seen. My stomach dipped: I hadn't forgotten about the roaring noise I'd heard the first time I had found myself in the mall.

'Ash!' I called, trying to keep the panic out of my voice. I didn't want him to think I was a wuss.

'Yeah?' he replied.

'Where are you?'

'Over here!'

I followed the voice, dragging my bag behind me. He was standing behind a counter in a small coffee shop attached to the bookstore. I'd been so absorbed by the books that I hadn't noticed it before. The aromatic scent of fresh coffee filled the air.

I sat on a stool in front of the counter and he pushed a cardboard cup of fresh black coffee towards me.

'You made this?' I asked.

He shrugged. 'Perks of the job. No milk I'm afraid, though.' He passed me several packets of sugar; they were hard and crystallised but I dunked them into the coffee anyway.

'How do the Guardians keep all this running?' I asked.

Ash shrugged. 'It used to drive me mad, thinking about it, but now I think, well, it is what it is.' He paused. 'Ginger says the Guardians must have kept one of the power stations running, maybe the one in Blouberg. Hester says it's way too dangerous to head out there and check it out, especially with all the new relocations, but we'll go one day. Besides, we're about due a trip to the beach.' He grinned at me.

I smiled back and took a sip of the coffee. It scalded my tongue, but I couldn't have cared less. It was delicious.

'Ash, what's wrong with Hester? I mean, I know she's really sick, but what's wrong with her exactly?'

'She's dying,' he said in a flat, emotionless voice. He looked up and stared straight at me. Again I was struck by his extraordinary eyes.

'Dying of what?'

'Cancer. Well, we think it's that, anyway.'

'But can't we get her something that will help?' I hadn't forgotten what she'd said about the Guardians and medicine, but this was a matter of life and death. 'Ash, I think we should try and get her some painkillers or something.'

'No!' he said. 'The last time we tried that . . .' His voice trailed away. 'We can't. The Guardians won't allow it.'

'But they aren't here.'

'You don't know for sure, Lele. Remember when you first came to the mall?'

I nodded.

'They were here then.'

'You saw them?'

'Yeah. Well, I heard them. We're pretty sure they must be watching us when we're in here.' He pointed up to a camera stuck on the ceiling. 'It's the only explanation. They leave us alone as long as we stick to the rules.'

I was beginning to put two and two together. 'Ash . . . is that what happened to the girl? Is that how you know they'd react if you tried to get medicine?'

His eyes flashed. 'The girl?'

'Ripley. The other Mall Rat. Is that what happened to her? Did you try and get medicine for Hester and they . . .'

He nodded and dropped his eyes to his cup. 'We don't know exactly what happened to her. All we know is that she's gone.'

'What do you mean?'

'We were all in the mall, and she decided to see if she could find something to help Hester – see if there was any morphine, or whatever. Saint and Ginger were doing the book run, and I was getting soaps and stuff, just one level up from where I knew Ripley was. She called for help on the walkie-talkie, but ... I was too late. I should have been with her. I shouldn't have let her go alone.'

'I'm so sorry.' I reached over and put my hand over his. 'Did they kill her?'

'I don't know. We found her stuff – her rucksack, her walkie-talkie – but she was gone.'

I took a deep breath. I knew I was prying, but there was something inside me that made me ask it. 'Were you in love with her? I mean, is that why you and Saint don't like talking about her?'

He looked up at me in surprise. 'I wasn't in love with her, Lele,' he said. 'I mean, we were friends, but love ... no.'

For some reason I felt a bright jab of relief.

He looked as if he was about to speak again, but then his walkie-talkie crackled into life: 'Ash, come in, Ash.' It was Saint.

'Ash here, over.'

'Better get down to basement level, over.'

'What's up? Over.'

'Ginger's up to his old tricks again, over.'

'Shit,' Ash hissed. 'Better get going.'

I tried to lift the rucksack over my shoulder, but I stumbled under its weight. Smiling slightly, Ash passed me his.

'No! I can manage,' I said.

'Trust me,' Ash said. 'It's a long walk home, and, knowing Ginger, there might be some running in our future, so be prepared.'

He had a point. With a rueful shrug I swallowed my pride and handed the rucksack over.

27

Saint was waiting for us at the bottom of the escalators.

'Well?' Ash said. 'He hasn't blown something up again, has he?'

'Not yet. Check it out,' she said with a half-smile on her face.

'Can someone tell me how to stop this thing?' Ginger yelled as he came barrelling towards us, wobbling on a skateboard, his arms outstretched. I couldn't help but laugh – he looked ridiculous – and I laughed even harder when he wiped out against one of the huge pot plants.

Leaping to his feet, Ginger brushed off his jeans and grinned at us. 'You want a go?' he asked, handing the skateboard to Ash.

I could see the conflicting emotions flicker over Ash's face. Part of him wanted to gripe at Ginger for messing around when he should have been working, but I could tell that he was also tempted to have a go on the skateboard.

'Okay,' Ash said. 'Just for a few minutes. But then we have to get out of here.'

'Awesome!' Ginger said before Ash had a chance to change his mind. 'I'll get all of us one. Wait here.'

'Typical Ginger,' Saint said, watching him jog into a nearby sports shop.

Seconds later Ginger was racing back towards us, three skateboards clutched in his arms. He handed them out, a look of childish excitement on his face. 'This is going to be *so* cool!' he said.

We spent over an hour on the skateboards, one of us keeping a lookout while the others practised, and by the end of it I was feeling pretty smug. It turned out that I was much better at it than Ginger – probably because I was smaller and lighter – and Ash and Saint were hopeless (they kept trying to go too fast before they had learned to balance properly).

The light was fading by the time we decided to leave the mall. A jostling group of Rotters was milling about outside the doors as if they were queuing up to get inside before the sales started.

Ash scanned them swiftly. 'All cool. They're totally rotted.'

'Yummy,' Ginger said. 'My favourite kind.'

'Gross, Ginger,' Saint said.

The light was taking on a bluish cast, the heat of the day settling, the mountain looking dreamy and unreal in the distance. The four of us strode through the fynbos that coated the highway, Ash carrying the bag of books as if it weighed nothing at all. Ginger's stomach rumbled.

'Hungry, Ginger?' I asked.

'Starving, mate.'

'Shall we stop for some chow?' Saint asked Ash.

'Yeah!' Ginger said. 'Let's have a barbecue!'

'A *braai*, Ginger,' Ash said. 'The word is *braai*. I can't believe you still say things like that. I'm going to confiscate all your British movies if you don't wise up.'

'Oh, yeah? You're not the boss of me.'

'Am so,' Ash said, pretending to punch Ginger in the stomach.

'Are not!'

Saint glanced at me and rolled her eyes.

We walked on for a while, until we reached a fairly large clearing, where Saint and Ash dropped their rucksacks from their shoulders with sighs of relief.

'I thought you were doing the underwear run?' Saint said to Ginger as his bag clinked to the ground.

He looked slightly shifty. 'Yeah ... So?'

She dived for his bag before he could whip it out of her reach. 'So, what sort of underwear clinks like that?' She searched through it. 'I knew it!' She pulled out several glass bottles of Coke.

'What?' Ginger said, trying to look innocent and failing.

'This stuff will kill you.'

He shrugged. 'Nice way to die, though, innit?'

'What are we going to braai?' I asked.

'Ash and I will sort that,' Ginger said.

'You want to help me get some wood?' Saint asked me.

'Sure.'

Ash and Ginger bustled off in one direction while Saint and I headed into a nearby copse.

'They're not going to kill a buck, are they?' I asked.

'Nah, there's a bunch of wild chickens around here,' she said. 'That's more Ginger's style.'

She knocked over a piece of dead wood and a baboon spider crawled out and scurried towards us.

'Ugh!' she said, jumping back.

I nudged the spider towards a clump of dried twigs, and within seconds it was gone.

'I can't believe the great Saint is scared of spiders,' I said.

'Believe it, Zombie Bait.'

'Do you mind not calling me that?'

For a second she looked as if she was about to snap at me, but then she relaxed and grinned instead. 'Sorry,' she said. 'I guess I've been a bit hard on you.'

I shrugged. 'It's okay.'

'It is not okay. I've been a bitch.'

'Total bitch is more like it.'

She laughed. 'But you handled it well, Zombie Ba – Lele.'

'Didn't have much choice,' I said. 'You're stronger than I am.'

'True,' she said.

'Can I ask you a question?'

'I'd be surprised if you didn't.'

'How did you become a Mall Rat?'

She looked down at the ground, and kicked her boots through a tangle of weeds. 'You really want to know? It's not a pretty story.'

I nodded.

She was right; it wasn't a pretty story. Saint had been living in New Arrivals when the Rotters had broken through the fence. She had watched as those closest to her had been mercilessly slaughtered before Hester had found her wandering, shell-shocked, through the streets, the only person in the area who hadn't been cut down or turned into a mindless Hatchling.

'So Hester knew that the Rotters couldn't sense you?'

Saint nodded. 'I don't know what I would have done without her. I'd lost everyone ...'

'I'm sorry, Saint.'

She looked up at me and smiled. 'Thanks.'

'And Ginger?'

She grinned. 'Can you believe it? Ash and Hester found him hanging around outside Ratanga Junction. He'd left the enclave, just wandered out after the Rotter break-in, and was planning on seeing if he could get the roller coasters to work.'

'Typical Ginger,' I said.

'But ... Look, thanks for being so good with him.'

'What do you mean?'

'I think sometimes people lose patience with him. Find him annoying.'

'I love Ginger. I mean, I love him like a brother.' I could feel myself blushing.

'And what do you think of Ash?'

Now my cheeks felt white hot. 'Nothing. He's okay.'

'Yeah, right.' She looked at me sideways.

'What about you, Saint? Why haven't you and Ash ever hooked up?'

She smiled. 'Because, Lele, I'm not into boys.'

'Ah.' It made sense: I hadn't forgotten what I'd overheard all those weeks earlier when I'd been hiding out in the kombi.

We wandered back, arms full of firewood.

The fire was already cracking and spitting when Ash and Ginger returned, each carrying a limp plump chicken.

Ginger immediately sat down next to the fire and started plucking them, feathers flying around his head, several getting stuck in his bushy hair and eyebrows.

I'm not lying when I say that I'd never tasted anything so delicious. Gran had kept her own chickens, which we'd been allowed to eat on special occasions, but I don't remember them ever tasting as glorious as the ones we ate that night. Finally we all sat back, wiping our greasy fingers on our jeans. It was now fully dark, the flames adding a glow to everyone's faces. Ginger handed round a bottle of Coke and Ash lit a cigarette.

'Go on, Saint!' Ginger said, with his usual look of adoration. 'Do your special trick.'

'What special trick?' I asked.

'You got to see this, Lele. Go on, Saint. Please?'

Saint rolled her eyes and sighed. 'I'm so stuffed I can hardly move, Ginger.'

'Go on, mate,' he said. 'Pretty please?'

Rolling her eyes again, she got to her feet and began to rummage in her bag. Pulling out a bottle of paraffin, she undid one of the bandannas tied around the strap of her rucksack and ripped it into strips.

I watched, fascinated, while she unwrapped the chains around her wrists and attached the spiked balls to the ends of each of them. Dipping the bandanna material in the paraffin she then tied it tightly around the metal balls.

'Ash? Chuck me your lighter,' she said as she made her way further away from the fire.

Moments later she lit the material, which flared instantly alight, and began to swing the chains around her head. She spun them faster and faster, the flames making impossibly bright, blurred lines against the dark canvas of the night. It was the most beautiful thing I'd ever seen.

I glanced over at the others, to check out their reaction. Ginger was completely enthralled, his eyes not leaving Saint for a second, but Ash caught my eye, and for several seconds we stared at each other. I didn't know what to think, so I dropped my eyes and concentrated on the whisper of the chains as they swept through the air.

I know what you're thinking: But what about Thabo?

Truth was, I didn't know.

28

'Hi, guys,' Ginger said, looking expectantly around the breakfast table.

'Oh, hi, Ginger,' Saint said.

'It's a lovely day today, isn't it?' Ginger said hopefully.

'Is it?' Ash said with a yawn.

Saint looked at me and winked. It was Ginger's birthday and the plan was to pretend we'd all forgotten, send him off to the market for some honey, and then surprise him when he got back.

I'd stayed up the previous night creating a sketch for him in the pad I'd slicked from the bookstore, hiding it from Saint as best I could. I'd drawn it movie poster-style, sketching a likeness of Ginger as I knew he saw himself in his mind: part action hero, part clown. Around him lay a pile of decapitated Hollywood-style zombies, and a woman clutched at his arm, gazing into his face adoringly. She was based on Angelina Jolie, but she had more than a passing resemblance to Saint.

The look on his face when he returned from the market and we all yelled, 'Surprise!' was classic.

Ash gave him the copy of *World War Z* we'd taken from the bookstore, Saint handed him a *Zombie Flesh Eaters* DVD, and Hester had baked him a cake, complete with a Lara Croft action figure toy in the middle of it.

'This is awesome!' Ginger said. 'You guys are the best!'

While Hester cut the cake, I snuck into my room and ripped the drawing out of the sketch pad.

'Here,' I said, handing it to him.

He unfolded it and laid it out on the table. 'What?' he said. 'No ways! That's me!'

Saint stared at me, eyes wide. 'Where did you get that?'

'I drew it,' I said.

'Whoa, Lele,' she said.

Ginger stood up and gave me one of his huge bear hugs. 'It's the best present ever, Lele,' he said. 'It must have taken you ages.'

'Lele,' Hester said, 'I cannot believe that you have kept this talent secret from us for so long.' She smiled at me and squeezed my shoulder. I felt a brief stab of guilt. Of course, the sketch wasn't the only secret I was keeping from everyone, but there was no way I could come clean about my plans to get Jobe out of the city enclave.

Ash was watching me, a strange look on his face. He was the only one who didn't comment on the drawing. But I could feel the blood rushing to my cheeks all the same.

29

It had been more than two weeks since I'd seen Thabo, and I decided that I had to risk it. I told myself that I needed to see him because he was the only link I had to my old life, and I missed him, which was true. But there was another reason, of course – my confusion about my growing feelings for Ash. I needed to put them in perspective, especially as I still had no clue where Ash disappeared to on his frequent mysterious errands, and apart from the occasions when I'd noticed him watching me, I didn't have any proof that he thought of me as more than just another Mall Rat. So, when Hester next asked one of us to make a run to the market, I jumped at the chance, praying that Ginger wouldn't offer to come with me. Fortunately he was lost in a British comedy series called *The Office*, and he barely glanced up as I left.

I knocked on Lungi's door, and this time she opened it

herself. 'Ha!' she said. 'It's the princess from the party.'

'Everything's better with –'

'It is fine, sisi,' she said. 'Thabo is here.'

She stood back to let me in, looking me up and down as I passed her.

'Lele!' Thabo said, jumping up from where he had been sitting slumped in one of the armchairs. He folded me in his arms and squeezed me tight. He smelled of camp fires and sweat, and when he drew back I had to smother my gasp of shock. He'd lost at least five kilos; his cheekbones stood out and there were huge rings around his eyes. He looked five years older than when I'd seen him last.

'I am so glad to see you,' he said, leading me into a small room attached to the kitchen area.

I sat down on a battered wooden chair in the corner. I could feel myself already breaking into a sweat (there were no windows and the heat from the kitchen had nowhere to go). 'What's going on, Thabo?' I asked. 'You look finished.'

'Bad week,' he said, pacing up and down the small space, running his hands through his dreads. 'Three of our members were taken, Lele. The Resurrectionists are really clamping down. There's talk that they're going to try to register everyone. Check exactly who is for and who's against them.'

'Seriously? I haven't heard anything about this!'

'It's not common knowledge.'

'So how do you know?'

'We've got someone inside the embassy.' He spoke without thinking – clearly so hot up that he'd forgotten about not telling me too much. 'Lele, this is seriously bad news. They'll start with the other sectors first, of course, but New Arrivals won't be left for long.'

'But they're not welcome here,' I said.

He shook his head. 'Now that they've started putting in the infrastructure for the electricity they're getting more and more support, and not just from the elite. Now the people are joining them, too.'

'But people aren't stupid, Thabo. They can see what they are.'

'Can they?' he asked. 'Don't be so sure. The Resurrectionists are smart. They're providing the people with what they need. With what they want.'

I pulled the robe over my head. Sweat was dribbling down my back and I fanned out my T-shirt to try to get some air on my damp skin.

'Lele, I need your help.'

'Of course, Thabo.'

He grinned, a trace of his old self shining through the new worry lines scored on his face. 'You don't know what I'm going to ask you yet.'

'We're friends, Thabo. If I can help you, I will.'

'Lele,' he said in a voice so soft I had to strain to hear it, 'I know you're with the Mall Rats.'

I jumped. 'How?'

'I keep my ear to the ground.'

I didn't know what to say to that. I knew his dream had been to join them, and I wondered how he felt, knowing that I was part of their group.

'Lele, listen. There are things we need that you can get for us.' He paused. 'Is there a chemist shop intact out there in the city?'

So he didn't know everything if he still thought we went out into the city. But what confused me was his lack of interest in *how* we managed to leave without being attacked by the Rotters, or, for that matter, arrested by the fence patrol. He either knew more than he was letting on, or it didn't matter to him.

I opened my mouth to answer, but he hadn't finished. 'We have to have medicine – especially insulin, and antibiotics, of course. And we need condoms.'

'Condoms?'

'Birth control. Not everyone wants to breed, you know.'

I couldn't stop the blush. 'Right. But you don't get it, Thabo. The Mall Rats aren't allowed to ... it's too dangerous. We can't get medical supplies. Surely you must know this?'

'Lele, you're the one who's not getting it. We need this stuff. Our members are dying needlessly. Now's your chance to do something that matters.'

I felt a lurch of panic. 'But if the Mall Rats find out –'

'They won't.'

'But Lungi – she's one of their contacts.'

'Lungi will keep quiet. *Her* loyalties lie where they should – with the people.'

'What do you mean by that?' I asked.

'You know what I mean, Lele. The Mall Rats are the only ones who can leave the enclave, yet all they do is bring back luxuries,' he shook his head in disgust, 'kak we don't need.'

I opened my mouth to defend them, but I couldn't deny that he had a point. A good one. He handed a list to me. 'Look,' he said, 'I realise most of this would have expired by now, but we're desperate.'

I scanned the list: insulin, condoms, gentian violet, morphine, bandages, micropore film, burn salve, sulphur and several items I'd never heard of.

'What's potassium chlorate for?' I asked.

He dodged the question. 'Listen, Lele, if you help me, I'll help you.'

'What do you mean?'

'I'll arrange transport for you and your brother.'

I stared at him in shock. 'How?'

'Don't worry about that now. Bring this back for me and I'll make sure you and Jobe get safely to the Agriculturals.'

30

I threw myself into my training that week, doing my best not to obsess about what Thabo had asked me to do.

I was having trouble sleeping, torn as I was between two loyalties: the safety of the Mall Rats and Thabo's promise to help Jobe and me escape to the Agriculturals. The Mall Rats had become my friends, and I practically thought of Hester and Ginger as family. Could I really go against the rules and put them in danger? I knew I couldn't allow my brother to be carted off to an institution, but was there another way? Could I find a place for him to hide out in New Arrivals? Or would that bring even more trouble down on our heads?

In the end something else made up my mind. Hester was getting worse by the day; she'd lost weight – her skin seemed stretched over her bones – and some mornings she didn't even have the strength to get out of bed. On more than one occasion, Ash had insisted that he would bribe a doctor from the posh enclaves to help her, but she refused to take the risk. The Resurrectionists may have been turning a blind eye to the stuff we were bringing into the enclave, but as Saint had said when I'd first joined them, who knew what they'd do if they brought one or all of us in for questioning and found out about the existence of the mall?

The night before the next mall trip I didn't sleep a wink. I spent the hours tossing and turning and sketching compulsively, the drawings morphing into terrible nightmarish images: raggedy Rotter bodies, spirals of that creepy spaghetti stuff and faces with dead staring eyes.

I was up and dressed before any of the others. I made the porridge for everyone while they showered, although I knew I wouldn't be able to eat any of it. My stomach was a hard knot.

'So, Lele,' Ash said, 'no prizes for guessing what you want to shop for today.'

I knew he was expecting me to say that I'd go for the book list again, but if I remembered correctly, the shop I'd slipped into on my first solo excursion (the shop where I'd seen the wheelchairs and herbal medicine) was next to the Woolworths store where the Mall Rats sourced the underwear – at the other end of the mall.

'I'll do the underwear run,' I said.

A flicker of disappointment flashed over Ash's face and I wondered if he had been planning on offering to accompany me again.

The walk to the mall seemed to take no time at all. Fortunately no one seemed to notice that I didn't say a word during the trek through the Deadlands. Ash, Saint and even Ginger seemed to be lost in their own thoughts, Hester's worsening condition on everyone's minds. Plus, with the increase in relocations, we were all on edge, expecting to be attacked by Hatchlings at any moment.

We paused to check out a group of Rotters milling around outside Ratanga Junction. 'You've been dead quiet, Lele,' Ginger said, nudging me. 'You all right, mate?'

'I was just thinking that I never got the chance to ride the roller coaster before the War.' I hated to lie to him, but there was no way I could tell him what I was actually thinking.

'I did,' he said.

'You did? What was it like?'

'Awesome, Lele,' he replied. 'It's like your tummy flips inside out.'

That was a feeling I could relate to. My stomach had been roller-coasting for hours. I knew what I was about to do could put the Mall Rats at risk, but how could I say no? Thabo was right. I'd be helping people. Doing something worthwhile for once instead of just bringing back luxuries for spoilt rich bitches like Zyed and Summer.

'Okay,' Ash said. 'Let's make it quick. Meet back here in an hour. I don't want to leave Hester alone any longer than we have to. Everyone got their walkie-talkies switched on?'

'Yeah,' I said. I couldn't swallow; the saliva had dried in my mouth.

'Want me to tag along with you, Lele?' Ginger asked.

'Nah, I'll be okay,' I said too quickly.

Saint gave me a sharp glance. 'You sure?'

'Yeah,' I said.

I headed off, moving as fast as I could without giving the game away. As soon as I was out of sight, I broke into a run, praying that I was going in the right direction. Thankfully, as I headed down the escalators, I saw the familiar signage. I slipped into Woolworths and grabbed as many bras and socks as I could. I didn't even check the sizes or bother to take from different racks to mask the amount I was shoving in my bag. My hands were shaking. It was now or never.

Checking both ways to make sure the Mall Rats were nowhere to be seen, I headed towards the shop I remembered from my first time in the mall (it was actually opposite, rather than next to Woolworths). I walked straight to the far end, heading for a counter above which hung a *Prescriptions* sign.

The shelves behind the counter were packed full of a confusing array of medicines, pills and tubes. I paused briefly at the condom display, grabbing a handful and shoving them into the bottom of my bag, before I finally spied a section that was helpfully labelled *Pain Relief*. Leaping over the counter, I scanned the shelves, comparing the items with the list. I randomly selected several co-proximal packets, and threw a bunch of aspirin and paracetamol bottles on top of the underwear.

This was going to take me forever. The names on the list didn't match the bottles on display.

Barely keeping the panic at bay (I knew I was fast running out of time), I scanned the packaging on the shelves once more. Nothing. And no sign of the other stuff on the list. Then I saw a door leading into the back of the store – presumably where the hard-core medication was kept. I tried the handle, but it was locked.

Refusing to give up now that I was so close, I started searching the drawers under the counter, scattering their contents everywhere, desperate to find the key.

I should have been more careful, more vigilant, kept the noise down, at least. The first I knew of the dire trouble I was in was when I heard the words: 'Just what in the *hell* do you think you're doing?'

31

I stood up so fast that I banged the top of my head on the shelf overhanging the drawers. Saint was peering at me from the other side of the counter, her eyes wide with shock. 'Tell me you're not doing what I think you're doing, Lele,' she hissed, her voice laced with fury.

In one fluid leap she jumped over the counter, and before I could react she'd grabbed my right arm and bent it sharply behind my back. The pain was immense. 'Do you have any idea what you've done?' she asked.

I struggled against her, but she wasn't going to let me wriggle away. 'I can explain!' I said.

'Save it, Zombie Bait,' she hissed in my ear. 'I knew you were planning something. How could you be so stupid?'

She yanked my arm up behind me even higher and I yelped in pain. With her free hand I heard her fumbling in her pocket as she pulled out the walkie-talkie.

'Ash, Ginger,' she said. 'Come in, guys. Emergency. Meet me outside Woolworths, now! Over.'

'Saint! Listen!' I said.

'No, you listen! You might have killed us all. We have to get out of here fast!'

She practically threw me over the counter and frogmarched me out of the shop.

Ash jogged towards us, looking from me to Saint in confusion. 'What's going on?'

'You won't believe what this ... this ... idiot has just done, Ash!' Saint said, grabbing my bag and throwing it towards him.

'It's not what you think!' I said. 'I was just getting some painkillers for Hester!'

Ash rooted through the bag, pulling out the underwear and chucking it onto the tiles. The condoms and painkillers spilled around us.

'Oh, yeah?' he said, picking up a condom box and raising an eyebrow. 'What sort of painkillers are these?'

Saint dropped my arm and snorted. 'Lele, Lele, Lele ... You got a boyfriend? Is that it?'

I shook my head and tried to meet Ash's eyes. I'd never felt so mortified. 'No!' I said. 'I was just –'

'Where's Ginger?' Saint said to Ash.

'On his way.'

'Good. We'd better get moving, if they've –'

But it was then that the lights went out.

I'd never experienced darkness like it – a flat, impenetrable blackness. There were no windows in the lower levels, no source of natural light, and I couldn't even see my hand in front of my face.

Seconds later the muzak cut out. The silence was almost as

terrifying as the darkness. 'Oh, shit,' Ash whispered. 'We're done for.'

The sound of roaring – the same sound that I'd heard the first time I was in the mall – floated towards us from another level, sounding louder by the second.

'Guardians!' Ash said. 'Saint, you got a torch?'

'Somewhere,' she said. I heard her swearing under her breath as she searched through her bag.

'Look!' I said. Ahead of us there was a light bobbing our way – the beam of a torch.

'Guys!' It was Ginger. 'Um ...' he said. 'You might want to run right about NOW!'

From behind us came a series of ear-splitting bangs and pops, followed by a long drawn-out whistle that made my ears ring. Showers of colour and blasts of shimmering light blazed around us, punctuated by the *rat-a-tat-tat* of what I later found out were cherry bombs. We were right in the centre of a huge indoor fireworks display.

'Ruuuun!' Ginger yelled.

We didn't need telling twice.

We didn't stop running until we reached the clearing where we'd shared the braai on the previous mall run. All of us were completely out of breath, and we threw our rucksacks down on the ground and slumped down next to them.

Ash lit a cigarette, and Ginger cracked a can of Coke. Behind her sunglasses, Saint's face was impassive, but I knew she was still seething. Not even Ginger would meet my eyes.

No one spoke, and the silence hung heavy. I knew it was up to me to break it. 'I'm sorry, guys,' I said, knowing that this was woefully inadequate.

'Just don't talk,' Saint snapped. 'We'll let Hester decide what to do with you.'

'I was only trying to help,' I mumbled.

'Help who? Yourself? If it wasn't for Ginger's quick thinking we would all be dead!'

'How cool was that, though?' Ginger said. 'I've always wanted to do that. And, like, I was at the Game store, getting the paraffin, and I thought –'

Saint cut across Ginger, jabbing a finger in my direction. 'Stupid, selfish *bitch*.'

For the first time in weeks I was hit by a familiar jolt of anger. I didn't plan my next words. They shot out by themselves. 'You're pathetic,' I spat. 'All of you.'

Saint yanked off her glasses. '*What* did you just say?'

The look of surprised hurt on Ginger's face was awful to see, but I hardened my heart.

'I said, you're pathetic. Hester is dying and you do nothing!'

Saint stood up and strode towards me, and I sprang to my feet to meet her. She grabbed the front of my jacket and pushed me backwards. I let her think she had the upper hand and then I grabbed her wrist and twisted it around, forcing her to let go.

'You know the rules, Lele!' Saint snapped. 'What you did was unbelievably stupid and selfish!'

'You're the selfish ones!' I kicked at a rucksack. 'You bring back all this kak that people don't really need. There are people dying! Hester's dying! We need to do more! We need to help!'

'Help who?' Saint spat. 'And why? The people chose to be ruled over by the Resurrectionists, Zombie Bait. *They* voted them into power, not us.'

'I know ... but look what's happening! First the relocations, now the Lottery. What's next? We have to do something.' The anger had fizzled out as fast as it had come upon me.

Saint shook her head. 'Yeah, right, Lele. But what have they ever done for us?'

33

We gathered around Hester's bed and Saint wasted no time filling her in on what I'd done, punctuating her tirade with vicious glances in my direction.

Hester listened carefully, her expression steady, her eyes never leaving Saint's face.

When it looked as if Saint had run out of steam, Hester nodded and turned to me. To my surprise she smiled and reached over to take my hand. 'Lele's heart was in the right place,' she said.

'But she put us all in danger!' Saint said.

Hester nodded. 'Yes, she did. But maybe she has a point. You would do well to listen to her, Saint.'

'Why? The people are stupid! Why should we do anything for them? If they want to believe that the Guardians are their saviours, then let them. We know better.'

'Yes. But things are different in the enclave now, Saint. It is no longer a case of a small minority of believers supporting the Guardians and Resurrectionists. Now they are impinging on everyone's rights.'

'I don't believe this!' Saint said, standing up and throwing her arms out in exasperation. 'I don't believe you're taking her side!'

'There are no sides here, Saint,' Hester said. 'Lele was trying to help me. She says she wanted to help the sick, of which there are many among us. That she wanted people to be able to be together without being forced to have children. Things have changed very quickly. You know this. Now the Resurrectionists are making the people's choices for them. Remember, I have seen this happen before in the past. It does not bode well for the city, or for the people in it.' She paused to smother a cough.

'What if the Guardians ambush us when we go back to the mall?' Saint asked.

'That is a chance you have to take,' Hester said. 'But I think it is time that we began to think of a way in which we can help.'

'We can't!' Saint said. 'You know what happened to Ripley. You *know*.' And suddenly I understood. It wasn't Ash who had been in love with Ripley. It was Saint.

'Oh, Saint,' I said. 'I'm so sorry. I didn't know.'

She looked at me, and then something happened that I never thought I'd see in a million years. Tears started to fall down her cheeks. 'You don't understand!' she said. 'None of you do.'

I walked up to her and gave her a hug. She stiffened and tried to pull back, then finally relaxed. 'I do,' I said. 'I really do.'

I looked at all of them in turn. 'I'm sorry, guys,' I said. 'If you want me out, that's fine. But I had to do it, and I can't promise I won't try and help in the future. I'm sorry.'

Ginger nodded and gave me a thumbs-up. ''S'cool, Lele,' he

said. 'You're all right with me.'

Ash nodded, but his mask was still in place.

'Saint?' I said.

She stepped away from me, wiping her cheeks with the back of her hand. 'Next time,' she said, 'at least tell us so that we know, okay?'

I nodded.

Ginger clapped his hands, clearly relieved that the tension had passed for now. 'So, guys,' he said, 'who's in the mood for a bromance?'

34

After three days of slightly frosty treatment, the Mall Rats – even Ash – seemed to forgive me. Of course they didn't know that I'd put them in danger because of Thabo – as far as they were concerned I'd acted mainly for Hester's sake – but eventually things returned to something approaching normality. Ginger joshed and joked and tried to get me to watch *Diary of the Dead* with him, Saint went rigidly on with my training, and Ash was his usual quiet self, though occasionally I was sure I caught him looking in my direction.

But I knew I'd screwed up. I couldn't risk putting them in danger again, even for Jobe's sake, even if I *was* helping other people.

Hours would speed by as I sketched in my room, lost in my thoughts, desperate to figure out what to do next. I really didn't want to face Thabo and break the news to him that I'd failed miserably, that it didn't look hopeful that I could *ever* get him what he wanted. And there was something else. The same intense thoughts whirred and whirled around my mind. I'd betrayed the Mall Rats, yes, but the Resurrectionists had betrayed the people they were supposed to serve, and if Thabo was right, it was only going to get worse. I thought back to the funeral, to Rickety Legs and his followers. Back when I'd thought the Resurrectionists were just some crazy harmless cult. Before I knew how dangerous they actually were.

My thoughts turned more and more often to Jobe. I wondered what he was doing, what he was feeling. I needed to get some perspective in my life. I needed to see my brother.

So, one night I waited until I was sure that Saint was fast asleep, pulled on my clothes as quietly as I could and tiptoed through the training room and into the lounge. The generator was still humming in the background, and Ginger was snoring in front of the flickering television. He didn't stir as I grabbed a Resurrectionist robe and scuttled past him and out into the tunnel.

The night air was fresh and faintly chilly, and for once I was glad of the robe. The New Arrivals' area was deathly quiet – the market shut down, the streets oddly naked without their bustling hawkers, hollow-eyed street kids and musicians – but I didn't allow myself to feel even slightly scared. One thing about the Deadlands: Once you've been out there, surrounded by the dead, the living aren't anywhere near as scary.

Or so I thought then.

35

It took me well over an hour to reach Sector 6. The streets were lit only by moonlight, the houses blank-faced and dark, and I lost my way several times. I'd encountered only a handful of people on my trek: a few Resurrectionist guards who I'd avoided by slipping into the less-used thoroughfares; a couple of drunks, high on home-brewed pineapple beer and dagga; and a small group of teenagers, out on a night-time adventure.

Finally, I paused outside the front door, holding my breath to listen for any sounds within, but all the windows were dark and the only noise was the occasional moan from the Rotters behind the fence. I turned the handle and walked softly into the kitchen.

I should have thought ahead and brought a torch. I knocked my shin painfully on a wooden chair as I struggled to get my bearings. Praying that I hadn't alerted anyone to my presence,

I stood stock-still and counted to ten. Silence. Then, stupidly, I allowed myself to relax.

'Don't move,' a familiar voice said from the doorway behind me. 'Stay where you are or you're dead.'

I whirled around, fists raised. There was the sputtering hiss of a match and an oil lamp flickered into life. The Mantis was staring straight at me, her eyes wide, her usually rigidly plaited hair in disarray. She was clutching a huge kitchen knife in her right hand, the blade glinting in the light, and for the first time I saw a trace of the old warrior in her: she was holding it as if she knew exactly how to use it.

'There's nothing to steal here. Leave now or I'll call the guard.'

'Hello, Cleo,' I said, pulling the hood back from my face.

'Lele!' she said, and then her body seemed to sag as if her muscles had suddenly decided to stop working.

'Surprised?' I asked.

Her mouth opened and closed almost comically, and then a single tear glimmered and ran down her cheek. That threw me. I hadn't been expecting *that* reaction. I waited for the anger to take over, but it didn't come. All I felt was an overwhelming tiredness.

There was the thump of feet in the hallway, and Dad appeared at the door. 'Lele?' he said, his voice cracking with emotion. 'Is it really you?'

He walked towards me as if he couldn't quite believe what he was seeing. In the poor light he looked years older. New lines were etched around his mouth, his clothes hung off his frame and grey stubble peppered his cheeks. He wrapped his arm around me. It had been years since he'd given me a hug – more years than I could remember – and I found myself hugging him back. When I stood back his eyes were wet.

But I couldn't let my emotions take over. I turned back to the Mantis. 'So, Cleo,' I said, doing my best to keep my voice level. 'Your plan didn't work. I'm not that easy to get rid of.'

'What are you talking about, Lele?' Dad asked, looking from me to the Mantis and back again.

'Why did you do it?' I asked. 'Was it because of Jobe?'

'Do what?' She stared at me with what appeared to be genuine confusion.

'Made sure that I won the Lottery, of course.'

'I would never do such a thing!'

'I don't believe you, Cleo. No one else could have done it.'

She sank into a chair. 'But, Lele, it was a huge mistake.'

'What do you mean?'

'Afterwards, Comrade Xhati – he told us that your name had been entered into the draw by mistake. Comrade Nkosi started a whole enquiry. It was just a horrible misunderstanding.'

'A misunderstanding! How could something like that happen by mistake? It was my life!'

'Lele!' Dad said, looking around the kitchen nervously. 'Keep your voice down.'

I watched the Mantis closely. She really did look relieved to see me. Either she was a brilliant actress or I had, in fact, got it wrong. 'It really wasn't you?'

'Of course not! I know we had our problems, but I would never do something like that. Send you out ...' She shuddered.

I slumped down into a chair opposite her.

'Lele,' Dad said, his voice soft, 'what happened? How did you get away?'

'I can't tell you that.'

The Mantis opened her mouth to speak.

'Cleo, really, don't ask me again.'

Dad moved to the stove and started fussing over it, trying to light a match with his trembling hand. 'Where have you been all this time, Lele?' he asked. 'Why didn't you come back to us?'

'Why do you think, Dad? What do you think the Resurrectionists would do if they knew I'd got away from the Guardians? That I was back in the enclave?'

The Mantis opened her mouth again as if to argue with me, but then she just nodded. 'Lele is right. The less we know the better.'

'Look, all I want to do is see Jobe and you'll never have to see me again, okay? I don't want to cause you any trouble.'

Dad and the Mantis glanced at each other but when I tried to catch their eyes they both looked down at the table.

'Where is he?' I asked. 'Where's Jobe?'

'Lele, he –'

They didn't need to say more. I knew.

I was too late.

Part Three

1

I spent the next few days doing little else but moping around in a depressed fug.

I know I'm probably coming across as some giant crybaby, but I couldn't help it. I mean, I'd joined the Mall Rats in the first place (or so I'd told myself at the time) so that I could save up and build a better life for Jobe and myself; so that I'd be able to get us out of the city. And now Jobe had been whisked away to Mandela House, and I had no clue what to do. There was a part of me that wanted to rush right over there and bust him out, but then what? For a start, I didn't even know where Mandela House *was*. And, let's face it, at that stage I hadn't exactly managed to tie up all the loose ends of my vague plan. Without the medicine and other stuff Thabo had asked for I couldn't trade for transport, and I was pretty sure I didn't have nearly enough credits to hire a wagon or bribe an official.

And there was something else too. The more I thought about it, the more I was convinced that it wasn't the Mantis who'd engineered my Lottery win. Either it had been a near-fatal mistake or I had another enemy out there.

I spent hours sitting in my room, sketching continually, not really seeing what I was drawing. Ginger did his best to entice me out with promises of a movie called *Shaun of the Dead*, and although it looked like something I'd normally have loved, I knew I wouldn't be able to take in what was happening on screen. Sick as she was, Hester also tried to cheer me up with anecdotes about her life before the War. And even Saint went out of her way to bring me books and graphic novels she thought I'd like. I was so clearly in a bad way that none of them – not even Ash or Saint – gave me a hard time for sneaking off to Sector 6 in the middle of the night.

'Come on, Lele,' Saint said as the days stretched into a week. 'I'm sure your brother's fine.'

'What would you know about it, Saint?' I snapped at her.

She sighed and left the room, a hurt look in her eyes. Now I could add guilt to the rest of the crap I was feeling.

I turned back to my drawing. I was sketching the contours of the bone pile – accentuating its horrible shape – and the ghastly sight seemed to mirror my mood.

Minutes later I heard the door opening again.

'Just leave me alone, Saint,' I said.

'Lele.'

I turned around to find Ash standing over me.

'What do you want?' I asked as he handed me a Resurrectionist robe. 'What's this for?'

'Come on,' he said.

'I don't want to go out,' I said, probably sounding like a four-year-old.

'I believe you'll want to see this,' he replied, holding my gaze with those unusual eyes of his.

'Where to?' I asked.

'You'll see,' he said with a small smile. 'And I won't take no for an answer. Ginger's trying to rope me into watching *Zombie Flesh Eaters* again. You have to save me.'

I couldn't help but smile back. I rubbed my face with my hands. 'Do I look awful?'

For a couple of seconds he seemed to really look at me. 'No,' he said. 'You could never look awful.'

He reached out as if to touch my cheek, and then seemed to think better of it. 'Come on,' he said, turning away.

Doing my best to deal with the hectic rush of mixed emotions, I followed him out of the bedroom.

'This? *This* is Mandela House?'

'Yeah,' Ash said.

It was located in the far reaches of New Arrivals, right up against the fence, and seemed to exist in its own little pocket of beforeness. It looked just like the houses I remembered from my childhood. It had a large wrap-around porch, huge picture windows, and, amazingly, it was nestled in the centre of a sizeable lawn. Next to the house there was even a colourful climbing frame and sandpit. But as we approached, I could see gaps in the paintwork where the plaster was crumbling and there were large dead spots in the lawn.

'This was one of the only buildings left complete after the war,' Ash said.

'And the Resurrectionists handed it over to kids like Jobe?' I said. 'Why? I would have thought they'd want it for themselves.'

'Yeah,' he said, 'but most of them wouldn't be seen dead in this part of town, Lele. Surrounded by scum like us.' He grinned at me. 'Want to go in?'

'Can we?'

'Of course.'

I followed him up on to the stoep and watched as he knocked on the heavy wooden front door. Several seconds later it was opened by a large woman with a mass of light brown hair, dressed in a bright pink overall.

'Yes?' she said, slightly apprehensively.

Ash removed his hood. 'It's me, Naomi,' he said.

Her face softened. 'How lovely to see you!' She gave him a hug, and I hid my smile behind my hand. He towered over her.

Ash pulled his backpack from his shoulder and passed it to her. 'I brought you this.'

'Oh, Jack, you shouldn't have!' she said with a wide grin as she pulled out several colouring books, cans of tinned peaches and packets of lime and strawberry jelly. 'How lovely!'

'Jack?' I said to Ash.

He shrugged. 'Naomi, this is Lele. I believe you know her brother.'

'His name's Jobe,' I said to her. 'Is he here?'

'Oh, yes,' she said, standing back to let us inside. 'What a wonderful little boy. Come in, come in, please!'

The house was warm and cosy, the wide windows allowing the sunlight to bathe every inch of the interior.

'They're in the playroom,' Naomi said. 'Go on through.'

I followed Ash to the back of the house – down a hallway that was painted a cheery yellow, rows of bright handprints stuck all over the walls – and watched as he disappeared through a doorway.

'Go on, Lele,' Naomi said, seeing me hang back. 'Take a look.'

But I was suddenly nervous. My palms were sweating and my heart was thudding in my chest.

Finally, taking a deep breath, not sure what I was about to find, I stepped into the room. There were five or six children sitting on a sheepskin rug in the centre of the floor, all of whom seemed to be Jobe's size or slightly smaller.

I didn't recognise Jobe at first. His hair was longer, and he was smiling.

My brother was *smiling*.

I walked towards him slowly.

'Jobe?' I said.

He looked up at me, and his smile widened. 'Gogo,' he said as I dropped to my knees and gave him a hug, trying to swallow the tears.

There was a mewling sound from behind me, and Chinwag, who was now almost a fully grown cat, stood up from the sun-bathed cushion she was sitting on, stretched and ambled towards me. She curled her body around my feet.

'I can't believe it!' I said, wiping my face and looking up at Naomi. 'Jobe seems so . . .'

'Happy?' Naomi asked, beaming down at us.

I looked over at Ash, who was sitting next to a small dark-haired girl.

'This is Sasha,' he said as she looked up at me. Her eyes were large, and I noticed that one was dark brown, the other grey. 'She's my sister.'

3

Ash and I sat side by side in the garden, watching Jobe and Sasha crouching in the sandpit, both of them trailing their fingers through the sand. Although Jobe was still subdued, he seemed more at peace than I'd ever seen him, even in the Agriculturals.

I knew he was happy. He was home.

'I can't take him away from this,' I said to myself.

Ash looked at me sharply. 'Why would you want to take him away?'

I shrugged. 'He's my brother. I miss him. I had some crazy plan for both of us to go back to the Agriculturals.'

'You did?' Ash said.

'Yeah,' I replied. 'I thought this place would be awful. I had no idea he would actually be happier here than at home.'

He nodded. 'I know what you mean.'

We sat in silence for a while.

'Ash, can I ask you a question?'

'Fire away.'

'Do you ever wonder what they did to them? What the Guardians did to the kids?'

Ash sighed. 'All the time.'

'And isn't it a weird coincidence,' I said. 'Us both having ... rejects as twins. I mean, what are the chances?'

Ash looked slightly uncomfortable for a second. 'Life's full of coincidences, Lele,' he said.

Of course, as I'm sure you've probably figured out by now, it wasn't a coincidence at all.

Ash and I stayed with Jobe and Sasha until the light started to die and Naomi began to get the children ready for bed.

'So, this is what you do with the money you make?' I asked as we strolled out of the gate together. 'Pay for your sister to stay at Mandela House?'

Ash nodded. 'Naomi would let Sasha stay for free – she's like that – but I like to help out.'

We both stood for a second, watching the last of the bright light dancing over the roof. 'We'd better get back,' he finally said.

I turned to face him. 'Thank you for doing this, Ash,' I said. 'I needed to see him like this.'

'I know,' he replied, taking my hand and snaking his fingers through mine. I tried to make out his expression, but the shadow under his hood hid his face. 'Is this okay?' he asked.

I didn't know what to say. I just found myself nodding. I know what you're thinking – and I hadn't forgotten about Thabo – but at that moment, being with Ash ... it just felt natural. But other than that, I haven't got an excuse.

We strolled through the alleyways hand in hand, cutting past groups of people also making the most of the last of the day's light. Someone nearby was playing guitar, and we stopped to listen for a few seconds. We didn't speak. We didn't need to. I felt at peace. It was a feeling I wasn't used to, and I remember thinking that I wouldn't care if the evening stretched on forever.

But this is my life, and nothing ever seems to run smoothly.

One second I was strolling along contentedly, the next I found myself being yanked roughly into an alleyway.

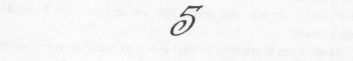

5

My reactions kicked in too late. Spinning around, I forced my arm out of the grasp of whoever was holding me, but my hood had already been snatched off my head and the more I struggled the tighter the collar of the robe dug into my neck, choking me.

'Get away from her!' Ash yelled. Neither of us had any weapons, but Ash had years of fighting experience behind him, and I almost felt sorry for whoever had grabbed me. I let my body go limp, felt the hold on my hood loosen slightly, and then slammed my heel down on top of the foot of whoever it was behind me.

There was a muffled 'oof', and then the grip on my hood loosened completely. I whirled around, ready to face my assailant – a tall figure in a Resurrectionist robe.

'You are so going to regret doing that,' Ash said, clenching his fists and taking a step forward.

'Don't be so sure.' The figure pulled back his hood, revealing a familiar bunch of dreads.

'Thabo!' I said.

'What the hell do you think you're doing?' Ash asked.

'I was worried about Lele,' Thabo said, shooting a bitter glance in my direction. 'But I can see I shouldn't have bothered.'

'Thabo,' I said, reaching out a hand towards him.

'Don't bother, Lele,' he said. 'It's pretty clear where your priorities lie. So you and pretty boy are an item, eh? I should have known.'

'Hey!' I said, starting to feel the first familiar stirrings of anger. 'I'm not some possession, Thabo. Ash is my friend.'

He gave me a withering glance, but I could see the hurt beneath it. 'What happened to "I'll try to help"?' he asked. 'I haven't heard from you in days. *Days*, Lele.'

'I did try,' I said, afraid to check out Ash's reaction to this. 'It was dangerous.'

'Dangerous? You think what I'm doing isn't dangerous?'

'Leave her alone, Thabo,' Ash said. 'You're going about things the wrong way.'

'Hang on,' I said. 'You two *know* each other?'

'We've met,' Ash said. 'Still blowing up civilians, Thabo?'

'Still ripping off civilians, Ash?'

Ash took a step forwards again, but Thabo held his ground.

'Why didn't you tell me you knew the Mall Rats personally, Thabo?' I asked.

'I don't know them,' he spat. 'I don't *want* to know them.'

'We met at Lungi's,' Ash said.

'Yeah,' Thabo said. 'When he came to get his pound of flesh.'

'You've made things worse for all of us, Thabo,' Ash said. 'You and those ANZ stunts.'

Thabo shook his head in disgust. 'At least I'm doing something other than lining my own pockets. At least I'm working towards a better future.'

'How? How is hurting innocent people going to do anything other than bring the Resurrectionists down on us?'

Their argument sounded almost rehearsed and I got the impression right then that they'd been through this before.

'Don't worry about it, pretty boy,' Thabo said. 'You just carry on bringing back useless *crap* for everyone. As long as the Mall Rats are getting rich, who cares about the rest of us?'

'You are so misguided, Thabo,' Ash said.

'Yeah? I'd rather be misguided than a coward.'

Ash's face darkened, and I was pretty sure that if I didn't intervene they'd attack each other with more than just words. I stepped in between them. 'Ash, Thabo, just chill out, okay?'

Thabo turned to me. 'You don't need to be around useless parasites like him, Lele. They're just using you. Come and join us. Join me.'

'Thabo,' I said, reaching over to touch his hand. 'I can't. You don't understand.'

He snatched his hand away from me. 'I understand more than you know, Lele.'

My stomach was beginning to feel hollow. 'Let's just go,' I said to Ash. 'Come on.'

'Ask him,' Thabo said. 'Ask your boyfriend.'

'Ask him what?'

'Ask him how come you won the Lottery, Lele. Ask your boyfriend who betrayed you.'

Ash jerked back as if he'd been pushed.

'What are you talking about?' I asked Thabo, but already I could feel the blood running cold in my veins.

'Ask him,' Thabo said.

'Ash? What's Thabo talking about?' But in my gut I knew he

was telling the truth.

'They planned the whole thing, Lele,' Thabo said. 'It was your precious Mall Rats who almost got you killed.'

And with a last hate-filled glance at Ash, he stalked off into the main thoroughfare.

6

'Is it true, Hester?'

She nodded. She was so weak that she could barely sit up in bed, but I needed to hear the truth from her. 'Lele,' she said, 'I'm so sorry. I didn't want you to find out this way.'

The shock of betrayal was so great that for a second I was sure I was going to throw up.

'Are you okay, Lele?' Ginger asked as I steadied myself against the bed.

'Of course I'm not bloody okay, Ginger!' I snapped. He flinched, but I didn't allow myself to feel guilty for sniping at him. I waited for the furious anger to take me over completely, but it didn't. All I felt was a weird calmness.

'But I don't understand, Hester. Why didn't you just *ask* me to join you? Why make sure I won the Lottery?'

Hester reached over to take my hand. 'We misjudged you,

Lele.'

Then it struck me. 'You needed me to need you!' I said. 'You needed to make sure I had no choice but to join you.'

She closed her eyes and nodded.

'But that's so cruel!' I said. 'I could have been killed! Or worse!'

'We wouldn't have let that happen, Lele,' Saint said.

'Oh, really?' I said. 'How would you have stopped the Guardians from doing whatever they had planned for me?'

Saint shifted uncomfortably. 'We had a plan.' I'd never seen her look so ill-at-ease.

'A *plan*? What kind of plan? How could you have a plan to beat the Guardians?'

'We were going to bust you out of the wagon – but things changed. You did it yourself.'

'So you let me wander around the Deadlands by myself? Go into the mall without trying to help me?' Now the anger was starting to build, and I welcomed it.

'We were watching you.'

'Thanks a lot. Watching to make sure the Rotters actually couldn't see me, right? Making sure I had the right *skills*!'

Saint nodded.

'And then you pretended that you guys had just been shopping, so that I'd think you'd rescued me. So that I'd be *grateful*.'

'Ash did rescue you, Lele,' Saint said. 'We didn't expect the Guardians to be –'

'Save it,' I said.

Ginger was staring at the floor, scuffing his feet like a little boy being scolded.

'Ginger?' I said. 'Please tell me you weren't part of this as well.'

'Sorry, Lele,' he mumbled. 'Really, I am.'

'But how did you know beforehand that I might be able to move around in the Deadlands without the Rotters attacking me?' Ash glanced at me, and then I had it. 'It's something to do with Jobe, isn't it? Have you all got twins who were taken?'

Saint nodded.

'Where's your twin, Saint?'

She shook her head. 'I do not know. He was sent to a different school from me.'

'And you Ginger?'

'Not me,' Ginger said. 'I'm just a freak of nature.'

'You can say that again,' Saint said, trying to make light of the situation. But it was too little too late.

My brain was racing. 'Okay, so you found out that I had a twin who was rejected by the Guardians during the War. But how did you actually fix the Lottery? Are you in cahoots with the Resurrectionists or something?'

'No ways!' Ginger said.

'But you must have had someone on the inside! Who? Comrade Pelosi? Zyed's father?'

'Who's Zyed?' Ginger asked.

Then it clicked. 'Comrade Xhati!' I remembered the book list from my first official trip to the mall, and what he'd said about being a poetry professor before the War.

He'd sold me out for a couple of poetry books.

Ash spoke up for the first time. 'Lele, we would have told you sooner or later.'

'Yeah, right!' I spat. 'You've all been pretending to be my friends. All this time!'

'Lele, we *are* your friends,' Ginger said. 'Come on, let's grab a Coke, hang out and watch a movie. Hey, how about *Zombieland* again or *28 Days Later*? It's set in London, and it's, like, so –'

'You're not my friends, Ginger,' I said. 'Friends don't do things like this to each other. Friends don't lie and cheat and ... and ... try to get someone killed!'

Hester struggled to pull herself up to a sitting position. 'Lele, truly, we made a terrible mistake. And I think you know what that is like, *nè*?'

She had a point, but all I could think of right then was that they'd lied to me. They'd planned it down to the last detail. And I'd been stupid. I should have figured it out sooner.

At that moment I decided that Thabo was right. That they *were* just using me.

I pulled the hood of the Resurrectionist robe back over my head and ran for the exit.

No one tried to stop me.

7

I walked for ages, not caring where I was going, not thinking about anything other than what the Mall Rats had done to me.

No longer worried about who saw or recognised me, I flipped the hood back from my face, letting it fall to my shoulders. I almost pulled the robe off entirely, but decided at the last moment to keep it on, just in case.

'Hey, sisi!' a man catcalled to me. 'Hey! Come and save me, girl!'

The men with him all laughed raucously, and I increased my pace. For the first time I sensed an aura of threat in New Arrivals. But what did I care? What was the worst that could happen? I'd thought the Resurrectionists were the enemy. But they weren't. It was those closest to home.

It was then that I knew what I had to do. My whole reason for being part of the Mall Rats – to rescue Jobe – had fallen away.

He was happier at Mandela House than I'd ever seen him. And now I'd discovered that the people I'd thought were my friends had betrayed me. So why shouldn't I join the ANZ? Do some good for a change. And this time, for the right reasons.

I didn't recognise the street I was in, but after a few wrong turns I managed to locate the market area. I got my bearings, and hurried towards Lungi's place.

A group of ten or so people were milling around outside her pink house. A fire was flickering in a half-drum, and an elderly woman was preparing to slaughter several chickens that were squawking in a pen next to her.

Lungi was squashed into a faded deckchair, chatting to the guy with the hectic scar on his face.

'What you want here, sister?' Lungi asked as I strode up to her.

The chattering stopped instantly as everyone turned to check me out – even the chickens seemed to be watching me distrustfully. 'I need to see Thabo,' I said.

'Why?'

'I just do.'

'Does Hester know you have come here?'

'Look, just tell me where he is.'

'How do I know you are not some sort of spy, nè?'

'You know I'm not a spy, Lungi,' I said.

The scarred guy grinned and winked at me. 'You can spy on me anytime, cherie,' he said, looking me up and down.

'Shove it, scar-face,' I snapped.

The men and women roared with laughter, and blood rushed to my cheeks.

'Oh, just forget it,' I said, turning on my heel to stalk away.

'Wait, sisi,' Lungi said.

'What?'

She sighed and looked at me carefully for several seconds. Then she seemed to come to some sort of decision. 'Come with me. I will take you to him.'

Lungi led me into the house and through the kitchen. She unlocked the back door and I followed her out in to the night. We trekked through a labyrinth of byways and backyards, Lungi calling out to her neighbours as we ducked under lines hanging with damp washing, traipsed across smallholdings where mealies struggled to grow, and climbed over fences made out of bits of old wire and rusted hubcaps.

We were heading closer and closer to the fence, but just before we reached it Lungi stopped outside a large army tent. I could hear the sound of voices within, and then a burst of applause. There was a hand-drawn sign outside the tent that read *Soup Kitchen*, and a few feet from the entrance an elderly man was stirring something in a metal pot placed precariously over a fire. Two women and a chunky teenage guy were sitting on the ground just behind him. They were dressed in rags and were passing a bottle around, but none of them seemed to be even slightly drunk. One of the women put her hand in her pocket and tensed up as we approached.

'You know what you are getting yourself into?' Lungi asked me.

'I think so,' I said, holding her gaze.

'Then all I can say is good luck, princess.'

She nodded to the elderly man, and he pulled the flap back so that I could sneak inside.

There had to be fifty people sitting close together on the ground, and I had to edge around the side of the tent to avoid causing a disturbance. It was stifling inside, the air thick with the stench of nervous sweat and unwashed bodies. Thabo and a tall middle-aged woman with cropped blonde hair stood in front of the crowd, and every eye was fixed on them.

'My friends, it is indeed getting worse,' Thabo said, running a hand through his dreads. 'Last week, seven of our members were relocated. Relocated! I like how they use their words!' The crowd murmured appreciatively. 'I ask you, when did the dead stop being our enemies? When did the living start to be the ones we fear most?' Thabo spoke unhurriedly, his words ringing out over the people in front of him, his demeanour inspiring the same kind of attention as Comrade Nkosi. His eyes strayed to mine and he paused, but he didn't change his expression. 'How long will we put up with this? What other secrets are they keeping from us? And then there is the Lottery. Sure, at the present time it is only Resurrectionist teenagers who are taken, but for how long? Who knows what deals they are doing with the Guardians behind our backs? We demand transparency! We demand to know our future!'

Now the crowd roared, and several people raised their fists.

Thabo waited for the cheers to subside, sweeping his eyes through the crowd, as if he was fixing his gaze on every individual there. 'That is why we are asking you to join us,' he finally said. 'It is time to fight back and gain what has been lost: our freedom!'

The crowd stood up and started clapping. I caught Thabo's eye again, and this time he gave me a small nod of acknowledgement. The applause went on and on, but then, under the noise of stamping feet and cheers, I heard another sound – a scream.

It all happened so fast that at first I didn't even have time to feel scared. 'They're here!' someone shouted. 'Get out! Run!' And, within seconds, the cheers turned into panicked screams as the crowd tried to push its way out of the tent. I couldn't see clearly through the panicked throng, but it looked as if a group of people wearing Resurrectionist robes and brandishing clubs were trying to fight their way inside. I heard the dull thuds as the clubs landed on heads and bodies, and although I was relatively safe at the edge of the crowd, I could see that it wouldn't be long before they reached me. I pulled the robe's hood over my head, in the hope that it would camouflage me for long enough to sneak out, but then I felt someone grab my hand.

'This way!' Thabo said, dragging me towards the back of the tent.

Following him through a gash that had been cut into the canvas, I found myself right next to the fence.

'Come on!' Thabo hissed as the head and shoulders of a robed Resurrectionist began to appear through the gap.

I've never run as fast as I did then – even when Ginger had set off the fireworks in the mall. Thabo and I sprinted down the narrow muddy pathway next to the fence, angry shouts pursuing us.

We dodged and sprinted through the crevices between shacks and tents and caravans, keeping to the shadows as much as possible and choosing our direction at random. Soon the screams and chaos were left behind, but fuelled by adrenalin we kept on going until both of us were completely out of breath and almost sick with exhaustion.

Finally, dragging in lungfuls of air, I followed Thabo into an alleyway between two rows of connected shacks.

'Are we safe?' I asked.

'I don't know,' he said, leaning over to catch his own breath. 'There were so many of them. I've never seen so many.'

He rubbed his head and a small dribble of blood snaked over his forehead.

'You're hurt!' I said.

'Duh, Lele,' he replied with his old lopsided grin. 'I'm cool. Don't worry about it, it's nothing. Look, I have to get back, see if I can help anyone else. You stay here.'

'No ways!' I said. 'I'll come with you.'

'It's not safe, Lele.'

'What will the Resurrectionists do to them? To the others who were there?'

'They'll be relocated, of course,' he spat.

I caught his sleeve. 'I want to join you,' I said. 'You were right, Thabo. I want to do what I can to help stop this.'

He smiled again. 'Good.'

'I'm sorry about Ash, about –'

He wound his fingers through mine. 'It's cool, Lele,' he said. 'But we'll talk about this later, okay? Right now I must go and –'

'Hold it!' a voice said from behind us.

Three robed Resurrectionists were blocking one end of the alleyway.

'Come on!' Thabo said to me, eyes wide. We darted towards the other end, but as we did so a couple of shadowy figures moved to block that exit as well. All five would be on us in seconds.

'We're going to have to fight our way through them,' Thabo said. 'Stand back and get behind me.'

'Thabo,' I said, forgetting my exhaustion as I was hit with another blast of adrenalin. 'You might actually want to get behind *me*.'

'But –'

The three Resurrectionists at the other end were approaching fast. 'See if you can stop the other two,' I said, and he nodded.

The three came at once, holding wooden clubs aloft as they ran towards me.

I floored the first with an uppercut from my elbow, finished him off with a kick to his stomach and ducked as the second swiped with his club. I let it slam into my back, trying to absorb the pain, and then hooked my leg under his and tripped him onto his back. I slammed my foot into his crotch and he let out a hiss of agony.

Behind me, Thabo was tussling with the two guards, but apart from the third Resurrectionist facing me – a ginormous blonde woman with icy eyes – the way ahead was clear.

'Hang on, Thabo!' I said, lashing out with my right leg.

'Nice try, girly,' the woman said, jumping back with way more agility than I was expecting. 'But that won't work with me.'

'Oh, really?' I said.

She leapt towards me, club held aloft, but at the last second I dropped to my hands and knees and rolled my body into hers, sending her flying. Then, kicking the club out of her reach, I slammed my foot down on her hand. She screamed in rage, swung around and lashed out with her leg. The woman was fast and it was all I could do to jump out of the way. Stumbling over the guy I'd knocked out, I almost lost my balance, and by the time I recovered she was on me. I let her punch me in the face. I'd been punched by Saint before, and it wasn't anything I couldn't handle. Letting my body go limp – feigning concussion – I dropped to a crouch and swept my leg out, hooking the back of her knee. This time she fell backwards, jarred her head on the ground, and was still.

'Lele! Run!'

'Thabo!'

He was being dragged away down the alley, and behind him I could make out the shadowy shapes of yet more Resurrectionists. More than I'd ever be able to defeat. I could still escape at the other end – that way was clear – and I had a split-second decision to make. Fight on for Thabo, or get the hell out of there before both exits were blocked.

I could hear the sound of more running feet, and the shrill shriek of whistles being blown.

There was no way I could fight them all off.

I had to run. I had no choice.

But I swore that I would help him another way.

I needed to come up with a plan.

And I had to hurry.

8

'Leletia!'

The Mantis's tea cup slipped from her grasp and splintered on the floor.

Dad came thudding through from his study. 'Cleo, are you okay?'

He caught sight of me and a mixture of emotions flashed across his face – shock, relief and worry.

I pulled the curtains across the kitchen window.

'Lele!' Dad said. 'You can't be here! It's too dangerous.'

'I need your help, Dad. A friend of mine – he's been taken by the Resurrectionists. I need to know where they've taken him.'

Dad and the Mantis glanced at each other.

'Who is this friend?' the Mantis asked.

'He's ... Look, you don't need to know that.'

'Why was he detained?'

'It doesn't matter – what will they do to him?'

'It does matter,' the Mantis said. 'The punishment fits the crime.'

'Look, he's a member of the ANZ, okay?'

'Leletia, you shouldn't be involved in this,' the Mantis said.

'I am involved!' I said, swallowing hard to stop the tears. 'I have to help him. Please! Will they take him to the embassy first?'

'Lele, you must break ties with this traitor.'

'What? He's not a traitor! A traitor to whom? A traitor to what? To the Resurrectionists? Come on, Cleo, I know you don't believe in all that crap.'

She sighed. 'Look, Lele, even if I wanted to help you, I can't. I don't have access to that sort of information.'

'What happens to them, the people who are arrested?'

'Well, usually they are taken to the embassy and questioned. But you will never get in there. Not even with an army.'

'When is the next relocation scheduled?'

'I do not know.'

'Cut the crap, Cleo!'

'The only person who would have information like that is Comrade Nkosi. He makes those decisions.'

'I need to speak to him. Just tell me where he lives, Cleo,' I said.

'You can't go to see him … You don't understand. He's …'

'I know. He's a bastard.'

'Lele!' Dad said. 'Language!'

The Mantis and I shared a look that basically said 'as if we need to worry about swearing right now'.

'But I think you should know, Lele,' the Mantis said, 'if this friend is part of the ANZ, it is possible that he might be relocated immediately.'

'What? No!'

'There's been a clampdown, Lele. The embassy has been forced to take a hard line against these dissidents.'

My hands had started shaking violently. Dad poured me a glass of water and handed it to me. I swallowed it down in one go.

'Lele,' Dad said. 'You must let this go. It is all for the greater good, you will see.'

'How can you say that, Dad! How can you support these people? Look what they're doing to the city! To the kids with the Lottery. Dad, how can you be on the Guardians' side after what they did to Jobe?'

'That was years ago, Lele. And there's no proof that the Guardians did anything to him –'

Now I didn't bother trying to stop the tears. 'No proof! But he changed, Dad.'

'Yes, Lele. But you didn't.'

'What do you mean?'

He paused and ran his hands over his face. 'They took you, too. And you didn't change.'

'No they didn't,' I said, my voice sounding hollow.

'They did, Lele,' he said. 'The memory is trapped in there somewhere.'

I sat down on the chair behind me so hard that my jaw clicked. I wasn't sure if I could handle another shock that evening without my skull splitting open. My mind was reeling. I had no early memories of the Guardians except for the few times I'd seen them at the edge of the Agriculturals, collecting the vegetables and livestock. I had a vague recollection of being in the soccer stadium, but that was it. Like I said, my memories of the War and its immediate aftermath were seriously sketchy.

'You never told me this,' the Mantis said to Dad.

'And Gran never said anything about it either!' I added.

He sighed. 'She didn't want to worry you.'

'So, what are you saying?' I asked. 'That just because they didn't do anything to me they didn't screw up Jobe's brain?' I couldn't think about the other implications of what he'd said right then. It was just too much.

The Mantis was watching me carefully. She stood up, opened one of the kitchen drawers and took out a piece of paper and a pen. 'Lele, please,' she said as she scrawled something on it and handed it to me. 'I'm begging you not to do this. He's a very dangerous man.'

'I don't have a choice. Don't worry, I'll keep you out of it.'

She nodded. 'I cannot do more,' she said. 'It's not just me and your father I have to consider now.'

'What do you mean? Jobe's in Mandela House.'

Dad and the Mantis shared another glance. 'Lele, I'm pregnant,' she said.

9

The Mantis's directions were clear, and it wasn't hard to find Comrade Nkosi's home. It was two streets down from the embassy, a couple of blocks from Malema High. It was way smaller and scruffier than I was expecting – a two-storey house not much larger than Dad and the Mantis's place. Comrade Nkosi clearly wasn't stupid. He didn't want to be accused of using his power for his own personal gain. At least one politician had learned from history.

I knew I was taking a hell of a chance, but what choice did I have?

As I stared up at the darkened windows I caught sight of the silhouette of a feathered dream catcher. Picking up a pebble from the road, I took aim, and lobbed it towards the window. It thunked against it, sounding far louder than I'd been expecting. I looked nervously up and down the street, but it didn't appear to have disturbed anyone. I was about to try again, when the window cranked open and someone leaned out of it. A thick curtain of black hair was hanging over the figure's face, but I was almost positive it had to be Zyed.

'Zyed!' I hissed.

He jerked his head up. 'Who is that?' he called.

'Shhhh! Keep your voice down. It's me! Lele!'

There was a pause while he took this in. 'You're supposed to be a Rotter by now,' he said. I could see he hadn't changed his attitude while I'd been away.

'Yeah, well, I'm not.'

'What do you want?'

'I need your help.'

'What?'

'Come on, Zyed. Please! It's a matter of life or death.'

Without responding he slipped back inside his room, shutting the window behind him.

'Crap!' I kicked the gate in frustration and was about to turn away when I heard the front door opening. Zyed approached me. He was wearing a simple grey tracksuit, his hair and clothes for once free of the feathers.

'Did you tell your father I'm here?' I asked.

'No. He's at the embassy. Working late as usual.' He sounded bitter. 'So, are you a believer all of a sudden?' he asked, looking me up and down, taking in the robe.

I snorted. 'What do you think?'

'How did you get back into the enclave?'

'That's not important, Zyed. Look, I need your help.'

'Why should I help you?'

'Because it's not actually *me* who's in trouble. It's Thabo.'

'What about him?'

'He's being relocated.'

Zyed's face slackened in shock. 'Oh, no! Why?'

'That doesn't matter. I'm going to try to save him, but I need to know where they're going to take him and when. Can you help me with that?'

'I don't know.'

'Your dad would know, though, right?'

'Sure. But he's at the embassy.'

'Could you get to him? Think of an excuse?'

'I never visit him at work. That would make him instantly suspicious.'

'Crap.'

'But I could sneak into his office when he gets back, I guess. He always brings paperwork home. But he might be a while. Apparently there's been some trouble in the poorer sectors.'

'Tell me about it,' I said. 'If you could do that, I can wait.' What choice did I have?

'Where will I find you?'

I told him and then, rummaging under the robe, I pulled off the tie I was still using as a makeshift belt. My jeans slipped to my hips, but thankfully didn't fall down. I passed it to him. 'Here. It's yours.'

'What's this?'

'Let's just say, if you help me out, there'll be way more stuff like this coming your way.'

He glanced at me. 'Okay, Farm Girl. You've got yourself a deal.'

10

I hunkered down in the alleyway where Thabo and I had sprayed slogans across the dumpsters all those weeks before, not caring about the stench of garbage and rotten food. It had to be heading towards midnight, and in the quiet of the sleeping city the Rotters' moans sounded louder than usual. I desperately hoped that Thabo hadn't already been taken out into the Deadlands, or that if he had, he'd found a way to escape somehow. I knew he was a fighter, a survivor, but he'd be no match for a pack of Rotters, or even worse – Hatchlings.

I don't know how long I waited there, but it had to be an hour at least. I had plenty to think about – too much to think about and digest, really – but I wasn't ready to deal with it. I allowed myself to doze for a few minutes at a time; the only way I could stop myself going insane with worry about Thabo, obsessing over what Dad had said, fretting that Zyed would turn me in or thinking about the Mall Rats' betrayal. At least my body wasn't too sore after the run-in with the Resurrectionists. My face was no longer tender from where I'd been punched and even my back had stopped aching, although the guy hadn't held back when he'd whacked me.

But I was wide awake when I saw a figure slip into the alleyway.

'Psssh! Lele!' Zyed called.

I pulled myself up, stretching my stiff muscles.

Even in the poor light I could tell that the news wasn't good. 'Well?' I said.

'You're too late,' he replied.

'What do you mean?'

'He's already been processed.'

'What does that mean?'

'That they're going to relocate him immediately. If they haven't already done so.'

I fought to control a surge of nausea. 'Do you know where?'

Zyed shrugged. 'The east gate most likely. That's where most of them leave from.'

That was miles away – where Gran's funeral had taken place.

'I have to go,' I said.

'But what can you do to help him? He'll be with the Guardians now.'

'You don't need to know that, Zyed,' I said. 'Thanks for this.'

'Good luck,' he said. 'And tell Thabo ...' his voice trailed away.

'I will, Zyed,' I said, already moving off into the night.

Whatever my next move was, I knew couldn't do it alone.

11

'Hello?'

With the generator off, the kitchen and lounge were deathly quiet and almost completely dark. A paraffin lamp flickered on the kitchen counter, and I lit a couple of candles to banish the worst of the gloom. I couldn't remember ever seeing the place so deserted.

'Anyone here?' I said, trying again.

'Over here, Lele,' a voice croaked.

Hester was lying on the couch, her small shape covered with a blanket. Even though I had seen her merely hours before, it was clear that she'd deteriorated further. The scar tissue on her face stood out starkly against the papery skin that stretched over her cheekbones.

I took her hand. It felt way too hot. 'Hester?'

'I am glad you are home, Lele,' she said. 'I have been worried.'

'Where's everyone?'

'Out looking for you,' she said, attempting to smile. 'We do care about you, Lele. I know what you think of us.' She sighed. 'Ash – I have never seen him in such a state. When you didn't return, he went out searching, even though the enclave is overrun with guards.' She coughed a horrible wracking cough. 'Please, you must forgive them.'

'That doesn't matter now,' I said and quickly began to fill her in on what had happened to Thabo.

'I have to go after him, Hester,' I finished. 'He's my friend.'

'It is not safe for you to go alone, Lele.'

'I know,' I said. 'But I don't have a choice.'

She leaned over and coughed again, the sound rocketing up from her very core.

'Can I get you anything, Hester?' I asked.

She shook her head. 'It is too late for me, Lele,' she said. 'But it is not too late for you. Your friend – if he has gone in to the Deadlands, then there is nothing you can do. You must not risk it.'

'I need to try.'

She struggled to sit up, and pointed towards the corner of the room where Ginger stored his massive collection of DVDs. 'There is a small carved wooden box underneath the television. Can you bring it to me?'

I nodded and did as she asked.

'Open it,' she said.

Inside there were loads of palm-sized metal square and star shapes. Thin as a blade, each one had a hole in its centre and razor-sharp spiked edges.

'You know what these are?' Hester asked.

'No.'

'They are called hira shuriken. Or, as Ginger would probably

287

call them, ninja throwing stars.'

I picked one of them up and weighed it in my hand. It was heavier than it looked. I ran my thumb carefully over its edges.

'These are weapons?' I said, although it was obvious that nothing this sharp could be anything else.

'Yes, Lele. But it is unlikely that you will be able to destroy an attacker with one of these. Traditionally, they were used to distract the enemy, before going in for the kill.' She coughed again.

'Hester –'

'I haven't finished,' she said. 'I want you to take these with you.' She smiled at me. 'I used ones like these during the last battle, when I found Ash. Take them for luck. They may just save your life. They helped save mine.'

I leaned over and kissed her on the cheek. 'Thank you,' I said.

'Take care,' she replied, her voice now cracking with exhaustion. 'And, please, forgive them.'

I chucked the Resurrectionist robe on the ground, grabbed my backpack and shoved the throwing stars into it, careful not to cut myself.

Hester's breathing had slowed as if she'd fallen into a deep sleep, but I gave her a hug anyway, her body feeling insubstantial under her clothes, just like Gran's in her last hours.

Wiping away the tears that rolled down my cheeks, I headed towards the tunnel that led into the Deadlands.

I didn't look back, and I didn't say goodbye, and I regret that now.

It would be the last time we'd ever speak.

12

Even with the full moon bathing the Deadlands in a bluish light, I'd be lying if I said I wasn't seriously spooked. My pulse was jackhammering and my feet sounded way too loud as I crunched over the dried leaves and fynbos, but I knew I couldn't afford to slow down.

I came across a large group of Rotters crowded together around a tree, their heads bowed together, almost touching, as if they were leaning up against each other. Their low doleful moaning sounded way eerier than I was used to, and from then on every gnarled tree trunk, every twisted branch and every elongated shadow seemed to morph into the figure of a Hatchling or Guardian. I had to fight to stop my imagination getting the better of me.

A few hundred yards from the bone mountain I slowed my pace, now doing my best to move through the undergrowth with as little noise as possible. I knew that this was where the Guardians took the bodies of the dead to reanimate them, but I had no way of knowing how many people had been relocated or if I would be forced to fight the thing that Thabo might have become. I pulled the shuriken out of my bag and shoved as many as I could into my pockets, deciding at the last minute to keep one at hand. Holding it made me feel calmer, more confident. Even if I was gripping it so tightly that it almost sliced through the skin of my palm.

I crept closer. The edges of the mountain glowed in the moonlight, the stripped bones gleaming whitely in contrast to the deep shadow of the bushes that surrounded them. I stood as still as I could, listening for any signs of life – any indication that there were Hatchlings around – but all I could hear was the ragged sound of my own breath, the guttural call of a plover and the low distant moans of the Rotters.

Then, a few metres away from me the undergrowth began to rustle. I readied myself to chuck the throwing star, but it was only a porcupine and it quickly melted back into the myrtle trees behind it.

There was no sign of the wagon.

I had to decide what to do next, but that decision was taken out of my hands.

A branch broke behind me, and this time I was sure that whatever had made the sound was a lot larger than a porcupine.

I weighed the throwing star in my hand, and prepared myself to fight as a shadowy silhouette emerged from behind a plumbago bush.

'Lele!' the whisper cut through the night, and I only managed to stop myself from throwing the star at the last moment. There was no mistaking who it was.

'Ash!'

He jogged over to where I was standing and threw his arms around me. Without hesitating I hugged him back. Right then I decided that whatever the Mall Rats had done to me was in the past. We'd betrayed each other – me by putting them in danger in the mall, the Mall Rats by fixing my Lottery win – and there were more important things to consider right then. Thabo's life, for one.

Ash was also out of breath, and when he drew back, his sweaty hair hung damply over his eyes. 'Are you okay?' he asked.

I nodded. 'Yeah, but, Ash ... Thabo isn't. The Resurrectionists, they've –'

'I know,' he said. 'Hester told me.'

'I have to find him,' I said. 'I have to go after him.'

I waited for him to argue, but he didn't. Instead he just nodded.

'Where are Saint and Ginger?' I asked.

'They've gone to the west gate,' he said. 'We weren't sure where you were headed.'

'And Hester? Is she ...?'

He shook his head. 'No. But it won't be long.'

In the moonlit darkness I could see that his eyes were glistening with unshed tears. 'Ash, you must go back and be with her.'

'No, Lele,' he said, wiping a hand furiously over his eyes. 'Hester would want me to be with you.'

He spoke with finality, and I could tell that it was no use arguing with him.

'Let's follow the wagon tracks,' he said. 'See if we can cut them off.'

I nodded. 'It's our only option. It doesn't look like the wagon stopped here, after all.'

But I'd spoken too soon.

We'd barely passed the bone mountain when we heard the crack of splintering branches and the sinister whisper of grass brushing against fabric.

The first Hatchling came at us with the same terrifying speed as the ones Ash and Saint had fought when I'd first met them. With all of my senses heightened by the adrenalin pulsing through my system, the moonlight seemed to light up the scene as bright as day, and I recognised her immediately. Even with her eyes rolled back in her head; even with the snarl that cut across her face. It was the short-haired woman who had stood next to Thabo in the tent.

I took aim and threw the star I had been clutching in my hand. It hit its target as I knew it would, and the woman stopped dead and twisted her head, giving Ash enough time to lash out with his panga.

But she wasn't alone.

They rushed towards us, only momentarily held back by the thicket of thorn trees. I dug in my pockets, pulling out the other shuriken and throwing one at the closest Hatchling – this one a woman wearing the remnants of a sari – but moments later the rest of them were upon us.

We moved so effortlessly it was if Ash and I were part of the same person. I would throw one of the shuriken, distract the Hatchling, and Ash would step forward, spin around and slice its head from its body. Apart from the crunch of their running feet, the Hatchlings made no sound, and all I could hear was the steady pulse of my heart, the *shwick* of Ash's panga, and the sound of bodies crashing to the ground, one after the other. I don't know how many there were that night, but despite their numbers it seemed as if it was over in seconds.

After we felled the last attacker, both of us stood absolutely immobile for the next couple of minutes. Finally, I sensed Ash relaxing.

'I think that's all of them,' he finally said in a low voice. He pulled a torch out of the bag slung over his shoulder and swept the beam around the undergrowth. The silver spheres of a mongoose's eyes flashed in the beam, but otherwise the light hit dead shadow.

Stepping towards one of the fallen bodies, he picked up one of the shuriken. It glinted in the moonlight. 'Did Hester give you these?' he asked.

'Yes,' I said.

'Did she teach you how to use them?'

I shook my head.

'I've never fought that many before,' he said. 'I wouldn't have been able to do it without you.'

Normally I would have felt thrilled to hear him say something like this to me, but there was something else on my mind right then. Something awful.

They'd come at us so fast that I hadn't been able to see all of them clearly.

And I had to be sure.

Ash helped me do it. It was grisly work, checking each one for those familiar dreadlocks. But he wasn't there. I remember hoping that he might have escaped after all, perhaps climbed out of the wagon as I had done, that he was somewhere out in the Deadlands, hiding from the Guardians.

'He's not here,' I said, stating the obvious and unable to stop the sob of relief that followed.

Ash slotted the panga back into its holder. 'Then let's find him,' he said.

13

In the end we almost walked straight into it. We were about half a kilometre from the mall and about to step onto the highway – the birds around us flitting from tree to tree and welcoming the dawn as if nothing out of the ordinary was happening – when we heard the creak of wood and the snort of horses behind the bushes parallel to where we were walking.

Ash put his finger to his lips, and both of us crept forward slowly. The wagon was rumbling along at a steady pace, but I still easily made out the shadowy shapes of two Guardians sitting side by side at the front of it.

We had no way of knowing if Thabo was actually in the back of the wagon, but I was determined to find out, whatever it took.

It was heading straight for the mall and we jogged after it, the sound of our footsteps muffled beneath the rumble of the wagon's wheels and the jingle of the horses' harnesses.

We hung back, watching as the horses clopped their way up the ramp to the parking area. Then, keeping as quiet as we could, we sprinted from car to car, using their fynbos-swathed bodies as cover. Creeping up the ramp, Ash pointed to the rusted shell of a Woolworth's delivery truck, and we scuttled behind it, just as the wagon came to a stop.

I watched, fascinated, as the Guardians climbed down and unhitched the horses – one of them leading the animals around the side of the wagon and back down towards the highway. I held my breath as it came uncomfortably close to where we were hiding, the horses shying slightly as they no doubt sensed our presence. Thankfully the Guardian leading them didn't falter, and within seconds they were out of sight.

Meanwhile the other Guardian had made its way to the back of the wagon, and was busy unlatching the high wooden tailgate.

'You think he's in there?' I whispered to Ash.

'Shhhh,' Ash said, his eyes fixed on the Guardian. He had drawn his panga and I could sense that he was steeling himself for a fight.

As the tailgate dropped to the ground a figure emerged from the back of the wagon, shielding its eyes against the sun.

It was Thabo.

Instinctively, I moved towards him, but Ash grabbed my arm and held me back. 'Just wait,' he hissed in my ear.

I knew he was right, but it hurt just to watch as Thabo stumbled down onto the ground. Even from where we were hidden I could see that he'd been badly beaten: his face was caked in blood and he was favouring his right leg.

The Guardian motioned Thabo to follow him, but instead he lurched forward as if his legs couldn't hold up his body – a move that I suspected was a feint. It was, and as soon as the Guardian took a step towards him, Thabo rushed at it. But what happened next took us all by surprise.

One minute Thabo was moving in for the kill, the next the Guardian simply held up a hand and stopped him dead in his tracks. Worse, Thabo then began backing up, his hands in the air. As he did so I saw the early morning sunlight flashing off something metal that was poking out of the sleeve of the Guardian's robe, but it took me what seemed like forever to realise that it was holding a gun.

I didn't even stop to consider why a Guardian would need a weapon. They were supposed to be all powerful, after all. I didn't even hesitate. I took the last throwing star out of my pocket – the one Ash had retrieved – and threw it as I ran forward. The star hit its target, and the gun zinged out of the Guardian's hand and skittered underneath the wagon.

Ash was right behind me, but even in his bloodied state Thabo didn't need his help. As we approached, he lashed out a leg and slammed it into the Guardian's stomach. It reeled backwards, arms cartwheeling, and fell to the ground, thumping its head against the back of the wagon.

Panga raised, Ash headed straight for it, but I didn't stop to see what he was going to do. I was too busy throwing my arms around Thabo. I couldn't believe that we'd actually found him. I needed to touch him, to get the fact that he was alive through to my brain.

'My hero,' he said in my ear.

'We're not out of this yet,' I replied, pulling back and checking him over. 'Are you badly hurt?' He was definitely going to have a couple of black eyes and it looked as if his nose might be broken.

'I've been worse,' he said, giving me his lopsided grin. Then he looked around at the mall. 'Is that really what I think it is?'

'Thabo,' I said, 'you haven't seen anything yet.'

'Guys!' Ash called to us. 'I think you should see this.'

The Guardian still lay where it had fallen, Ash staring at it with a mixture of shock and disbelief. Using the tip of his panga, he had lifted one of the robe's sleeves, and as Thabo and I joined him I caught a glimpse of human skin where a hand – a human hand – peeked out.

Then, with absolutely no warning, the body shifted and sat up, moving with a horrible sinuous speed. Ash moved as if to slice it with his panga, but then it was still again.

'Hello, Lele,' a human voice – a guy's voice – said from beneath the hood. Bizarrely, the voice sounded familiar, but I couldn't place it.

Ash and I stared at each other.

'We knew you would be back,' the Guardian said.

'Who are you?' I asked, still struggling to remember where I'd heard the voice before.

Shifting the panga to the Guardian's throat, Ash reached down and pulled the robe's hood completely from the its face. It took me less than a second to download who was in front of me, but far longer to actually believe it.

'You!' I said, trying to make sense of what I was seeing.

'Me,' he replied.

It was Zit Face – Paul – although the cruel nickname I'd given him didn't fit anymore. His skin was smooth and clear, and his once permanently greasy hair shimmered in the sunlight where it curled over his forehead.

'If you run now, you might just get away,' Paul said, and I knew then why I didn't immediately recognise his voice. There was something dead about it. Emotionless.

'Look at his eyes,' Thabo said, his voice flat with shock.

At first I couldn't see what Thabo was talking about. The sun was now so bright, and I had to lean in closer to see properly.

I couldn't hold in the scream.

Paul's irises were no longer the faded blue I remembered. They were just dense black spheres that didn't seem to reflect the light.

'But ... you're a Guardian? *You?*' I said.

The Paul thing smiled a cold, fake smile. 'Me,' he said.

'This is what the Guardians – you – do with the teenagers?'

'Yes.'

I glanced at Thabo and Ash. They were both staring down at Paul, their expressions a mix of fascination and horror. I knew that it was neither the time nor the place to ask questions, but I couldn't help myself.

'You were going to do that to Thabo?' I asked. 'Change him?'

'Yes.'

'But ... why teenagers?'

'Teenagers are the only humans that can survive the change without it destroying their system, disrupting their minds. Without the need for death. This kind of human system is receptive: it is grown, but not fully grown. A body in transition.'

I thought then of Jobe, and shrugged away the thought of what Dad had told me – that I'd also been taken away by the Guardians.

'So you're kind of like a Rotter?' I said. 'Like a mix of Rotter and human?'

'In a sense. Yet, unlike the dead ones I will never grow older and decrepit. This body will never rot if I take care of it.'

'How do you control the Rotters?' Ash asked.

'We are all connected, the walking dead ones and us. We share a common thread. What I know, they know.'

'But you're nothing like the Rotters!'

Paul stared at me with his blank eyes. 'In the enclave, you have workers – people who pull you along the streets like horses, others who pick up the rubbish. That is what the dead are to us.'

'You use them to keep us under control,' Ash spat.

'Yes,' Paul said, again without changing his expression. It was almost like talking to a robot in one of Ginger's movies.

'The Resurrectionists are going to *freak* when they find out about this,' Thabo said.

'So, you're aliens?' I said.

'No, Lele.' Paul smiled again. '*You* are the aliens.'

'What should we do with him?' Ash said. He glanced at Thabo, who shrugged.

'Well, you can't kill him,' I replied. 'It's Paul!'

'It's not Paul, Lele,' Thabo said. 'Not anymore. It's just a shell.' And I knew he was right. It looked like Paul; it presumably had his memories (he'd recognised me, after all), but there was something sinisterly alien about the eyes, about the way he didn't seem to blink or show even a glimmer of emotion.

Then Ash asked the question we'd all been wondering. 'Why did you – the Guardians, I mean – leave the mall intact?'

'Because it is your god.'

'*What?*' I said.

'We couldn't destroy the thing you love most. Before we came, we watched you carefully. Places like this are where you spent most of your time and energy.'

'But ... the shopping mall isn't our god!' I said.

'What is then?'

Good question. 'I suppose, for the Resurrectionists, you are.'

The Paul thing let out a low cold chuckle again.

'Shall we lock him in the wagon?' Ash asked.

'We've got to do something,' Thabo said. 'There were two

of them, remember? The other one could be back at any time.'

But that observation was too little too late.

The shot rang out, sounding impossibly loud in the quiet of the morning, the bullet splintering the wagon's wooden side, missing Thabo's head by inches.

'Into the mall!' Ash yelled. We didn't have another option; we needed to get under cover fast. A tall figure was walking unhurriedly towards us from the direction of the highway. It had removed its robe, and its tall shape looked vaguely familiar, but I wasn't about to waste any time trying to figure out who it was.

Another shot rang out, and the three of us hunched over to make ourselves as small as possible as we sprinted towards the mall's entrance. The glass doors had never looked so welcoming.

'You won't get far!' the Paul thing called after us in that same lifeless voice.

We all ducked again, as a puff of plaster smoked off the mall's wall next to my head.

'Come on!' Ash grabbed my hand, and the three of us pushed through the entrance doors, tumbling on to the hard marble tiles, just as another shot shattered the glass next to us.

14

The three of us hared along the corridor.

'Where to?' I asked Ash.

'We're going to have to get hold of some weapons,' he said. 'I'm thinking we head to Game – get our hands on some of Ginger's fireworks.'

'At least we know the Guardians aren't unstoppable,' I said.

I realised that Thabo was falling behind, and slowed my pace. My stomach twisted when I noticed the bright spots of blood glistening on the white tiles behind him. He was holding his side, and his eyes were bright with pain.

'Ash! It's Thabo! He's badly hurt. He's bleeding!'

'I'll be okay, Lele,' Thabo said, trying to grin. 'I think they just nicked me.'

Without a word, Ash slung one of Thabo's arms around his

shoulders and I did the same with the other. I was a good head smaller than both of them, but it didn't look like Thabo would make it much further without help from both of us.

'You going to make it?' I asked.

'Yeah,' he said. 'So you came after me, huh?' He glanced at Ash. 'You too? I didn't expect that.'

'That's your way of saying thank you?' Ash asked.

'Yeah,' Thabo said, trying to smile again, although the pain he was feeling turned it into a grimace. 'Seriously, guys, it's just a scratch.'

Ash pulled out his walkie-talkie. 'Ginger! Saint! Come in, over!'

But in reply there was nothing but the empty buzz of static.

'You think they'll know to come here?' I asked.

'Yeah,' Ash said. 'Where else would they go? I'm betting that they'll head this way when they don't find you at the west gate.'

'I just hope they don't run into the Guardians outside. Why didn't Paul and the other one follow us in here?'

'I don't know,' Ash said.

We hobbled along, Ash glancing back every now and then to check that we weren't being followed.

'So this is where you get all the stuff from?' Thabo said, struggling to speak between laboured breaths.

'Yeah,' I replied.

'So that's why you're called Mall Rats ...' he said. Then, his legs seemed to lose all of their strength and he slumped forward.

'We can't stop now!' Ash said as we both staggered under Thabo's weight. 'Come on, guys, it'll be plain sailing when we get to the escalators.'

But Ash couldn't have been more wrong.

15

We'd just turned the corner into the main aisle and were a tantalising five metres or so from the escalators when we saw the first bunch. The Rotters were congregated in front of a lingerie emporium, two of them doing their best to sweep the floor while the others milled around as if they were doing nothing more than cheering them on.

'Oh, shit,' Ash said.

I'd been so used to them not seeing us that I'd completely forgotten that they could sense Thabo.

A broom-wielding Rotter was the first to react. Its head jerked up, and it opened its skinless jaw wide, letting out a desolate moan. The others immediately stopped what they were doing and twitched their heads around. Then they started shuffling towards us, slowly at first, but then one of them – a hunched figure missing one of its arms – suddenly lunged forward, moving with that same jerky surreal speed I remembered from Gran's funeral.

'Come on!' Ash yelled. 'Back the way we came!'

We backtracked, but another knot was approaching from that direction, as if drawn by the moans of the others. Both routes were blocked, and from the sounds of the clumping feet behind us it seemed that their ghastly moaning was summoning more and more of them. Ash and I were now practically carrying Thabo between us and I knew that we wouldn't be able to continue much further. Ash stopped dead and unsheathed the panga. 'No choice but to fight!' he said.

The roar cut through the moans, followed by the most welcome sound I'd ever heard: 'Yippee-kai-yay, zombie suckers!' Ginger yelled.

Heads bounced towards us, spewing that strange spaghetti stuff, as Ginger cut a path through the dead.

'Get inside!' Saint shouted at us, appearing from behind Ginger and pointing us towards the bookstore, its entrance just metres away.

'We'll be trapped!' Ash yelled back.

'No choice! There's too many!'

Saint, Ash and Ginger sliced and hacked at the tide of bodies, while I manoeuvred Thabo inside. I helped him stumble towards the back of the store, but his strength was failing fast, and we only just made it to the children's section.

I raced back to the front of the store and started edging the heavy glass door shut, its hinges screaming from disuse. At the last moment, Ash, Ginger and Saint slipped inside.

Ginger shut off the chainsaw, and we were left listening to the sound of the Rotters moaning outside, several of them bumping against the glass in a vain attempt to get to us.

'Now, that's what I call cutting it fine,' Ginger said.

I jogged back to Thabo, Saint and Ginger close behind.

Saint slumped down in exhaustion. 'What the hell have you got us into now, Zombie Bait?'

'It's my fault,' Thabo said, trying again to grin. Sweat was beading on his forehead, and, more worryingly, his skin was taking on a greyish tone. 'Blame me.'

Saint took in his injuries for the first time. 'What happened?'

'The Guardians shot him,' I said.

'Wait ... *What*? Why would the Guardians need guns?'

'We've seen them, Saint,' I said. 'We know what they are.'

'And what are they?'

Thabo and I shared a glance. 'Teenagers,' I said.

'Teenagers? What have you been smoking?'

'It's true.' Ash said, returning from the kitchen with a pot of water and several clean tea towels.

'And the first ones that came? You think they were also teenagers?'

Ash shrugged. 'Who knows, but I'm pretty sure it's why they did all those experiments on the kids. Trying to find hosts that would take whatever that spaghetti stuff is without it destroying their bodies.'

I shuddered again.

'How many are there do you think? Guardians, I mean?' Saint asked.

'There are the ones from the Lottery, I guess,' Ash said. 'Lele, you knew that Guardian outside. Was he one of the Lottery winners?'

I nodded.

'There must be shedloads if you think about it,' Ginger said. 'All the ones that bring building materials and food into the city. Weird to think they're, like, our age, innit?'

Thabo groaned, and his eyelids fluttered.

'Guys!' I said. 'Thabo needs help.'

'We're going to have to stop the bleeding and clean that wound,' Ash said to Thabo.

Thabo looked up at him and nodded, but his eyes were turning glassy.

Slowly, I helped Thabo out of his jacket. I bit back the gasp of shock – his black T-shirt was sodden with blood.

'Ooooh, *mate*,' Ginger said as I rolled Thabo's T-shirt up as gently as I could. The wound looked surprisingly small, nothing but a dark hole just beneath his ribs, but the blood that oozed out of it was black.

Ash tried to hide the dismay on his face – but he didn't do a good enough job of it. He must have seen countless wounds during the war, and the fact that he was horrified didn't bode well for Thabo.

'It's bad, isn't it?' Thabo said.

'Just try to relax,' Ash replied.

Ash crouched next to me and started to clean the wound, the water running bloody instantly.

Thabo took my hand. 'Lele,' he said. 'You must get out of here. Just leave me.'

'No ways! Don't even say that.'

He looked up at Ash. 'Tell her. Get her out of here.'

'We're not leaving you, Thabo,' Ash said, taking off his jacket and making a pillow for his head. 'That's non-negotiable.'

Thabo settled back and closed his eyes, his breathing becoming steadily more laboured.

There was a banging sound on the windows. Ginger got to his feet and peered around the bookshelves.

'What's going on?' I asked.

'There's even more of them,' Ginger said, shoving a hand through his ginger curls. 'It's just like *Dawn of the Dead*, innit?'

He looked down at Thabo. 'Don't worry, mate,' he said, 'we'll get you out of here.'

'How though?' I asked. 'I mean, say we get out of the mall, how will we get him through the Deadlands?'

'We'll need some kind of vehicle,' Ash said.

'The wagon?'

Ash nodded. 'But we'll need to get the horses.'

We shared a glance. Both of us knew that the odds were heavily stacked against us.

'First things first,' Saint said. 'We've got to get him past those things outside.'

'I've got an idea,' Ginger said.

'You have?' Saint said. 'What?'

'You'll see,' he replied. 'There's a Coke machine back there, right?'

'Is that all you think about, Ginger?' Saint asked.

Ginger winked at her, grabbed his bag and his chainsaw and jogged off in the direction of the coffee shop.

The banging on the glass had intensified and it sounded as if the Rotters were now using more than just their fists.

'You think they can break through?' I asked.

'I doubt it,' Saint said to me.

'Should we move Thabo to the storeroom just in case?' I pointed towards the back of the shop.

'I don't think we should move him anywhere right now. At least not until the bleeding has stopped,' Ash said. 'That wound looks –'

The sound of shattering glass swallowed Ash's words.

It happened so quickly that a bunch of Rotters were inside the store before Ash and Saint were on their feet. I squeezed Thabo's hand and hared after them.

Ginger ran through from the kitchen, revving his chainsaw,

feet thumping across the carpet tiles. Ash was slicing away with his panga, but more and more Rotters were crashing through the splintering glass, kicking paperbacks out of the way, their sightless gazes seemingly fixed in Thabo's direction.

Ginger sliced his chainsaw in an arc, sending several scattering at once, but then it sputtered and died.

'You run out of petrol?' Ash yelled at him.

'Kind of,' he said, 'I – watch out!'

Another wall of bodies lurched forwards, stumbling over the Rotters Ginger and Ash had just cut down. They didn't fight – they acted as if Saint, Ash and Ginger weren't actually present – but their shrunken eyes seemed to be fixed on where Thabo lay.

I flung my knife, hitting a Rotter square in the chest (it didn't even falter), and quickly looked around for another weapon. There was nothing but books. I grabbed a bunch of *Twilight* graphic novels from a display table and started chucking them at the heads of the Rotters. To my right, Saint was doing her best, but she was being forced back as wave after wave of the dead surged forward. I caught sight of her head disappearing as she stumbled backwards, and then, as the crowd of the dead parted, I saw her being pushed to the ground, her leg caught behind one of the shelves at an awkward angle.

Her scream melded with the Rotters' moans.

'Ginger!' I yelled. 'Saint's down!' But he was too busy trying to fend off the Rotters with the blade of his chainsaw to do anything.

Ash was now a one-man shield between Thabo and the Rotters, and he couldn't wield the panga fast enough to stop them. The *Twilight* display depleted, I grabbed a hardback book about Nelson Mandela and threw it like a frisbee. It conked off the head of the Rotter closest to me, but there were way too many. I skirted around Ash and flung my body on top of

Thabo's, wrapping my arms around him, waiting for the Rotters to get to us.

But they never came.

An immense roar shattered the air, and at first I thought that Ginger had managed to fire up his chainsaw again. I stood up and edged forward in time to see two motorbikes crashing through the empty display window, scattering paperbacks everywhere, wheels crunching over shards of broken glass. They skidded in a tight arc, sending Rotter bodies flying, the stench of burning rubber and exhaust thick in the air.

As the engines cut out, I recognised Paul astride one of the bikes, and it was then that some part of me realised that this was the source of the ear-splitting sound I'd heard in the mall when I'd first met Ash.

Paul's robe was gone, and he was dressed in a slim-fitting black silk suit, blindingly white starched shirt and a black tie. Leaping from his bike in a single movement, he gestured dismissively to the Rotters. One of them snapped its toothless maw at him, but it shrank back when he approached, and then, one by one, the Rotters stumbled out of the store. But to be honest I wasn't really watching them anymore; my attention had been caught by the other Guardian.

'Jamale,' I said, my voice escaping in a whisper. But it wasn't the terrified Jamale I remembered from the back of the wagon; the Jamale who hadn't been able to control his bladder. This version was standing with his back straight, his face emotionless, oozing confidence and self-control. Like Paul he was dressed in an expensive silk suit – although his was white – and the handle of a gun stuck out of his belt.

'Guys!' Saint called from behind a bookshelf. She tried to get to her feet, but her leg wouldn't hold her up. 'Ow!' She crawled forward, eyes wide as she took in Paul and Jamale.

'They're Guardians,' I called to her.

'Yeah,' Ash added, still struggling to catch his breath, 'Guardians with guns.'

'My knee,' Saint said, voice trembling with pain and shock. 'I think it's dislocated.'

'Just stay there, Saint,' Ash said.

'Don't you touch her!' Ginger roared as Jamale pulled out his gun, but instead of moving towards us he walked over to stand by the shattered display window. He showed absolutely no sign that he recognised me or had heard Ginger's warning; his dead eyes stared straight ahead.

'Please, Paul,' I said, the tears now falling freely down my cheeks. 'Thabo's badly hurt. We have to get him back to the enclave.'

'I can help him,' Paul said moving as if to approach me.

'Don't take another step,' Ash said, weighing his panga in his hands.

'You can't stop us.'

'Oh yeah?' Ash replied, taking a step forward. 'Just watch me.'

'Stop!' I yelled to Ash. 'He'll shoot you!'

For a couple of seconds I was terrified that Ash wasn't going to listen, that he'd go for Paul anyway. He didn't drop the panga, or lose the look of cold anger in his eyes, but he stayed where he was. I took a deep shuddering breath and turned back to Paul. 'What do you mean you can help Thabo. How?'

'How do you think, Lele? He can become one of us, as we had planned.'

'What? No!'

'Then he will die,' Paul said, again in that same lifeless tone. He waved his hand towards the shop's doorway. 'And he will join the dead ones.'

'But I can't let you do that to him!'

The Paul thing cocked his head on one side in a gesture that was more alien than human. 'Why not?'

'Because you're ... you're monsters!' It was the only word I could come up with right then to describe them. What else *were* the Guardians?

'It is not us who are the monsters, Lele.'

'What do you mean by that?'

Paul laughed his empty laugh. 'People kill each other, brutalise each other, do far worse things to each other than we ever could. Like what is happening in the city now. It is not us sending people out of the enclave to become the living dead. We are not the ones filled with hate.'

'But ... people aren't just all about hate!'

'That is not what we have seen.'

I glanced at Ash, who was watching me carefully. 'But ... what about love?'

'Love?' Paul said, and for a second I thought he was going to smile. 'There is no such thing.'

Although the Rotters had scattered, I could still hear their moans in the background. 'If Thabo dies he will become one of the dead ones. Let me save him, Lele,' Paul continued.

I didn't know what to do. I thought about what had happened to Gran, and the thought of Thabo turning into a Hatchling was too much to bear. I looked over to Ash, Ginger and Saint.

'What should I do?' I whispered to them.

'You don't have a choice,' Paul said.

Thabo let out a moan of agony. The carpet beneath him was sodden with his blood.

'It is now or never, Lele.'

'No!' I said. But when Paul glided over to Thabo, I didn't try and stop him. 'Watch,' he said.

I didn't really want to see what Paul was going to do, but something compelled me to lift my head.

Paul bent down, picked up a sliver of glass and nicked his finger. A bright bead of blood bubbled at the top of it.

'You can bleed?' I said.

'Yes,' he replied. 'We are more like you than you think, Lele. Or, should I say, you are more like us.'

He sank to his haunches and pressed his finger to the wound in Thabo's stomach. Thabo winced, but he didn't open his eyes. It was clear he was past feeling much of anything.

Paul stood up.

'That's it?' I asked.

'Watch,' Paul said again.

I moved closer, and caught a flicker of silver deep in the depths of the wound. I couldn't make much sense of what I was seeing at first, but as the blood dried and clotted, I could make out fine tendrils, glinting silver versions of the spaghetti stuff I'd seen on the bone mountain, twirling and knitting together inside the wound.

'What is that stuff?'

'It is what we are,' Paul said.

I watched as Thabo's body shivered, the hairs on his arms standing up. For a second his eyes opened wide, and then they shut again, and he was still.

'It will take time, but he will heal,' Paul said.

'He'll live?' I asked.

'Not quite as you mean it, but yes, in a sense, he will live.'

'So what happens now?' Ash asked. 'Are you going to kill us?'

'Kill you?' Paul said, his blank voice for once sounding almost human. 'No. We have been watching you for some time. We know what you are. You must join with us. We can help you fulfil your true potential.'

'You serious?' Saint asked, face still vivid with the agony she was feeling. 'I'd rather die.'

'If that is your choice,' Paul said. 'Then you must die.'

'Why can't you just let us go?' I said. But even as I said it I knew why. We knew who they were, *what* they were. There was a reason they covered their bodies and faces with the robes. Thabo had been right: if the people in the enclave knew what the Guardians actually did with the teenage bodies, who knew how they would react?

Paul looked over at Jamale, and without hesitating Jamale aimed his gun at Ginger's head.

'Don't do this, Paul!' I said. 'Please! There must be another way. We won't say anything, please, just let us go!'

He stared at me through those soulless eyes. 'No.'

'Wait!' Ginger said.

Paul jerked his head in Ginger's direction.

'Mate,' Ginger said, 'we can't stop you doing what you're going to do, but can I ask you a favour?'

Paul glanced at Jamale, and again they seemed to communicate without words. 'What is it you want to do?'

'Well, like, if you're going to kill us or whatever, I was wondering if I could have a last request.'

'What?'

Ginger held up his bag, which clinked as he opened it up.

'I'd like a last drink of my Coke if you don't mind. And I think Ash would probably like one of his smokes.' Ginger looked over at Ash. 'Isn't that right, mate?'

Ash narrowed his eyes slightly, but then nodded at Ginger. 'Yeah,' he said. 'I could do with a cigarette ... sure.'

Ginger pulled a couple of Coke bottles out of his bag and flipped off the lids. He glanced at Saint. 'You know how you're always saying this stuff is bad for me?' he said, looking down at the two bottles filled with unusually yellow liquid.

'Yeah,' she said, still dazed.

'I don't think it's me it's going to harm.'

It took a split second. Ginger threw the bottles as hard as he could at the science fiction section, where they smashed into pieces, the whiff of petrol engulfing the shop as almost simultaneously Ash threw his lighter. There was a whoosh as the petrol ignited, the rainbow shimmer of fumes blossoming into flame.

Jamale moved to shoot, but Saint was too quick for him. She lashed out with her chains, catching him around the neck, and Ginger whirled around and kicked him so hard that the Guardian's body tumbled backwards and out of the window.

Taking advantage of the distraction, Ash sliced at Paul with his panga, whacking him in his side. But, bizarrely, Paul didn't bother to fight back. Instead he let his body crash into the bookshelf behind him.

'You'll be back, Lele,' he said, shooting me a brief, cold smile, and then, with an eerie alien speed, he got to his feet and ran to the front of the store.

The flames were eating through the books faster than I would have thought possible. The sprinklers hissed and sputtered into life, but they were no match for the thick smoke, and within seconds the water dried up – a casualty of ten years of disuse.

'Ginger!' I said. 'Get Saint out of here!'

He nodded, his face grim, and picked Saint up as if she weighed nothing at all.

The fire was raging now, dancing down the aisles. 'Lele!' Ash called as Ginger headed towards the door.

'Don't worry about me. Help Ginger!' I said. 'I'm coming!'

Ash and Ginger were at the doorway, Saint in between them,

when we heard the sound of roaring.

We were too late.

Another bike skidded to a stop at the doorway, blocking our exit.

A figure dismounted and stepped forward. Despite the smoke that was causing tears to course down my face, I couldn't take my eyes off her. Her long dark hair shimmered down her back, the silvery T-shirt she was wearing accentuated the rich brown glow of her skin, and although her eyes were shielded by mirrored shades, her beautiful face showed not the faintest trace of emotion.

'Ripley?' Saint said in shock, and if Ginger hadn't been carrying her, she would probably have slumped to the floor.

Holding his side where Ash had sliced through his jacket, Paul moved to stand next to her. Ripley looked at Saint, her perfect face still expressionless, and pointed out into the mall. 'Just go.'

'You ... you're a Guardian?' Saint said.

'Go,' she said, her face still betraying no emotion.

I couldn't see Ginger's face, his back to me, but I could tell by his body language as he carried Saint out of the store that he was as shocked as she was.

'Lele!' Ash shouted as I turned back into the store. 'What the hell are you doing?'

'I'm right behind you!' I said, but all I could think about was getting back to Thabo. I couldn't leave him. Guardian or not, I just couldn't leave him.

Taking a deep breath, and pulling my T-shirt up over my mouth to keep out the worst of the smoke, I staggered blindly back into the store, stumbling towards the children's section. Thankfully there was a break in the smoke and I sank to my knees where he lay. 'Come on, Thabo,' I said. 'We have to get you out of here.'

He still lay motionless, even when I shook his shoulder as hard as I could. There was no way I could carry him out of there.

'Thabo!'

His body shuddered, and he grasped my hand.

'Don't worry about me, Lele,' he said, and I knew from the dead sound of his voice that I was too late. 'Everything's better now.'

'You don't understand, Thabo – you have to fight it. There's something inside you, you have to –'

'I understand everything perfectly,' he said. He smiled, but it wasn't his usual lopsided grin. This one was as fake as Paul's. 'I know everything. Nothing hurts anymore, Lele.'

As I watched, his dark brown eyes seemed to liquefy and swim, and then they merged into a black, blank nothingness. He was gone.

I tried to yank my hand out of his grasp. I could barely breathe now, my lungs were burning, but he wasn't letting go.

'You know, Lele,' he said. 'You're more like us than you know. We are all connected.' There was the flash of something in his other hand, and then I felt a sharp burning pain in my palm.

'What?'

'Look,' he said.

I looked down at my hand. The wound was deep, blood welling up where he'd sliced it open with a shard of glass.

I tried again to pull my hand out of his grip, but he held fast.

'Look deeper.'

It was hard to see through the roiling smoke, and I couldn't make out anything at first, but then the breath froze in my lungs. Way down deep in the wound, barely noticeable silver strands curled and glistened under the welling blood. They were fainter and finer than the ones that had knitted Thabo's wound together, but they were still there.

'You see?' he said. 'You have the potential to be like us. The seed was planted long ago. When you die, you will live. You see?'

'Lele!'

I could make out Ash's shadowy figure staggering towards me, and then, suddenly, Thabo released his grip and I was free.

I backed away from him, holding my hand out in front of me, vaguely aware that Ash was dragging me towards the exit. I moved like an automaton as Ripley and Paul stood back to let us pass, horror, nausea and disbelief melding as the last piece of the puzzle fell into place.

No wonder I had never had any lasting injuries whenever I was hurt.

No wonder the Rotters didn't try to attack me.

Why would they attack one of their own?

16

So now you know my big secret. Sorry I didn't warn you at the start that it was going to end like this, but would you have believed me anyway? I barely believe it myself.

But I didn't hide everything. I told you in the beginning that this story would end with a funeral. And it does.

The four of us are standing around the pyre Ginger has made in the Deadlands, watching as the flames engulf Hester's body. There'll be no crappy Resurrectionist funeral for her. She won't end up as one of those shambling things she'd fought so hard against.

I make a fist and shove my hand deep in my pocket. It's been three days since Thabo sliced into it, and there's nothing but a faint scar to be seen on my palm. Sometimes I try to convince myself that I just imagined the silvery tendrils that glistened deep down in the wound, but that's just wishful thinking. Still,

I haven't told the others what I know in my heart: That we're even more different from the people in the enclave than we assumed. That something happened to all of us a long time ago that's changed us forever, something connected to our other halves – our twins. That we're not entirely human, not entirely Guardian, but something in between. That there's a reason Saint's knee healed so quickly. That there's a reason the Rotters ignore us.

Saint's taken to wearing her dark glasses all the time, and although I can't see her eyes, her cheeks are wet. She may have recovered from her knee injury, but she hasn't recovered from seeing Ripley again, from knowing what she's become. What she'd *chosen* to become. Because I have to assume that Ripley was the same as us; that for some reason she'd chosen to join the Guardians. Yet, I can't forget Thabo's final words to me: 'When you die, you will live.' So perhaps I'm wrong. Perhaps Ripley didn't have a choice, after all. Perhaps when she encountered the Guardians in the mall, when she was trying to get medicine for Hester, she was mortally wounded and had no choice but to change. It's not a comforting thought.

I want to tell Saint that the Guardians were wrong, that Paul was wrong. I want to tell her that there *is* such a thing as love, and that Ripley proved it by letting us go, that we all prove it daily by sticking together. And that not even the Guardians can destroy it. But now's not the time. I'll wait until later, until we've finished making the journey to the Agriculturals – the only place we can go now.

Ginger stares straight ahead, tears rolling unchecked down his cheeks as Saint moves nearer to him and he takes her hand. All of us know that whatever we do, we can't go back to the mall. And, at least for now, Ginger will have to live without his DVDs, his comic books and his endless bottles of Coke. But of all of us I think he's the strongest. Even now he's rubbing his hands over his cheeks, wiping away the tears. And when I look over to catch his eye, he manages a small smile.

Next to me Ash stands with his head bowed. He puts his arm around me and I rest my head against his shoulder. As I watch the smoke from Hester's pyre curl upwards I think about Jobe in Mandela House, about Dad and the Mantis working for the Resurrectionists back in the enclave, the half-brother or sister who will arrive in the months to come. I hope I'll have a chance to meet him or her one day. I wonder if Thabo made it out of the flames unscathed, and if that matters now that he's no longer who he used to be. I think about Zyed and the others at Malema High, playing into the hands of the Resurrectionists, whose hold over everyone is growing daily. I think about the future of the city. And I think about the funeral all those weeks ago – Gran's funeral – where this story began.

A mournful Rotter moan floats towards us, and, as if on cue, it starts raining.

But there's a flicker of hope alive inside me, even now. You see, this is the end of my story, but somehow I've kind of got the feeling that it could actually just be the beginning.

Read on for an extract from

Death of a Saint

A Mall Rats Novel

Available in October 2013 from

www.constablerobinson.com

LELE

We smell it before we see it.

'Oh, man, not another one,' Saint says, propping herself up on one elbow. 'Whose turn is it?'

We both look over at Ginger, who's lying nearest to the fire, his orange hair curling out of the top of his sleeping bag. He rolls over and snores, but I can tell he's faking. I grab my sketchbook out of my rucksack and chuck it at him. 'Nice try, Ginger, but I know you're not really sleeping.'

'Am so,' he mumbles.

'Seriously, Ginger, it's your turn. And get a move on – it's stinking up the place.'

'All right, all right.' He sits up and kicks his sleeping bag off his legs. The Rotter is stumbling towards the campfire, its raggedy arms hanging at its sides. 'Yuk,' Ginger says. 'It's one of the soggy ones. I *hate* the soggy ones.'

It reeks of that old book odour that all the Rotters stink of, and something else, something *dead*.

'Just get on with it,' Saint sighs, flapping a hand in front of her face. 'It's rolled in something disgusting.'

Grabbing a smouldering log from the edge of the campfire, Ginger prods the Rotter in the leg, herding it away from the clearing. It turns its head in Ginger's direction and blindly thrashes out one of its bony arms. The suit it must have died in clings to its limbs, but its eyes are nothing but holes in its skull. 'Go on, fella,' Ginger says. 'Go and find your mates.'

The Rotter lurches out of camp, but it doesn't go far before it throws back its head and lets out a low, mournful moan. The sound echoes through the bush. There's a pause of a few seconds, and then there's a louder, answering chorus. *Crap.* There must be a pack close by. I know they won't harm us, but still, it's not really what you want to hear in the dark. It was one thing coming across a bunch of the walking dead on our excursions to fetch supplies from the mall, quite another to encounter them staggering into our camp. Saint thinks they must be attracted to the warmth of the fire, which creeps me out. I don't like to think of them as still human, as things that might have feelings or whatever.

Saint groans. 'I'm getting *so* sick of this crap.'

'Really, Saint? I never would have known, you only mention it every single day.'

'*Whatever*, Zombie Bait.'

I don't really blame her for whingeing. Being at one with nature is all very well, but it's not much fun waking up with a wolf spider inches away from your face. Not to mention the fact that we all stink – it doesn't matter how often we wash in the freshwater streams, the odour of wood smoke seems ingrained in our pores.

I shiver and shuffle deeper into my sleeping bag. We've been out here for weeks, and although summer is on its way the nights can still be chilly. We should really scrounge some tents from the mall, but there's no way we can risk going back there.

Another group moan floats towards us from the direction of the enclave. It's louder this time, and Saint and I share a glance. The Rotters are usually only this vocal when they sense there's going to be a relocation or a funeral – fresh meat to add to their numbers.

'What time do you think it is?' I ask.

'Dunno,' Saint says. 'Four, five a.m., maybe?'

I wriggle out of my sleeping bag, check my boots for scorpions and pull them on.

'Where are you going? You've already done lookout duty.'

'Yeah, I know. Can't sleep.'

Ginger nods knowingly at Saint.

'It's not like that, Ginger,' I snap at him. 'I'm just going to see if Ash needs anything.'

'Yeah, like some *lurrrrve*,' Ginger says.

'Ha ha, guys. We're just friends. How many more times?'

Saint stretches her arms behind her head and yawns. 'You might be fooling yourself, Zombie Bait, but you're not fooling us.'

'What's that supposed to mean?'

'Hurry up and get it on already. There's only so much lovesick *Twilight* crap me and Ginger can stand.' She holds out a hand and Ginger slaps her palm.

'Whatever. Give me your torch, Ginger.'

He leans forward and I snatch it out of his hand. 'Come on, Lele, don't be like that,' he says.

Giving them both the finger I start pushing my way through the fynbos and head towards the lookout point. I hate it when they tease me about Ash. It's a seriously sore point and they know it.

Early-morning light bathes everything in a bluish glow, and

I don't actually need the torch's beam to light my way. The top of Table Mountain appears in front of me and the occasional light from the enclave below winks through gaps in the trees. A porcupine snuffles out from behind a bush and bumbles across the path.

Ash is leaning against the large boulder that provides the best vantage point up here, and for a second I'm able to watch him without him being aware of me. It looks like he's reading something by torchlight. But that's nothing new. He's always reading.

I take a step forward and a branch cracks under my boot. He whirls around, shoving something into his pocket.

'Sorry! It's only me … What's that?'

The shadow cast by the rock hides the expression on his face. 'Nothing. Why aren't you sleeping?' He sounds exhausted.

'Another Rotter came into camp. Woke me up.' In fact, it's been ages since I had a good night's shut-eye. *Thanks, guilty conscience.*

He sighs and runs a hand through his hair. It's growing long, and flops over his forehead. I can't remember the last time he smiled at me. Or smiled at all. Hester's death took its toll on all of us, but it hit Ash the hardest. She'd been a mother figure to every one of us, but he'd known her since he was seven years old, and they'd had a bond that the rest of us didn't – and couldn't – share.

I climb up onto the boulder and perch next to him. From this distance it's easy to pretend that the enclave is a peaceful place, all its citizens happy and equal. I swing round and let my legs dangle. It's a long way down, but we chose this spot on purpose. Saint had wanted us to camp out on the beach at Blouberg, but an oil tanker had run aground there, a decade's worth of pollution still clogging up the sand. And none of us wanted to find refuge in the crumbling, overgrown buildings that used to make up Cape Town's metropolis. The blackened shells of the hotels and convention centre are way too spooky and dangerous.

So we'd set up camp on a koppie with a good view of the enclave, and far enough away from the mall to feel safe. Looking down at the lights makes me feel closer to Jobe, and I know Ash feels the same way about his own twin, Sasha.

'You think they're okay?' I ask.

'Who?'

'Jobe and Sasha.'

'They have to be.'

Sometimes I think that Jobe and I share some kind of mental twin connection, but I know it's only wishful thinking. It sucks not being able to see him whenever I want to, but Ash and Saint insist that we should give it some time before we dare return to the enclave.

'So how will we know?' I ask.

'Know what?'

'When it's safe to go back?'

He shrugs. 'I don't know, Lele.'

'But we can't stay out here forever –'

He turns on me. 'I *said* I don't know. What more do you want from me?'

'Sheesh, sorry, okay . . . '

He scrubs a hand over his face. 'Yeah. Me too. I didn't mean to snap at you.'

I'm reluctant to leave, but it's pretty clear I'm not wanted here. Ash has never been one to witter on about kak – that's Ginger's forte – but since the fire at the mall an awkwardness has crept in between us. And after what happened with Thabo, I'm not sure he even thinks of me in that way any more. If he ever did.

The worst of it is that it's partly my fault. Ash isn't an idiot, and I reckon he knows I'm keeping something from him.

And he's right.

I *am* keeping something from him. I'm keeping something from all of them.

The secret burns inside me, but I've left it so long, *too* long, and I don't know how to even start to tell them what I know.

Ash suddenly reaches over and grips my arm. 'Did you hear that?'

'What?'

'Listen!'

All I can hear are the moans of the Rotters and the hoot of an eagle owl. Then I catch it – a faint rumbling sound. A wagon? This early?

'You think it's Guardians, Ash? They don't usually –'

But my words are cut off as a piercing scream carries towards us. A human scream.

Oh *crap*.

'Come on!' Ash holds out a hand to help me down – I don't need it, but take it anyway – and together we hare through the bushes, back to camp.

Ginger and Saint are booted up and waiting for us. Saint has tied a bandanna over her wild mop of hair and is attaching spiky metal weights to the chains wrapped around her wrists; Ginger is hefting the axe he's been using since he lost his chainsaw. I can barely lift it, but it looks like a toy in his hands. He swings it once around his head. 'Sounds like it's time to party!' He grins.

Another scream cuts through the bush.

'Save your breath, Ginger,' Ash says, sliding his panga out of the holster on his back. 'Sounds like you're going to need it.'

'This isn't a relocation,' Saint says. 'What do they think they're doing?'

We're hiding behind a thatch of wattle trees, twenty metres from the enclave fence, and the scene in front of us is made even more chilling by the shadows the Port Jacksons are casting around the clearing.

An elderly man, a woman about the same age as Dad and a teenage boy are cowering on top of the roof of a high, covered wagon. The family – if it is a family and not just a random bunch of escapees – are clustered in a tight, terrified bunch. There's no sign of the horse – it must have panicked and broken free of its harness. And who could blame it? There are at least twenty Rotters surrounding the wagon, bashing their bodies against the cart's sides and rocking it dangerously. And more are heading towards it, moving with that eerie speed they always find when they get the scent of blood in their manky nostrils.

Ash peers around us. 'See any Hatchlings?'

'Doesn't look like it, mate,' Ginger replies. 'We'd know about it if there were.'

'Okay, guys,' Ash says. 'Ginger, you go first – cut a path through to them. Lele, you hang back, check for Hatchlings and catch the stragglers. Saint, you're with me. Let's go!'

Ginger doesn't need asking twice. Raising his axe above his head he runs towards the pack. 'Come and get it, zombie freaks!' he yells as he swipes his axe in a clean arc, and heads tumble and bounce over the fynbos. But the Rotters aren't even slightly deterred. They seem intent on only one thing – tipping over the wagon.

I watch as Saint shakes out her wrists and throws her arms forward, her chains rocking through the air and wrapping around the necks of the two Rotters closest to her, Ash slices through their necks with his panga, and another two bite the dust. Scanning the bushes for Hatchlings, I grip the throwing stars Hester gave me before she died. My heart rate speeds up, the familiar flood of adrenalin coursing through my veins. I know the Rotters won't attack us, but where there's a wagon there are often Hatchlings around, and our immunity against Rotter attack doesn't extend to the newly zombiefied. It takes days for their senses to dull.

The woman spots us first. 'Help us!' she screams.

'Up here!' the man yells. 'Help! Nceda!'

'That's what we're here for, mate!' Ginger calls to them, dispatching another Rotter. This one's head rolls towards me and I kick it away, trying not to look at the spaghetti tendrils twitching and curling out of its severed neck.

One of the Rotters has managed to find a foothold on the wheel of the wagon, its arms flailing up at the woman and the teenager. I pick out a throwing star, weigh it in my hand and skim it towards the wagon. My aim is true and it hits the sweet spot at the back of the thing's neck. It jerks forward, twitches, and then slumps to the ground.

Ginger is making short work of the Rotters with his axe and Saint and Ash are working together seamlessly, easily polishing off two particularly ripe specimens, but even as they do the moans of another pack float towards us. They sound close. 'Lele!' Ash shouts. 'Get them down from there!'

'I'm on it!' Ducking to avoid Ginger's flailing axe, I race towards the wagon, jump up onto the wheel and hold my hand out to the woman. 'Come on!'

'No! The dead ones will get us!'

'You can't stay up there!'

Another moan echoes through the bushes. She glances around her and the elderly man nods. 'Take Thokozani first!' she says to me.

Ignoring my hand the teenager slides his legs over the edge and then tumbles onto the ground. The elderly man follows. He is way more athletic than he looks, and before I can stop him he picks up a large branch and drops to a crouch, waving it in front of him. 'Get the others away!' he shouts.

'Get back,' I yell as the woman finally takes my hand. 'We can handle it!'

Ignoring me, the old man runs over to where Ginger, Saint and Ash are finishing off the stragglers. We don't have time for this – we have to get them all as far away from here as possible before the next lot catch their scent. Luckily Ginger notices the old man, grabs him around the waist and drags him out of the danger zone before the last of the Rotters can get to him – though for some reason they seem to be more intent on getting to the woman and the boy. 'Blimey, you were lucky, mate,' Ginger says to the old man as Ash and Saint dispatch the last two Rotters. 'You shouldn't have done that.'

'I thought I would distract them. Give the others time to get away.'

'Yeah, well, all's well that ends well.'

The boy shudders, eyes glassy with shock. Ginger smiles down at him. 'Don't worry, we'll look after you.'

Ash wipes the blade of his panga on the grass. 'That was close.'

'You're telling me,' Saint says. 'I think that's the lot –'

But she's spoken too soon.